"I owe you a lot," she said.

"Jamie, we haven't worked together in years."

"I'm talking about everything you taught me, Dan. When everything gets crazy, I can hear your voice inside my head. You've kept me alive m

Dear Reader,

Happy New Year! And welcome to another month of great reading from Silhouette Intimate Moments, just perfect for sitting back after the hectic holidays. You'll love Marilyn Pappano's *Murphy's Law,* a MEN IN BLUE title set in New Orleans, with all that city's trademark steam. You'll remember Jack Murphy and Evie DesJardiens long after you put down this book, I promise you.

We've got some great miniseries titles this month, too. Welcome back to Carla Cassidy's Western town of MUSTANG, MONTANA in *Code Name: Cowboy.* Then pay a visit to Margaret Watson's CAMERON, UTAH in *Cowboy with a Badge.* And of course, don't forget our other titles this month. Look for *Dangerous To Love,* by Sally Tyler Hayes, a book whose title I personally find irresistible. And we've got books from a couple of our newest stars, too. Jill Shalvis checks in with *Long-Lost Mom,* and Virginia Kantra pens our FAMILIES ARE FOREVER title, *The Passion of Patrick MacNeill.*

Enjoy them all—and be sure to come back next month for more of the most exciting romantic reading around, right here in Silhouette Intimate Moments.

Yours,

Leslie J. Wainger

Leslie J. Wainger
Executive Senior Editor

Please address questions and book requests to:
Silhouette Reader Service
U.S.: 3010 Walden Ave., P.O. Box 1325, Buffalo, NY 14269
Canadian: P.O. Box 609, Fort Erie, Ont. L2A 5X3

DANGEROUS TO LOVE

SALLY TYLER HAYES

Silhouette®
INTIMATE™ MOMENTS®

Published by Silhouette Books

America's Publisher of Contemporary Romance

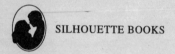 SILHOUETTE BOOKS

ISBN 0-373-07903-6

DANGEROUS TO LOVE

Copyright © 1999 by Teresa Hill

This edition published by arrangement with Harlequin Books S.A.

® and TM are trademarks of Harlequin Books S.A., used under license.
Trademarks indicated with ® are registered in the United States Patent
and Trademark Office, the Canadian Trade Marks Office and in other
countries.

Printed in U.S.A.

Books by Sally Tyler Hayes

Silhouette Intimate Moments

SALLY TYLER HAYES

lives in South Carolina with her husband, son and daughter. A former journalist for a South Carolina newspaper, she fondly remembers that her decision to write and explore the frontiers of romance came at about the same time she discovered, in junior high, that she'd never be able to join the crew of the Starship Enterprise.

Happy and proud to be a stay-home mom, she is thrilled to be living her lifelong dream of writing romances.

Writing has given me many wonderful things. The sheer bliss that comes from having a story to tell. The joy of having more time to spend with my children, and freedom from the 9-to-5 grind.

But the most unexpected gift has been the sisterhood. Friends who always understand, who care, who sympathize and celebrate each little step along the way.

This book is for my sisters:
Barbara Samuel, Liz Bevarly and Christie Ridgway.
Here's to many more years of sisterhood and success.

Chapter 1

An inky blackness settled over the District of Columbia in the aftermath of a hard-driving rain and gusting winds, which left downed power lines in their wake. But the man had eyes like a cat. He knew how to cut through the darkness and the elements to focus on his target, and it was second nature to him to take note of everything around him.

Parking his car two blocks from his destination, as instructed, he crept through the nearly empty streets. Arriving early as always, he used the time to familiarize himself with the area before moving any closer. Experience had taught him a man couldn't be too careful, and a familiar tightness between his shoulder blades had been nagging at him all day.

Something was going to happen tonight, something bad.

He circled the area, making detailed observations from the four corners, finding nothing amiss. But as he approached the building from the south, he caught a flicker of movement in one of the alleys and found himself slipping into the canyon created by the tall buildings on either side.

The deeper he went into the alley, the blacker it became. He stopped and waited, patient and still, heedless of the drizzling rain, until nothing moved and no sound came to him for a five full minutes. Had he seen something? Or was he just jumpy?

Working his way back to the main road, he watched and waited again, then found himself curiously disoriented in the darkness. Visibility was infinitesimal, the rain falling harder, the streetlights still out and all the buildings looked alike now. The one he sought had a recessed entrance, a high arching tunnel that housed fifteen wide stairs leading to the front door. If someone wanted to break in, the cover it provided was ideal.

The man slid his hand beneath his dark leather jacket to the weapon he kept, loaded and ready, in a shoulder holster that fit like a second skin after so many years of being strapped in the same spot.

Pausing, the man decided to check in on the radio before moving any closer. He'd already inserted a tiny earpiece before he left his car, and he had a small microphone clipped to his left shoulder, preset to the channel he needed. He touched a button to turn the unit on. But when he spoke softly into the mike, no one responded. That was definitely cause for concern.

He made a quarter turn to the right, planning to check the area again. But suddenly, the tightness between his shoulder blades was crushing, and he reconsidered the wisdom of moving at all. Standing perfectly still, he looked all around. Something wasn't right.

He backed to the edge of the nearest building. The hair on the back of his neck stood on end. Instinctively, he knew the barrel of someone's gun was leveled at his back. Too late, he reached for his own and whirled around.

"Don't do it," a voice warned.

His weapon never even cleared the folds of his jacket, and he found himself staring long and hard at the wrong end of a gun. It was pointed with deadly accuracy at the center of his chest.

He didn't so much as blink.

It took him all of five seconds, once the roaring in his ears receded, to realize he knew that voice, recognized something in the way she held her body braced, ready to shoot.

The man had the audacity to smile.

"Steady as a rock, Jamie. I'm impressed," he said, a hint of pride in his voice. After all, he'd taught her well.

"You should be impressed I didn't put a bullet through that hard head of yours." She took her time about lowering the weapon. "Damn it, Dan. Could you just stick to the plan and call us on the radio before you approach us?"

"I got distracted. And my radio shorted out for a second," he said, peering at her through the darkness, hearing her irritation rather than seeing it. "Sorry."

"Sorry? I could have killed you."

He laughed, because she *was* killing him, little by little, day after day. Even thousands of miles away, sneaking into his thoughts at the oddest of times, she was killing him.

Jamie kept right on giving him hell for sneaking up on her, and Dan tried not to smile—knowing it would only exasperate her more. He must have just caught some interference in the signal from his radio, because he could hear her voice echoing through his earpiece as well now. She could chew him out in stereo sound.

He took a minute to study her. Like him, she was dressed entirely in black, a silhouette of long limbs and shapely curves encased in snug pants and a dark, loose jacket that covered more than he would have liked. Still, he knew exactly how she looked. He'd memorized every detail years ago, then fought a losing battle to forget about her.

She had pale skin, flawless and luminescent, like the polished ivory keys of the baby grand piano his mother once played. Rich black hair; the last time he'd seen it loose, it had fallen to a point just past her shoulders. Eyes big and dark. Soft, generous lips that smiled easily. A voice that laughed beautifully. She was a woman who'd always seemed impossibly young and innocent to him, and he'd fought against ever letting her get too close to him.

Inside his head a voice taunted him with the knowledge that he could have had her years ago, could have forgotten her by now.

If it was possible for him to have her and forget about her. He'd fallen into the habit of needling her, just to keep her at arm's length. Which said a lot for the way he dealt with the women in his life. How was he going to handle her now?

"You scared me half to death," she complained, "and you have the nerve to stand here laughing about it?"

Dan wiped the smile off his face and wondered exactly what she would say if he admitted that she was just about the only person who could still make him laugh. He wondered if she'd care.

"How 'bout I stop laughing," he suggested, "and the two of us get out of the rain?" He didn't wait for her agreement, merely turned to walk with her toward the building. Feeling edgy and a little reckless, he brought his hand up to curl around her elbow, even though he knew better.

Because touching her, even in the slightest of ways, set off a chain reaction that rippled through him. It brought a tightness to his body that started in his throat, slid downward to do peculiar things to his breathing and his heartbeat, then tied his stomach in knots, sometimes sinking even lower, making itself embarrassingly evident in the changing contours of his body.

She did that to him, always had, probably always would, and he was tired of fighting both her and himself.

Give in to it, he thought recklessly. She was right here in front of him. All he had to do was reach out for her and pull her to him.

She'd wanted him years ago, still looked at him from time to time like a woman who was his for the taking. And there were so few things left in this world he truly wanted. At the moment, he could think of only one.

Her.

"Dan?" she said hesitantly.

He swore softly, the words carried away on the wind, absorbed into the darkness.

"Out of the rain, Jamie. I'd be happy to argue with you when we get out of the rain," he said, trying to ignore the impression of her body at his side, the gentle sway of her hips that he couldn't quite feel but somehow sensed, the narrow shoulders and hips, the top of her head that would fit perfectly under his chin if he ever let himself hold her cradled against him that way.

With the rain coming down, washing the air clean, he shouldn't be able to smell whatever it was she used on her skin, either. Too delicate to be perfume, it had come to haunt him. Soap, he imagined. Or scented lotion. Something she poured into her bathwater, maybe. Whatever it was ended up all over her body. He could swear that at various times he'd smelled it in her hair, on her hands, at the nape of her neck. She must drown in the stuff, and it made him want to drown as well, in her.

Too soon, they reached the arched entrance of the building and stepped out of the rain. Dan let his hand drop from her elbow, then brushed the worst of the moisture from his hair.

"Did you catch that?" Jamie called out, looking over his right shoulder. "I had a gun stuck in his face, and he laughed at me."

Dan turned and saw a tall, lean, smiling man with the face of a movie star and the demeanor of a diplomat, the latter a role he played quite regularly, in the line of duty, with great skill and success. "I heard," the Golden Boy said. "Good to see you again, Dan."

"Josh," he nodded, looking quickly from the too-good-looking man to the woman who so thoroughly tormented him, and wondered for the hundredth time if there was something going on between them.

"If I could trust you two not to fight, I'd go inside and get my walk-through done while we wait for Geri," Josh said.

"We'll behave," Jamie said. "You should, too, Josh."

Dan wondered about the look that passed between them. Was it the closeness that came from working together for a long time, or the intimacy of lovers?

"Hurry," Jamie called out. "Dan's scowling at me again."

Damned if he wasn't.

Josh punched a security code into the sophisticated system mounted at the side of the front door, then slipped inside, leaving Dan alone with Jamie once again. Without a word, they walked down the steps, to the front wall of the building, their eyes scanning the darkness stretched out before them.

"Sorry I spooked you," Dan said. It couldn't be that much of a risk to talk to her, and he just wanted to hear her voice, which still held a hint of her Virginia upbringing. "I thought I saw something in the alley," he explained.

"So naturally, you took off after whatever it was without telling anyone what you were doing."

"I tried the radio. Must have hit a patch of interference, because I couldn't hear anything for a few seconds."

"It's working now?"

He nodded, thinking he heard an edge to her voice tonight, wondering if she was still uneasy at having him creep up on her, or if something else was going on.

"Any problems tonight?"

"Not a one," she said.

End of conversation.

Dan eased back against the wall. This assignment had come up at the last minute. And ever since he found out Jamie was going to be here, he'd done nothing but think of her.

Dan didn't make a habit of obsessing over women. He didn't get rattled often, either. He couldn't remember the last time he'd been thrown off-balance like this over a woman. But he'd needed to see for himself that she was okay, after that nasty business in London last week.

"When did you and Josh get back?" he said.

"Late yesterday." She sighed. "Things....uhh. Let's just say things came together faster than we anticipated in London."

He supposed that was one way of putting it. Dan had heard about it—a bomb had gone off about fifty feet from her, and she was damned lucky to be alive.

A well-connected U.S. businessman had been shipping high-tech electronic circuitry to a group suspected of bombing popular tourist spots in London over the past year, and Division One had been trying to find out where the shipments were coming from and how to stop them before anyone else was killed.

Jamie had been trailing one of the suppliers when his clients decided to cut all ties with him and make a political statement at the same time. They blew the supplier to kingdom come while Jamie was standing across the street.

Ever since then, Dan had been asking himself how it would have felt to know he'd never see her pretty face again, or hear her hint-of-honey voice that had a way of skimming softly across his skin and setting his nerves on end.

Hell, he decided. It would have been hell.

So was imagining her in bed with Joshua Carter.

"About London," he began, unable to leave it alone. "It was good work. Tanner's giddy, thinking the agency's stock just shot through the roof with everybody in the District."

"So giddy he stuck us with baby-sitting duties?"

"No, this is…" Dan shrugged. "I don't know, Jamie. I don't understand what this is."

They seldom worked in the States, seldom took on anything as simple as a bodyguarding assignment. Tanner, their boss, had been quite cryptic about this one. They were told there'd been troubling security problems at the scientists' previous location, and temporary arrangements had been made to move them here until a permanent place was found for them. The agency had been called in temporarily because they had teams available in D.C. to take on the job immediately. But they'd been given pitifully few details about the three men inside or what they were doing.

Supposedly, the assignment would be over within forty-eight hours, which could account for them getting so little information about the situation. Still, it was odd.

"Have you seen these guys?" Dan asked.

"No. They're hermits. They haven't shown their faces to us or to anyone on the previous shift. Doc came on two hours ago. He's patrolling the corridor inside. He's talked to them through the intercom system, but that's it."

Dan glanced toward the door. He only had a few moments before Josh returned, and he didn't think he could afford to lose this opportunity. The way they worked, they could go their separate ways when this assignment was over and not see each other again for months. If ever.

She could walk into another explosion next week, and he'd never get the chance to say what he wanted to say.

"Jamie? About London?" He reconsidered. It was much more than that. "Not just London. The last four years. I wanted you to know, it's been good, solid work. You've turned into a damned fine agent."

She stared up at him, her eyes wide, her expression one of stunned disbelief that gave way to a hesitant smile. How long had it been since her face lit up with a genuine smile for him?

"I didn't think I'd ever hear you say that," she said.

Which left Dan feeling like a fool. But he deserved it. "It's true. You should be proud of yourself. I am."

"Dan..." She took a tentative step toward him, then stopped and slid back to her post against the opposite wall. "I had no idea you felt that way."

He turned back to the street, having a hard time keeping his attention on his duties. "I should have said it a long time ago."

She shook her head, looking genuinely pleased. "This from a man who didn't think women could hack it in the agency?"

He laughed a little. "You made me eat those words."

"From the man who did everything he could to make me wash out in Intermediaries?"

"No," he objected, thinking he should have realized what she'd read into his actions, should have corrected that impression long ago.

"You wanted me to fail," she insisted. "You were on me day and night for the whole twelve weeks, pushing me harder than you pushed any of the men. Because you didn't think I could take it."

"I didn't *want* you to fail." Hell, maybe he did, but not

for the reason she imagined. And it wasn't a distinction he
thought he could make her understand. But he could make
one thing clear. "I wanted to keep you alive out here. Think
about it, Jamie. Washing out as a trainee is one thing.
Washing out in the field doesn't always mean quitting and
walking away." He closed his eyes, thinking of the friends
he'd lost along the way in this business. "Sometimes it
means dying."

And he hadn't wanted her to die, hadn't wanted the responsibility for any agent making it through the program
who wasn't prepared for what he or she would face in the
field. She'd call him a chauvinist—or worse—if he admitted it, but he would have found it especially hard to accept
responsibility for the death of a woman.

He'd been raised to believe a man protected a woman at
all costs, particularly those he cared about. So it hadn't
been easy for him to accept the idea of having a woman
beside him in the field, with bullets flying. He'd seen with
his own eyes that women were capable of handling themselves in all manner of hair-raising situations; he just didn't
think they should have to when there were men around to
do the job for them.

Of course, no one forced a man or a woman into the
service of their country these days, and if a woman chose
this life, that was her decision. Begrudgingly, he'd accepted
that. But no woman made it into the field for the agency
when Dan was taking a rotation as an instructor unless he
was satisfied she could handle the job.

That was part of the reason he'd been so hard on Jamie.
The other part was much more complicated than that.
Glancing at her through the darkness, he could see he still
had a lot of explaining to do.

"It's not what you think," he began.

She folded her arms across her chest and glared at him.

"You want me to believe you were doing me a favor by making it so hard for me?"

"Could I?" he said lightly.

"No way," she protested. "It was because I'm a woman. Because you didn't think women could hack it in this program."

"Size and strength and speed still matter in this kind of work," he said, "and like it or not, men are bigger, stronger and faster."

"Some men," she corrected.

He smiled again and supposed he'd have to eat those words as well. "Okay. Some men."

She'd run circles around a number of men to make it here.

Looking as if she was thoroughly enjoying herself, she leaned back against the side of the building. "I know I shouldn't gloat, but…"

Dan laughed out loud, the sound coming from somewhere deep inside him. It was too easy to argue with her. "Go ahead," he offered. "Enjoy it. You deserve it."

"All these years," she said, almost wistfully. "I thought you hated me."

Dan froze, genuine regret washing over him.

Hate her? It was anything but that.

He'd never explained to her that she reminded him of a woman he desperately wanted to forget. A woman who'd once shared his bed and his name, one he'd made miserable in the short time they'd been married. He thought he'd gotten past that in the days the agency was in its infancy. He'd been a part of it from the beginning, helping select and train its first operatives. He particularly enjoyed the challenge of building something from the ground up when the rest of his life was falling apart around him.

Then he'd walked onto a field full of prospective agents and seen Jamie. And wanted her, wanted to protect her from himself and his life, as well. Put all that together, and he hadn't been in the best of moods from the first moment they met. But he'd never hated her.

He'd wanted her, but he knew she'd be much better off without him.

"Jamie," he said softly. "I never hated you."

Jamie stood there, staring at him, wishing she could see more clearly, relying on her memory to fill in the gaps left by the darkness. He was twelve years older than she was. His hair didn't have a hint of gray, but there were tiny lines at the corners of his eyes, more at the corners of his mouth when he smiled that sarcastically amused smile of his, which he often did around her.

She found him even more attractive and compelling with each year that passed. There'd been a time when she would have cut off her right arm in exchange for a kind word from him, a time when she alternatively wanted to wring his neck or have the satisfaction in throwing him flat on his back, just one time, when he stepped onto the mat in self-defense class.

She'd longed for his respect almost as much as she longed for him to show the slightest bit of interest in her as a person. *As a woman.* Which was silly, because he couldn't stand her.

She wanted to believe he was one of those men who didn't think women had any place in an agency such as Division One. But she'd lost even that bit of comfort when Dan, himself, had been paired with a woman, a petite dynamo named Geri Sinclair. They'd been working together for about a year now, and he seemed perfectly at ease entrusting his life to her, which was what a partnership meant in their line of work.

So, if it wasn't that Jamie was a woman, or that he didn't think she could handle the job, that left only one reason for the way he treated her. He must not like her, period.

And now he claimed he was proud of her and the work she'd done?

"I..." She had to stop and think before she really put her foot in it. He'd complimented her work and nothing else. "I appreciate you telling me that."

"As I said, I should have told you a long time ago," he said, looking unusually serious. "For a while after I heard about what happened in London, I thought that I wouldn't get the chance to tell you."

"Oh?" she said carefully.

"Not because I thought you couldn't handle the job," he said carefully. "Because I know how dangerous the job is."

"All the jobs are dangerous," she reminded him.

Looking like he was ready to spit nails, he said, "I was worried about you, Jamie, all right?"

This was getting more and more interesting all the time. Jamie just stood there, immensely satisfied by the turn of the conversation, immensely hopeful.

Worried about you.

God, if only he knew how many nights she had spent awake, worrying about whatever mess he'd gotten himself into, wondering if he would make it back alive and how long it would be before she saw him again.

They both traveled a great deal, coming and going on what at some times seemed directly opposite schedules. It wasn't unusual for weeks, even months, to go by before she caught a glimpse of him. Which was probably one of the reasons she hadn't already made a fool of herself over him.

"I'm supposed to be in town for a while after this job's done," he said.

"Me, too," she offered tentatively, thinking that either she'd gone mad or he was about to suggest they get together sometime.

"Jamie, it's probably none of my business, but what's going on between you and the Golden Boy?"

"Josh?"

All serious and stern-looking, he nodded.

Jamie fought not to give anything away in her expression, to keep it carefully neutral, while inside she was screaming for joy. Could he really be jealous of Josh?

"Josh is my partner," she said, thinking she should let him wonder another moment or two. "And a good friend."

"Okay," he said, accepting it, although she sensed he wanted a more definitive statement on the relationship.

It gave her hope. A dizzy, giddy kind of hope. Jamie thought just about anything could happen next, that all things were possible.

And then, through the earpiece of her radio, she heard Dan's partner announce that she was approaching them from the southwest. Dan heard it, too. They were all tuned to the same frequency. Looking frustrated and uncharacteristically uncertain, he stared at her for a moment, and she wanted to believe that he regretted—as much as she did— that their conversation had been cut short. Then he turned to greet his partner.

Jamie wondered if that would be the end of it, if she'd ever know what he would have said next. Through sheer force of will, she made it through the next few minutes as she and Josh turned over responsibility for the men inside the building to Dan and Geri.

The last item on their checklist of duties was a walk-through of the interior security setup. She took Dan through the building while Geri and Josh stayed outside. He didn't say a word to her, just listened, surveyed the area himself and followed her.

There was only one problem. He was much too close. Pausing at the far end of a deserted hallway, Jamie wondered if her mind was playing tricks on her, if she was simply too in tune with every move he made, every breath he took. Surely she was putting too much stock in a few simple words of praise for her work, one intriguing question about her relationship with Josh, and her own attraction to a man who for so long had been oblivious to her.

"Well," she said, her composure wearing thin. "I guess that's it."

She went to brush past him, but Dan snagged her with an arm like steel and pulled her to him.

"Not quite," he said, backing her against the wall in the darkened corner of the building and lowering his mouth to hers.

She gasped, her mouth opening beneath his. Her palms were pressed against his shoulders, her fingers splayed wide around the muscles bunched tightly at the top of his steely arms. Never in her life had she been so aware of the fact that she was pressed tightly against a man so much bigger and so much stronger than she was. But then she'd always gotten a little thrill out of the fact that he moved so fast and possessed such strength.

This close, she felt the broad muscles of his chest, the tightness of his stomach, the rock-solid muscles of his thighs. One of his hands settled into the indentation at the base of her spine, arching her against him, bringing their bodies intimately together. Against her belly, she felt the first stirrings of arousal in his, a growing pressure that had her gasping for breath once again. Dizzy with surprise and hope, she clung to him.

He held her up with his arms and with the pressure of his body, an object as immovable as the solid brick wall against her back. Yet, for a man who had moved so quickly, and used such strength to hold her there, he kissed with devastating gentleness. His lips were firm and sure against hers, his tongue like velvet as it slowly invaded her mouth, coaxing, stroking, enticing.

She shuddered against him. He held her more tightly, breaking away long enough to whisper urgently, "Jamie, I would never hurt you."

"I know," she answered, absolutely certain he wouldn't ever use his size and strength that way.

He gentled the kiss even more. Worried that he was going to pull away, that the moment would be lost, she pressed one of her hands to the side of his face and into his hair, still wet from the rain, and urged him closer.

So many times, she'd imagined how his body would feel wrapped tightly around hers, how he would move against her, how he would taste and the way his big, calloused hands would feel against her bare skin. But nothing she ever imagined equaled the devastating reality of him.

His tongue stroked its way through her mouth, against her lips, across her teeth. She whimpered a little, unable to help herself, when he started to back away, his touch growing lighter as he pressed a series of soft, sweet kisses against her lips, before he finally withdrew.

Dazed, she stood there pressed against the wall and gazed up at him. His massive shoulders were heaving in the effort it cost him to breathe, his dark eyes positively smoldering, his lips stretched into a sexy smile that spoke of satisfaction, then slowly gave way to concern.

He took her chin in his hand, his eyes dazzling, "Did I scare you?"

"No."

He didn't look convinced.

"Dan, I'm not afraid of you," she added.

Nothing could be further from the truth. She felt safer with him than she ever had with anyone else. It was his brash self-confidence, the sureness with which he moved, the ease he had with his body. There was strength and immense power inside of him, tempered with impeccable judgment and a scrupulous sense of responsibility.

She could easily entrust her life to him, could so easily give him her heart as well.

"I want to see you," he said. *See her?* The husky tone, the words that sounded more like a command than a request.

"In the morning?" she suggested, not willing to give him too long to think about it, possibly to change his mind. His eyes narrowed, and she thought she might have surprised him with her eagerness and impatience.

"You're done at seven?" she rushed on.

"Yes," he said.

Dinner was out of the question. She and Josh were pulling the evening watch until their mystery scientists were moved. And Dan had the nights. That only left the days.

"We could have breakfast," she suggested.

Breakfast sounded reasonable, like something two rational adults might do. It could be nothing more than sharing a meal together. Or it could turn into just about anything. She swallowed hard, fighting against the tightness in her throat. Fighting her nervousness and all her insecurities, she waited, wanting so desperately for them to have this chance.

Dan stood in front of her, using that uncanny ability he had to be so quiet, so absolutely still, people wondered if he was still breathing. He was silent long enough to make her panic just a little. And then he nodded, his lips curving into that satisfied smile again.

"I'll pick you up in the morning, as soon as I'm done here."

"I'll be waiting," she whispered.

His lips came down to hers once more, the kiss quick and hard and leaving her head spinning once again.

"If we don't get outside now, someone's going to come looking for us," he said.

"I know."

Amazed and so very hopeful, she turned and followed him down the hallway. Her legs were still weak, her hands trembling badly, her lips tingling, joy and wonder surging through her.

It felt as if she'd been waiting forever for him.

Chapter 2

Jamie was still in a daze five minutes later as she and Josh walked through the darkened streets to their cars. Half a block away from the warehouse, Josh said, "Well?"

"He wants to see me," she said, echoing Dan's own words.

"See you?" Josh repeated. "As in...call you into his office and chew you out over something he thinks you've done wrong?"

"No. *See me*. As in...get together. Talk. Share a meal. You know...like a date."

Josh laughed. "You can't stand him. Remember?"

"I know." He was the most frustrating man she'd ever known.

"He makes you crazy."

"I know."

"He'll break your heart," Josh said, sounding suspiciously protective, like one of her brothers.

"I won't let him," she promised herself. They walked

quietly through the rain for a few moments. Finally, she said, "I just can't forget him, Josh. No matter how hard I've tried, I can't get him out of my mind. I still remember the first time I ever saw him."

It had been one of her first days with the agency. Dan Reese, dressed all in black, his blondish-brown hair cropped close to his head in military precision, his eyes a dark, rich green, was an imposing study in grace and power and confidence as he marched onto the field and explained in the most softly intimidating voice she'd ever heard how few trainees ever made it through Intermediaries with him.

"That first day, he took me aside after class and told me in no uncertain terms there was no place in this organization for me, then he swore he wouldn't kick me out because I was a woman, but because I wouldn't be able to cut it."

Josh shook his head. "The man has a way with women."

Jamie laughed. "I hated him. As my father says, 'I wouldn't have bothered to spit on him if he was on fire.' But I worked harder than I've ever worked in my life because of him, and he taught me so much. I guess…I admire him for that. For a lot of things."

He showed her a wealth of determination and strength inside of her, and she knew if she succeeded within the agency, a great deal of the credit would belong to him.

On graduation day she tried to tell him, then watched in dismay as an old, familiar look came across his face. One that said he thought she was very young and inexperienced, that she had a lot to learn about the world in general and about what would be expected of her within the agency in particular. He managed to look cocky, condescending and amused all at once as he cut her to shreds with his wicked tongue, dashing her hopes that he'd changed his mind about her and her abilities. The hard part, he told her, hadn't even begun, and if she was smart she'd know she had to work ten times as hard in the field as she'd ever worked for him, if she simply wanted to survive.

Jamie looked up and found herself at her car. She punched the code into the door that unlocked it, then turned to face Josh again. He was a friend, a very good friend, who pulled her to him for a quick embrace.

"So, this is what a man has to do to get your attention? Annoy you? Insult you? Belittle you? You're a disgrace to liberated women everywhere."

"I know. Believe me, I do."

She was a smart woman, and it broke her heart to admit it, but no matter how mad Dan Reese made her, she'd always been aware of him as a man, a big, tough, gorgeous man. She suspected he'd been indulged by what he considered the weaker sex his entire life. It showed in the grin he wielded like a weapon, the one that cut right through her as neatly and efficiently as any knife she'd ever handled.

Jamie had seen women make absolute fools of themselves over men, and she'd always assumed they were just weak, pathetic creatures, somehow lacking in the common sense she possessed. And then Dan swept into her life, making her realize she could be as foolish as any other woman. All it took was the right man. Or the *wrong* one.

"Be careful," Josh said.

"I will," she promised. "Josh, do you know anything about his ex-wife?"

"Not much. I don't think I ever even saw her. Somebody told me she hated the military, hated the agency." He shrugged. "You know the kind of toll it takes on relationships—the danger, the long absences."

Jamie did know. She'd grown up in a military family.

"Somebody told me she gave Dan a choice, his job or her," Josh said. "He chose the job. That should tell you something about the kind of man he is."

Oh, she knew his kind of man, the kind who kept everything inside, who worked hard, lived dangerously, accepted the risks as a fact of life, one who never let anyone get close to him. Jamie wanted to break through all those barriers. She wanted to know the man inside.

Once again, Josh urged her to be careful. Then she climbed into her car and took off, thinking there was just one problem with being careful—it hadn't gotten her anywhere with Dan.

Her first truly rash decision was that she should fix breakfast for them at her apartment in the morning, because she wanted Dan all to herself for a while.

She wasn't exactly a picture of domestication, but the stores made it easy these days and she'd worked odd hours long enough to know where she could shop in the middle of the night. Jamie found fresh fruit, croissants and jam, two kinds of flavored coffee and some eggs she would scramble with some peppers and cheese. Shamelessly, she added fresh flowers and scented candles to her purchases, as well.

At home, she readied the food, found vases for the flowers. She lit one of the scented candles and took it into the bathroom, where she poured her favorite bath salts into the tub and soaked herself until the water turned cold. After drying her hair, she smoothed lightly scented lotion all over her body and, because she was ghastly pale, put on a bit of makeup. Then she dug through her closet, wondering what a well-dressed woman wore when she invited a man to breakfast on their very first date.

She had nice pajamas that weren't at all revealing, but still soft and smooth and shimmery. It would be presumptuous of her, but then there'd been nothing subtle about the way he kissed her in the hallway. Nothing subtle about her impulsively inviting him over the minute he got off work, either.

She set the pants aside to put on later, then slipped on the top of a pair of silky peach-colored pajamas, which fell to a few inches above her knees, and walked to the full-length mirror that hung on the back of her closet door. Once again, she remembered the rough, strained sound of his voice in the hallway. *I want to see you.*

Would he like seeing her in this?

Closing her eyes, she imagined that kiss one more time, except this time she was in whisper-thin pajamas. The heat of his body would sear right through her clothes. So easily, he could push the fabric aside, slide those calloused hands of his against the bare skin of her back or brush the collar aside to nibble on her neck. Heat started to rise from a point deep inside her. Her breasts felt full and heavy, aching for the touch of his hands. Her breathing wasn't quite steady.

She felt as if she was standing on the ledge of a building fifty stories high or the edge of a cliff, with no gear, no safety harness, no ropes. No plan. Just air under her feet, free fall in the making. Nerves came shimmering to life inside her. The reality of what she'd set in motion, what she wanted to happen in the morning, was starting to sink in.

Jamie would give him anything he wanted.

Anything.

She hoped that would be enough, that the night would be the beginning of something wonderful between them.

Too restless to sleep, she opened her patio doors. It was fairly quiet where she was, but in the distance, lightning still danced across the sky. She stood there listening to the rain. From the west, she heard a crush of sirens, which didn't alarm her. There was always some sort of trouble in the city. But a few minutes later, she heard something else. She could have sworn it was the distinctive, rhythmic strumming of a big, military helicopter.

Why would anyone be flying in weather like this?

Jamie felt a shiver work its way down her spine.

She was setting the table for two when her doorbell rang. Jamie turned to the clock; it was much too early for Dan.

Cautiously, she walked to the delicate-looking table in the hallway where she kept her keys, her purse and three novels between elegant, scrolling bookends she'd picked up in an antique shop in Georgetown. The book on the right had a false bottom with a keypad lock. In the hidden compartment, there was a gun. Just in case anyone ever came to her door like this.

The doorbell rang again as her fingers hit the last number in the coded lock. As she retrieved the loaded gun, she heard a voice calling to her.

"Jamie? It's Josh."

That was odd. He certainly didn't make a habit of showing up at her apartment at 3:00 a.m. And if they'd been called out on assignment, someone would have summoned her to the office, either by phone or through the high-tech pager she always kept with her. That was basic procedure.

With professional caution, she unlocked the door but didn't open it. Then she backed up three steps with the gun in her hand, keeping it trained on whoever was behind the door. "It's open," she called out.

The door swung inward, revealing only Josh, who, despite the hour, managed to look incredibly elegant and polished in a pair of jeans, a white button-down and a well-worn leather bomber jacket.

It wasn't until she took another look at his face that she knew something was wrong.

"Put the gun down, Jamie," he said gently.

Something in his voice stopped her cold. He ended up taking the gun from her hands himself, then closed the door, took her by the arm and turned her toward her bedroom.

"We have to go out. You need some clothes and some shoes."

"Why?"

It was all she could manage, but her mind was racing, rapidly considering possibilities, all of them bad, all of them personal.

Jamie stood silently by his side while Josh dug through her dresser drawers. She took the black leggings he put into her hands and tugged them on, took the warm wool socks he found in another drawer, slipped into the loafers he pulled from her closet.

"Find another shirt," he said, before he walked out of her bedroom.

Jamie did. She had a whole wardrobe designed around hiding a gun on her body. Automatically, she reached for something that would do just that. When she walked back into the living room, she donned her shoulder holster, tucked her gun inside, then pulled a loose jacket over it. She let Josh help her into her raincoat. When he held out her own ID and keys, she shoved them into the coat's deep pockets and followed him.

Once she thought she was prepared to hear the answer, she choked out the words, "It's Dan, isn't it?"

"Afraid so."

"Where is he?"

Josh put her into the car he'd left double-parked in front of her building. Hunched down on his heels in the open doorway, he looked her right in the eye and said, "On his way to Bethesda."

She nodded. Then she waited until he walked around to the driver's side, climbed into the car and started it. "The helicopter?" she asked.

As he accelerated down the road, he reached over and gave her hand a quick squeeze. "Somebody called you?"

"No. I heard it take off. Couldn't imagine why anyone

would be flying in weather like this.'' Of course, the answer
was obvious now. He was hurt, badly.

Minutes counted.

Seconds, even.

Much of the ride was lost on her, as was their arrival at
the hospital, where she kept quiet and stuck close to Josh.
Normally, nothing rattled her on the job. Not even a threat
to her life. But this was different. This was personal. This
was Dan. Clipped, intense conversation flowed around her,
which she didn't even try to comprehend, letting Josh handle it. He would do that for her, because he knew how
terribly afraid she was that Dan was dead or dying.

Josh steered her to a room at the end of the hall where
two military guards stood outside a glass-paneled door.
Josh flashed an ID and her reflexes took over. She pulled
hers out of her coat pocket and displayed it for the guards.

While Josh fired questions at them, Jamie glanced into
the treatment room and saw a man and a woman, doctors,
shaking their heads and pulling off latex gloves stained
bright red. It seemed as if an eternity passed before the
crowd clustered around the gurney shifted to give her a
clear view of the patient's face.

No, not a face. A white sheet draped over a face.

She closed her eyes and let the knowledge sink in. The
person inside that room was dead. A strangling sound of
protest slipped out of her throat. Josh turned to her, and
she gestured with a trembling hand toward what she'd seen.

Josh swore. ''It's not Dan, okay?'' He grabbed her by
the arms and held on. ''Jamie? Dan's upstairs in surgery.
He made it to surgery.''

Relief, swift and intense, spiraled through her. Josh was
quietly giving orders. He wanted two guards with the body
at all times. No one got close to it without his or her per-
mission. No one answered any questions about what had
happened, either.

So, the dead person was either a suspect or another agent. "Is it Geri?" she asked.

"No," he said.

She breathed a bit more easily, even though she and Geri weren't close. Geri was quiet and serious, highly competent, but she kept to herself. Dan had a great deal of respect for her. Maybe he felt even more than that for her. Jamie never felt she had the right to ask. But she didn't want to see her dead.

"Jamie," Josh said, nodding toward the body under the sheet. "It's Doc."

Doc was a living legend, affectionately known as the Old Man, because he was the most experienced agent they had. Rough and tough and intimidating as hell, but the first guy you wanted on your side in any kind of fight. He and Dan had always been the backbone of the agency, both of them in it from its beginnings.

Now Doc was gone.

"Hey?" Josh grabbed her by the arms and held her tightly. "I'm sorry. I know this is hard for you, but I don't have time to mince words right now. We've got work to do, Jamie, and I need you with me."

She nodded, knowing he'd sacrificed precious time by coming to her apartment himself to tell her the news about Dan, knowing he was through covering for her. She'd have to start acting like an agent again, and not a woman who—

She took a deep breath. "I'll get myself together," she promised.

His hand settled on her shoulder. "I know you will."

Jamie forced herself to think. Her friend and colleague had lost his life. How had that happened? Why? "Someone got inside?" she said, scarcely able to believe it.

"Yeah. The whole thing's blown wide-open."

Josh turned and headed down another hallway. She followed him, still struggling to decide what this meant. "The men we were guarding? The scientists?"

"One of them's gone," he said dryly.

"Gone?" She considered the possibilities. "Dead? Kidnapped? What?"

"I don't know yet. Tanner's at the scene trying to sort it out. And you and I have to work it from this end."

Jamie looked to the end of the hallway and saw yet another pair of military guards outside another treatment room and began to realize the scope of the disaster that had befallen Division One. In its illustrious five-year history, the agency had never lost an agent in the field. Until tonight.

Nodding toward the room in front of them, Josh said bleakly, "Geri's in there."

"All three of them?"

Josh nodded, then turned his attention to the new set of guards.

Jamie was stunned. How was it possible that three agents had gone down in one night?

True, the work they did was dangerous, and there'd been more close calls than usual of late. Some of the more cynical, more experienced agents said the agency was due—for disaster. Things had been too good for too long, and it couldn't possibly last.

But this? Despite her years in the military, Jamie had never seen a disaster of this magnitude hit so close to her, to people she worked with. Oh, God, she thought. She couldn't think about that. Not tonight. Not when she was feeling so shaky already. Work, she thought. This was about work. Doc was dead, Dan was in surgery, and Geri was hurt, too.

"What in the world happened out there?" she asked.

"That's what you and I have to find out," Josh said as he pushed open the treatment room doors. Inside, a burly male nurse stopped them. Josh flashed his ID and started explaining who they were and what they were doing.

"Josh?" A weakened voice called out.

Jamie turned toward the woman lying on the gurney. Geri's eyes were glazed with pain, her face incredibly pale, her speech slurred. Two people were working over her right shoulder, which was packed with blood-soaked gauze. Jamie went to the gurney and put her hand on Geri's other shoulder. "We're right here, Geri."

"Dan?" she said weakly.

"Upstairs. In surgery." Knowing the next question that would follow, Jamie pushed onward. "Doc is dead."

Geri's brows crinkled and her eyes worked to focus on Jamie's face. "They got inside?"

Jamie nodded. "Who? Who got inside?"

"Kids. Gang kids." Breathlessly, she gave a quick description of the colors they wore, the car they'd driven, the two teenage boys and the girl she'd seen.

It didn't make sense. A gang of teenage hoods coming after a trio of government scientists? Why? Before she could ask anything else, the nurse stepped in and motioned her away.

"Geri," Jamie added, "we're going upstairs. To check on Dan."

Tears seeped out of the corners of her closed eyes. "My fault," she said weakly. "Dan? It was all my fault."

Jamie felt a rush of anger. If that was true... If it had been Geri's fault... No, she thought. Geri was in shock. More than likely, she wasn't thinking clearly. There'd be time for questions later. Time for answers. For now, she had a job to do.

Jamie waited until she and Josh were alone in the elevator before she said anything else. She was running on pure adrenaline now, on her training, her determination and her sense of justice. She was strong and capable, and the man upstairs fighting for his life had trained her well. She wouldn't fall apart now.

"This doesn't make sense," she told Josh, thinking like an agent now. "A teenage gang? So intent on breaking into a government lab, they made it through three armed federal agents?"

"No way in hell," Josh said.

"No," she repeated. "No way."

Chapter 3

Bone-tired, Jamie sat in a straight-backed chair in the hallway. Bent forward at the waist, elbows on her knees, head in her hands, she stared at the floor.

She'd been waiting for hours. So much time had passed before they even knew Dan had pulled through surgery, so many more before the doctor could say with any confidence that he would make it through the night.

A bullet had ripped through his side and struck a glancing blow to his spine. Jamie had stood like a statue as she listened to the surgeons go through the litany of possibilities, all of them bad. Very easily, he could have bled to death in the alley near the warehouse. He had arrived at the hospital with no measurable heartbeat and no spontaneous respiration. His heart had stopped twice more on the operating table. A weaker man would have died already. But Dan Reese had never been weak. He was in top physical condition and possessed a will of iron.

It was nearly six o'clock in the morning, a little more

than twenty-four hours after the shooting. He'd made it this far, and she had to believe he would live.

Jamie had had someone pull his personnel file. His ex-wife was still listed as his nearest relative, and Jamie had called the woman, who hadn't sounded particularly upset. Her exact words had been, "It was bound to happen sooner or later." She wouldn't be coming to the hospital. Jamie had also left a message for his brother, who lived in California and hadn't yet returned her call.

Josh was out somewhere, using what little information they had and searching for the people who did this. Jamie had been shuttling back and forth between the hospital, the office and the scene of the crime, the pace frantic, her nerves frayed to the breaking point. She was worried, angry, and more tired than she'd ever been in her life.

At the sound of footsteps in the hallway, she sat up, pulling back her shoulders and lifting her chin as yet another doctor came out of Dan's room in an isolated corner of the surgical intensive care unit. Jamie stood on legs that still trembled and tried to read the expression on the doctor's face. She decided he looked every bit as grim as he had all night long.

"Still unconscious?" She hoped that was the extent of it.

"Yes." The doctor held up a hand to silence her. "No need to worry over that yet."

Of course not, Jamie thought. They had so many other things to worry about. The fact that he hadn't awakened yet was several points down on the list. But she couldn't wait in the hall any longer. "I need to be in there, doctor."

"There's no point," he said. "Your friend's unconscious—"

"He's not just my friend," she cut in. "He's my responsibility."

Jamie had already shown the doctor her government ID,

designed to look much like the ones the FBI used. It came in handy when working for an agency that didn't officially exist. Now she lifted one side of her jacket and showed him her weapon as well. "I'm here for his protection," she added.

It was the truth, even if it wasn't her primary motivation in wanting to be inside his room. There was no telling who had come after the government scientists, but they'd been skilled and organized enough to get past three federal agents, and no one was willing to take any chances at this point. If Geri or Dan recognized the shooters, or if they could give the agency some clue as to their whereabouts, someone might be coming after them. So from this point on, they would be under armed military guard.

The doctor sighed. He looked as tired as Jamie felt and not nearly as determined. "All right," he said. "Sit there with him. It can't hurt."

Bracing herself, Jamie pushed open the door and went inside.

Her feelings for this man were hopelessly complicated, but at the moment her desire to see him, to touch him, stemmed from one thing and one thing only—her need to reassure herself that he was truly alive. It hadn't been enough to hear the doctor say it. She had to see him for herself.

Jamie found a chair pushed against the far wall and dragged it to his bedside. Various monitors clustered around him were giving off all sorts of blips and beeps, but she wasn't at all reassured by the sounds. Instead she kept imagining what she would do if they stopped.

It was only when she was sitting down that she risked a glance at the man in the bed. She saw the impression of his toes against the thin sheet, the outline of his legs, one of his hands lying on top of the sheet.

Jamie reached out and touched him, her fingertips meeting his, then let out a shaky breath, relief flooding through her. She sat with her fingers laced through his cold ones, their palms pressed together as she listened to him breathe, the rhythm not as steady as she would have liked. It brought home to her once again that there were no guarantees in life, often no fairness or justice to the things that happened to people on this Earth.

She'd lost people she loved before, had grown up with a father who put his life on the line day after day in service to his country. He'd been wounded three times in his years with the military, and three times he'd survived. And she truly hadn't been afraid to see her brothers follow in his footsteps, hadn't feared for her own life either. She'd been a cadet at the U.S. Naval Academy during the Gulf War. Her father had been over there. So had her brother, Richard, who never made it back home.

Jamie closed her eyes, unable to think of Rich, even now, without crying, unable to think of the way the world simply continued on around them after he was gone, leaving an awful void in their lives, a hole that couldn't be filled. She'd wanted to make the world stop and take notice. Her beloved brother was gone, and she didn't understand how it could have happened—he was too important to her and to her entire family. They needed him, couldn't be expected to go on without him. But, of course, they did somehow.

Seeing Dan like this brought back those memories of her brother. Of losing him. Of feeling shaken to the core. Of wishing she could go back and have just one more day with him, one more hour.

They'd left so many things unsaid.

Her heart told her things simply weren't the same between her and Dan. She'd loved her brother without reservation, had admired him, had cherished him. She admired Dan as well. But she hadn't let herself fall in love with him. How could she? They'd never even been out on a date together. They didn't talk, hadn't gotten to know each other at all outside of work. She couldn't possibly love him.

The potential was there, the connection, the awareness, at least on her part. But they'd never taken the first steps toward each other. Until that kiss.

One kiss, she told herself. She and the man lying so frighteningly still in the hospital bed had shared one kiss. So why did she feel as if she'd nearly lost everything? As if she still could?

During the past twenty-four hours, she'd berated herself a dozen times for all the days they'd wasted, all the times she could have simply gone to him and told him how she felt—it would have been the simplest and the quickest way of finding out how he felt about her. Then she could have moved on with her life somehow, or she could have spent these past years with him. And she would never have found herself in this awful limbo. As it was, she slipped back and forth between a terrible grief over the thought of losing him and the knowledge that he'd never been hers to lose. That her sorrow couldn't possibly be this deep, this overwhelming, for a relationship that had never been.

But she couldn't help the way she felt, couldn't deny that her emotions were raw and exposed, as if someone had taken a knife and cut down to her heart, leaving it bare and totally unprotected against anything that might happen. She needed this man so desperately. Needed him to open his eyes, to give her one of those cynical, sexy smiles of his, and tell her she hadn't been imagining things the night before, when she'd stood in her apartment waiting for him to come to her, waiting for the best part of her life to begin.

It was silly, she told herself, but it was how she felt— the best part of her life would be gone if she lost him.

Jamie had no idea how long she sat there before she saw the expression on his face change, saw his jaw tighten, his mouth stretch into a grimace of pain. "Dan," she said, in case he could hear her now. "It's Jamie. Be still for me, all right?"

Worried that he'd wake abruptly, that training could kick in and he'd perceive her presence as a threat, she sat perfectly still, talking in a low, soothing voice, telling him over and over again who she was and that he shouldn't try to move.

Slowly, his head turned toward hers, his face etched with pain. As his eyes blinked open, she watched him struggle to focus. "Jamie."

"Right here." Forcing a weak smile, she let her hand close over his.

She had to lean close to hear him mumble something that sounded like, "Breakfast?"

Jamie felt hot tears stinging her eyes again and decided he must be half-asleep and dreaming. "You're hungry?"

"No. You and me. Breakfast."

"You stood me up." She nearly choked on the words, forced out in a light tone. The last thing he needed was to see how scared she was.

"Rain check?" he mumbled.

"Name the day," she whispered. "I'll be here."

Dan glanced around the room, saw that they were alone, then looked up at her, waiting. She didn't make him ask, didn't want him to have to expend the energy.

"You're at Bethesda. It's early Monday morning." Which meant he'd lost more than twenty-four hours. She waited and let the news sink in. "Do you remember what happened?"

"Bits and pieces," he mumbled.

"You were shot. In your right side." She'd carried the bullet to the lab herself. "It happened in the district. In an alley near a bunch of rundown buildings on Burns Avenue. We have a safe house there. It was dark and raining and cold. Remember?"

She didn't think he did, thought he'd drifted off again. But his eyes slid open again. "Geri?" he said urgently.

Jamie put her hand on his shoulder and let it rest there, told herself it was none of her business what was between the two of them, then answered his question. "She should be in the room next door in an hour or so. She took a bullet in her right shoulder. A couple of specialists have been working to repair nerve damage to her shoulder and her arm."

Looking relieved, he waited, considered, then said. "Why?"

"I don't know how this happened. Or why," she admitted. "I was hoping you could tell me. Tanner said you and Geri were found side by side, about twenty-five feet inside one of the alleys." Deliberately, she left it there, waited to see what he remembered.

Once the sun rose, it was obvious they hadn't been together when the shots were fired. Geri had been shot closer to the street, had apparently crawled to where Dan was found. And there was speculation they'd been shot with their own guns. The agency had been issued special prototypes of weapons that were being considered for use by the FBI, the CIA and some branches of the military. So far, the weapons had performed admirably, with deadly accuracy and force. The bullets they fired were prototypes as well, distinctive and powerful enough to cut through the protective vests agents wore. None of those weapons had been found at the scene, or among the agents' personal possessions.

Despite what the evidence said, Jamie couldn't imagine a suspect getting Dan's own gun away from him. "Why were you in the alley?" she asked him.

Why had they left their post in the shelter of the enclosed doorway for the vast open spaces of the street? If someone was trying to get inside the building, Dan and Geri would have gone inside and fought off the intruders from there.

Restless, Dan tried to shift his weight to the right just a bit. Jamie saw a quick stab of pain flicker across his face. An eerie stillness came over him.

"Jamie? Where did they find the bullet?"

Her eyes filled with tears. She squeezed his hand. This was going to be so hard on him. "Near your spine."

When she dared to look at him again, he was watching her, watching the tears roll down her cheeks, and she was the one who had to look away.

He was alive, she told herself. For hours she'd offered up hurried, desperate prayers for him. *Please, just let him live.* She hadn't asked for anything else, hadn't let herself think beyond his survival.

Jamie felt movement on the bed, heard a grunt of pain. Turning, she saw that he'd lifted his head off the mattress to stare down at his body. She put her hands against his shoulders and pushed him back down again.

"You had surgery," she said sharply. "You have stitches, and you're going to tear them loose if you try anything like that again."

He ignored her, gave his own orders instead. "Grab my toes."

Jamie froze. This was what she feared most, once she let herself believe he would live. "Dan, please."

"Move the sheet out of the way and put your hand on my toes."

"Listen to me. It's too soon to know anything for certain. The bullet hit one of the vertebrae in your lower back. It didn't sever the spinal cord, but it did chip the bone, and some of the bone fragments ended up in the cord. The surgeon said there's a lot of swelling in the area, and until the swelling goes down, there's no way to know whether you'll have any permanent damage."

"My toes. If you don't do it, I will."

He used the voice she'd come to hate when he was her instructor, the one she'd obeyed without question and had later been grateful to hear in her head when things got intense and instinct alone could save her. Sometimes it seemed as if he *was* her instincts, that the things he'd taught her were so deeply ingrained he might easily be beside her, guiding her through the worst of it.

He needed her now. If she'd wakened in this bed unable to feel her legs, she'd want someone to do this for her. She'd want him beside her, want him to be honest with her, as well. Jamie went to the foot of his bed. Pulling back the sheet, she found his right foot and clasped her fingers tightly around it.

"Got it?" he said tightly.

"Yes."

"Squeeze."

She did.

He showed no response.

"Dan, I would never lie to you. The doctor said just because you don't feel anything now doesn't mean—"

"Higher," he insisted. "Move your hand higher. My leg. My knee."

Sighing, her fingers trembling, she did.

"Higher," he insisted again.

Her hand slid to his thigh, tracing muscles she knew to be rock-solid and so very strong. He'd always moved faster than anyone she knew. He climbed higher, kept going when men ten years younger had given out. What would he do if he couldn't run or jump or walk anymore?

"Keep going," he ordered.

She pulled back the sheet carefully, because she suspected he wasn't wearing anything, found a strip of bare skin along the side of his hip and his abdomen, slid her hand along his side. In all the times she'd imagined touching him, it had never been like this.

"There," he said grimly, when her palm was pressed against his smooth, flat stomach. She let it rest there while she forced herself to look him in the eye once again. His features could easily have been set in stone.

"Nothing?" she asked.

He shook his head.

"Give it twenty-four hours. Maybe forty-eight. There's no way to know for sure until that much time has passed," she insisted, battling her own emotions now.

"Jamie? Your hand?"

"What?"

"You can take your hand away now."

She looked down at her fingers, pale against his sunbrowned skin, and felt again that this must be a bad dream. If she could only wake up, everything would be fine.

A day and a half ago, he'd held her body pressed against his, had kissed her as if he'd never get enough of her. He was going to come to her in the morning. Anything could have happened in the morning.

It still could, Jamie told herself, as long as she didn't let him push her away. She had always fought her feelings for him, instead of fighting to make him hers. She wouldn't give up so easily now. Jamie let her hand slide over his rib cage, dodging the pads and wires of the cardiac monitors attached to his chest, until her hand was right over his heart.

"Please," she said. "Don't shut me out now."

Dan swore softly and viciously.

"Sunday morning…" she began.

"Forget about Sunday morning," he said, catching her hand with surprising strength and shoving it away from him.

"I can't forget." She would never forget, wouldn't let him, either.

"It never happened, Jamie," he said harshly. "It doesn't matter, because it never happened."

"Which means what? That it never will? That whatever you were going to say was nothing more than some reckless impulse? That because you didn't get the chance to say it then, it's of no importance now? I don't believe that."

"I can't help what you believe."

She flinched, unable to help herself, because it hurt. Even knowing what he was doing and why, his words still cut into her.

"Jamie, get the doctor." His tone was softer now, weariness creeping in.

"I will, but…"

He shook his head, the look in his eyes as bleak and as determined as any she'd ever seen. Too weary to fight him any longer, too upset to hold herself together any longer, she turned and left.

Dan held himself rigidly under control until he forced her from his room.

Turning his head, he looked through the open door. He saw Josh standing in the hallway, opening his arms, saw Jamie go to him, saw the other man's arms close around her. Her shoulders started to shake, and Dan could hear the hushed sounds of her sobbing. He watched as Josh pushed her head down to his shoulder, as his fingers stroked through her pretty, dark hair. Dan watched until the door slid into place, mercifully blocking his view.

They looked good together, he decided. They seemed comfortable with each other, seemed to care for each other, as well.

He couldn't help but wonder if Josh ever kissed her like a madman and scared her half to death. If Josh had, Dan wondered how she'd responded. If her body could possibly have been as soft and yielding as it had been in his arms.

If she tasted as intoxicatingly sweet and made those sexy little sounds of pleasure deep in her throat—for Josh. As murderously angry as Dan felt at the thought of her and Josh together, he'd forget about her if he could, even if it meant pushing her right into Josh's arms. She would be better off with him, the pretty boy, closer to her age, who so readily made women laugh and charmed them with easy words. There was nothing bitter about Josh, nothing cynical, nothing inside him that was remotely old or worn down, and Jamie, who was so young and so beautiful, still untouched by the harsher realities of the life they'd chosen, deserved someone like that. Dan had felt that way long before he was shot, long before he ever contemplated the possibility that he might have to go through the rest of his life unable to stand on his own two feet.

He believed her when she told him there was nothing between her and Josh but friendship. But that didn't mean the relationship couldn't change into something more. That scene in the hallway had him wondering if it already had, at least on Josh's part.

For her sake, Dan would forget what might have happened between them if he'd made it to her apartment Sunday morning.

He felt a whish of air, saw that a man he suspected was his doctor had entered the room. Dan ignored him, his gaze moving unerringly to Jamie. She was staring right back at him, even as she stood there pressed against Josh's side. From the look on her face, he knew he'd hurt her. But no matter how much he wanted her by his side now, he wouldn't allow her to feel any misplaced sense of obligation toward him. After all, nothing had happened between them.

Tired, Dan turned his attention to the doctor. It was difficult to concentrate, to follow all the technical terms the doctor used, but Dan caught the gist of it. He had something called spinal shock. The force of the bullet had driven slivers of the chipped vertebra into his spine, bone chips the doctors had successfully removed. But the spinal cord had been nicked. It was irritated and swollen. There was a possibility that nerves had been damaged, a chance he would be able to feel his legs but not move them, a chance he could move them but not feel them. A chance that the swelling would go down and he would be fine. A chance that even with months of physical therapy his body would never again work the way it once had. And as Jamie had said earlier, there was nothing to do but wait to see what he could and couldn't do.

Other than that, the doctor said, he was lucky. The bullet had nicked a few other organs before digging into his back, but somehow he hadn't bled to death and the shock hadn't killed him.

Lucky? He couldn't feel anything below his belly button and didn't quite see how that made him lucky. But he didn't feel up to arguing with the doctor, either. So he closed his eyes and let himself drift away, half-asleep, half-awake. Dan thought he'd known what it was to be afraid. But he'd never felt more alone, never felt such stark terror.

If he couldn't walk...

Someone was with him, sitting beside him. There was a small, soft hand tucked into his. He thought he smelled a hint of scented soap or lotion that was hauntingly familiar.

Jamie.

Dan knew he should send her away, for her own sake. But he didn't have the energy. Maybe he didn't have the courage, either. Tomorrow, when he was stronger and not feeling so absolutely alone, he would send her back into Josh's arms, where she belonged.

Chapter 4

It was painfully apparent at the memorial service for Doc three days later that the agency was his family. He'd never married, never had children, had few friends outside his work. In the pouring rain, agency personnel and a few colleagues from his days in the army stood huddled together under a tent erected at the gravesite.

Jamie knew she didn't want to end up all alone like Doc. She wanted to have babies, a husband to grow old with. The agency was fine for now; she was young. She enjoyed the challenge, the excitement. But it would never take the place of her family.

She glanced down the rows of somber faces and felt the horror of the situation take hold once again. Doc was truly gone. Dan's life was still hanging by a thread, due to a post-operative infection that had proven especially difficult, given the shock his body had suffered. He'd lapsed into unconsciousness soon after the doctor told him the extent of the damage to his body and hadn't awakened since. Geri was going to be okay eventually, and the agency had screwed up its biggest case ever.

Abruptly, Jamie realized the crowd was moving, some people rushing for cars, others turning to talk to those around them. The service was over. Lost in thought, she'd missed the end of it. Pulling herself back to the present, she nodded at several of her colleagues. Andy Wade, a techno wizard affectionately known as the gadget master; Jack Malone, a communications expert; Chris Reynolds, an expert in acquiring and forging credentials allowing them access to just about any place in the world. She turned to head out the other way, thinking it might be less congested, and found herself face-to-face with Amanda Wainwright, who was on the secretarial staff.

"Jamie, how's Dan?"

She took a breath and forced out the words. "Hanging on."

With tears in her eyes, Amanda nodded. Standing next to her was a tall, slender man Jamie recognized. "Rob?"

"I'm sorry," Amanda said, turning to the man at her side. "This is my fiancé. Rob Jansen. Rob, you remember Jamie Douglass?"

"Of course," he said, shaking her hand.

He was with the FBI, but he'd spent the previous summer at Division One establishing a specialized, direct computer link between Division One and some of the FBI databases. And he'd been smitten immediately with Amanda Wainwright, and she with him.

Jamie had been the one who'd introduced them. It was something for which he claimed he would be forever in her debt. She hadn't seen him since.

"It's good to see you again, Rob."

"You, too," he said.

Jamie remembered that their wedding date was just

around the corner. "I hope the two of you will be very happy together."

"Thanks," Amanda said. "If there's anything we can do for Dan…"

"Pray," she suggested.

"Of course. I will."

Jamie excused herself. She was on the edge of the crowd, ready to make a run for her car, when she ran into the agency's director, John Mitchell. Instinct and a military background made her jump to attention. "Sir," she said.

"Anything new to report on our investigation?" he demanded.

"The lab has gone over the ballistics evidence twice more," she said. "They're confident their first findings are correct. Both agents outside the warehouse were shot with the same weapon, with one of the prototypes we're using."

"We still haven't recovered any of them?" he asked.

"No, sir."

"And we don't know which agent's weapon was used?"

"No, sir."

"Is your second agent conscious yet?"

"No."

He scowled. "You should know, Ms. Douglass, that except for the internal review of the shooting, we're off the case."

Jamie kept her expression carefully blank. She heard right before the funeral service began that Mitchell and her direct supervisor, Martin Tanner, had spent the morning in the Oval Office, getting a tongue-lashing from the Commander-in-Chief himself. Apparently, the president was so angry about the bungled mission, he'd stripped the agency of any responsibility in locating the missing scientist, whose fingerprints were on a Colt .45 found six blocks from the scene, the one used to kill Doc.

She hadn't wanted to believe it was true, that the agency

didn't have the right to go find the man who shot and killed their own colleague. But Mitchell had just confirmed it. He glared at Jamie for another long minute, then, in an intensely intimidating voice said, ''Don't screw up this investigation.''

''No, sir.''

Martin Tanner walked up to them a moment later, nodded, shook hands with Mitchell, then turned to her. ''I just spoke with one of Dan's doctors. His vital signs are improving. They think he's close to regaining consciousness.''

God, she'd give anything just to see him open his eyes.

''I'll get right over there,'' she said, then turned and fled.

Twenty minutes later, her expression carefully blank, chin up, shoulders thrown back, she flashed her ID at the two guards stationed at the first checkpoint just off the main corridor of the hospital.

''Any problems?'' she asked crisply.

''No, ma'am,'' they chorused, eyeing her curiously, still a little uneasy about following the directives of a woman.

She'd learned early on how to take orders, more recently how to give them. Calmly, authoritatively, without hesitation. If she expected the people under her to carry out those orders with any confidence, they had to believe she knew exactly what she was doing. More often than not, she did.

But this…

Jamie rounded another corner and found herself in a narrow, deserted corridor, bordered at either end by a ninety-degree turn. She was less than fifty yards from Dan's room when she put her back to the wall, sagged weakly against it and concentrated for a moment on simply breathing in and out.

The past four days had been crazy. Every time the phone rang, every time her pager went off, she wondered if that would be the message she'd been dreading. That Dan was gone.

And now she was going to see him—a man clinging stubbornly to life who seemingly wanted nothing to do with her. If she had any pride left, she would pull herself together, and he would see nothing but an agent doing her job.

Jamie heard footsteps coming down the hall toward her. She snapped to attention and found herself face-to-face with one of the legion of specialists working on Dan's case. "Dr. Richardson?" she said. "How is he?"

"He's awake, Ms. Douglass."

Her only reaction was a quick, deep breath. "And?"

"He's still weak, in a lot of pain and on a great deal of medication. I expect he'll be fading in and out of consciousness for another day or so."

"I have to see him," she said, the demand instinctive.

"Fine." The doctor nodded. "Make it quick. And don't wear him out."

"Yes, sir," she said, walking briskly toward the door to his room.

Another pair of guards snapped to attention at her approach. She flashed her ID, and at their nod, pushed open the door to Dan's room. Calling on every bit of her training, she paused just inside the doorway to steady herself, then walked slowly toward the bed.

Dan turned his head slowly at her approach, his only reaction to seeing her a tightening of his jaw before he looked away and his eyelids drifted down. She quickly took note of his ashen face; she was still afraid he might die.

But she got set to work. She'd come here with a job to do, one she truly hated at the moment. Clearing her throat, she sat down, opened the briefcase she carried, found a notebook and a pen. "Dan, I need to know what happened."

His voice weak, he rattled off an amazingly detailed description of two young men and a girl he'd seen that night. Jamie took notes, looking for discrepancies between his recollection of the suspects and Geri's, looking for additional details he remembered that Geri hadn't mentioned. Jamie would have preferred to let him work with a sketch artist on his own to come up with a drawing, but it might be days before he was strong enough to do that. So she pulled out the composites made from Geri's descriptions and held them up for him to see.

"Look at this," she whispered, thinking he might have drifted off already. "Is this one of the people you saw that night?"

His eyes opened, stared, then he nodded.

"And this one?" It wasn't nearly as detailed, but it was all they had.

"That's him."

"The girl?" She held up the final drawing, of a young, vulnerable-looking girl.

"Her hair's longer. Fuller. She had a small scar...." He touched his index finger to the right side of his mouth. "Here. She was too thin. Had a busted lip. A bruised cheek..."

"How old?" Jamie asked. "Sixteen?"

"Maybe. Maybe younger. Did you pick them up yet?"

"No."

As Jamie finished writing up her notes on the descriptions, she was dreading what she had to do next. She wasn't sure how much he had seen, how much he remembered, and she didn't want to be the one who told him about Doc. She also didn't want to sit in judgment of him and the actions he'd taken that night, but Tanner had put her squarely in the middle of it. She had no choice.

There was a slight tremor in her right hand as she pulled

a miniature tape recorder from her briefcase and placed it on the table by his bed.

When she looked down at Dan again, he was sleeping.

Two hours later, she was back in his room. She'd spent the time thinking about how to handle this, and decided that all she could do was steer clear of anything personal. Maybe, when the job was done, he would talk to her. Maybe he would let her be his friend, if nothing else.

She sank into the chair at the side of his bed. He looked better now, she thought, more alert, and not so very weak. Though still not glad to see her.

"Sorry I faded out on you," he said.

"It's all right." She found her pen, her notebook and her tape recorder again. There was no way to stall any longer. "Mitchell's ordered a Section 123 investigation into the shooting."

"One twenty-three?" he repeated, staring at her, at the tape recorder in her hand.

She nodded.

He knew exactly what that entailed. After all, he'd written many of the rules and regulations that governed the agency.

Section 123 was a rarely used formal internal investigation triggered when an agent or a civilian was seriously injured or killed during an agency operation. It was about deciding who was at fault, about laying blame—reviewing an agent's judgment or actions to discover whether orders were disregarded, basic safety procedures not followed, or the lives of others recklessly or carelessly endangered. It was the kind of investigation that had the power to end careers. Or worse, to find one person responsible for the death of another.

God, she didn't want to do this to him. Or to anyone.

Daring to look him in the eye, she saw that he was more

alert, more focused than she'd seen him at any time since the shooting.

"What happened?" he said tightly.

"You know how this works. You tell me," she said, clicking on the recorder. She could almost see the thoughts racing through his head, the questions he would fire at her as soon as she was done asking hers. He gave her what she needed, quickly, succinctly recounting the events of that night.

It had been 2:23 a.m. when a car, a four-door, late-model white sedan with darkly tinted windows, the stereo blaring, stopped at a traffic signal on the west side of the warehouse. The passenger-side door opened. A girl was shoved from the car. She screamed as she landed hard on the pavement. The first suspect climbed out of the car. He pulled her to her feet, smacked her across the face with his gun, then put it to her head.

"You thought they were going to kill the girl?" Jamie asked. That point was critical.

"Yeah. Geri and I took off to try to stop it."

"Both of you?"

"Yes," he insisted.

Jamie didn't believe him. It was the first discrepancy between his version of the events leading up to the shooting and Geri's, and it was a crucial point. "Both of you decided to leave your posts to try to save the girl?"

"Yes."

"But Geri got there first?"

"I took the time to call Doc on the radio to tell him what we were doing." The look Dan threw Jamie's way as he spoke told her she wouldn't shake him on that point. He knew exactly what she was getting at, and he knew the tape recorder was running. He wouldn't say anything else for the tape.

Frustrated, Jamie continued. "When you told Doc what you were doing, he acknowledged that message?"

"Yes."

"You're sure? You're sure it was his voice you heard?"

Dan's arm came out, shoving the recorder aside. It tumbled off the bed and clattered to the floor. His voice dangerously quiet, he growled, "What the hell happened out there?"

Jamie could tell by the look on his face, the worry in his eyes, that he knew something terrible had happened, something worse than the injuries he'd sustained. To give herself time to think, she bent over to find the tape, checked to see that it was still working, then carefully placed it on the bed beside him again.

He and Doc had been close. They'd worked together off and on for fifteen years. There was no way to spare him, no way to cushion the blow.

"What happened, Jamie?" he said, more forcefully this time.

"You know I can't tell you that until you tell me everything you know first."

He stared at her. Four years ago, the fiercely determined look on his face would have left her shaking in her shoes. Even today, if it came to a test of wills between them, she would lose. And it was silly to go up against him when she knew she would lose.

"I'm sorry," she added, not knowing what else to say. "I hate this as much as you do. Please, just answer the questions and then I'll tell you everything I know. Doc acknowledged the message?"

"Yes," he said tightly.

Jamie started the tape again. "What happened then?"

In a clipped, dry tone, he told her. Jamie closed her eyes, envisioning the alley as she'd seen it near dawn, about twenty-four hours after the shooting. It would have been even darker the morning he'd been there, the sky covered with thick clouds, the rain falling, the streets slick and all but deserted. She could see Geri running, Dan chasing after her. Geri tackled the man holding the girl, had him pinned to the ground. The girl got up and ran into the alley, and Dan went after her. He tried to reassure her that she had nothing to fear from him, that she was safe. And then a figure appeared through the fog and the rain, a gun in his hand. The girl they'd gone to rescue disappeared into the early morning darkness, and Dan felt something slam into his side, felt his head connect solidly with the pavement, and then everything went black.

Jamie had been to the scene, had seen the traces of blood on the pavement that the rain hadn't washed away, had reconstructed it in her mind the way she thought it happened. But listening to it now, in his own words, it was even more real.

So close, she thought. All of them had come so close to dying. And she was supposed to make sense of it all somehow.

They ran through it three times, and she still hadn't been able to get him to admit that Geri had been the one to take off after the girl, leaving Dan with the difficult choice of watching her run headlong into danger or going to help her. Geri readily admitted it, but even when Jamie told Dan, it didn't sway him on his version of the story. He knew what was at stake, and he'd decided to protect Geri, even though it might mean his career.

Jamie turned her attention to the weapons. "When you took off after the suspects, where was your weapon?"

"In my hand."

"And when the second suspect emerged from the alley with his gun drawn? Where was your weapon then?"

"At my back. The girl was hysterical, and I didn't think I had a chance of calming her down with a gun in my hand. So I tucked it into the waistband of my pants, at my back, so she wouldn't see it."

"So the second suspect—"

"Walked right up to me. He would have put a bullet between my eyes if Geri hadn't drawn his attention away from me for a second."

"She took the first shot?"

He paused. "I'm not sure."

"Think about it," she urged. "Did Geri have a shot? Did she take it?"

He shook his head back and forth. "She was behind me. There's no way for me to know whether she had a shot or who fired. I was too busy watching a kid shove his gun into my face. Something drew his attention away from me for a split second. I think it was Geri. I dived to the left, in case I was blocking her shot, and grabbed for my gun. But it was too late. I heard shots, felt a kick in my right side. That was it."

"Two shots? Three? How many?"

"Three, I think."

"From behind you? Or in front of you?"

"I'm not sure."

"Dan—"

"It was over in a split second," he cut in. "I heard shots. I felt a bullet digging into my side, and everything went black. There's nothing after that."

"Nothing?" she said again.

He looked directly at her, somehow seeming less like the agent and more like the man he so seldom let her see. Something eased inside of him, the tight control slipping, a warm, gentle heat coming into his eyes.

His voice softened, the hard edge all but gone, as he added, "Not until I looked up and saw your face."

She wanted to believe it, wanted to believe he'd let down his guard and told her something he didn't intend to admit. All of a sudden, the situation took on an intimacy that had no place here. He'd made this personal, when before he'd fought to make it anything but that.

Why, she wondered?

He didn't do anything by accident, and he so seldom made mistakes.

She felt his hand close over hers, the touch gentle and warm and somehow terribly intimate. It was welcome, but so very out of character, as well.

Why?

She could guess. That he'd done it deliberately, calculatingly, would use any means available to him to influence the investigation. Even by using the way she felt about him?

She flinched. Because it hurt to think he'd use her that way. To think he was so good at playing games, he nearly got away with it. She wanted so badly to believe he cared about her that he nearly got away with it.

Angrily, she shut off the tape again, heedless of the fact that she was destroying the credibility of the interview. Maybe she could get one of their audio experts to edit out the breaks in the sequence, so that if she ever had to produce her copy of this interview for one of her superiors, it wouldn't be obvious they'd started and stopped the tape again and again. At this point, she didn't care. She just wanted to get through this, hopefully without screaming at him.

"Tell me what happened, Jamie," he said softly, playing with her again.

Closing her eyes, she heard that same seductive voice, low and compelling, from lips so close to hers. She was remembering the night before disaster struck. She felt the hot brush of his tongue sweeping through her mouth, finally knew how it felt to be cradled close to that big, powerful body of his. Felt the full-blown force of his masculine charms focused intently on her.

Did I frighten you? he'd whispered intently.

He'd meant it then, she told herself. That night had been real. He'd kissed her hungrily, greedily, because he hadn't been able to help himself, and he'd honestly worried he'd somehow frightened her.

Today, lying here battered and bruised, he'd used the same tone of voice deliberately to distract her from the business at hand. To throw her off-balance by letting her think it meant something to him to wake up, after nearly dying a half-dozen times, and find her sitting by his side. To have her face be the first he saw.

He was willing to use her feelings for him, because that was the kind of agent he was. It was the kind of agent he'd trained her to be.

Jamie could still see him so clearly in class that day so long ago. Being a woman in this business put her at a disadvantage in terms of strength and quickness, and she had to compensate for those disadvantages any way she could.

Use it, he'd whispered, standing much too close, crowding her with his body, sending an unmistakably sexual heat sizzling toward her. *Use everything you have. Everything you know. Everything another person might have the misfortune to feel. Because your first objective is to get the job done. Any way you can.*

It had been amazing, seeing him turn on the power of his masculinity like that, all in the name of making a point and teaching her a lesson.

Fine, she thought bitterly. She'd show him his lessons hadn't been in vain.

She leaned close, let herself smile at him, let herself wish she had the right to press her lips against his, to let him set her body on fire.

"I can play this game just as well as you can," she said softly, then let the anger come into play as well. "Because you taught me how to do it. So if you want to go at this as adversaries, that's how we'll do it."

Chapter 5

"Jamie," he began, giving a credible portrayal of a man who regretted what he'd just done.

Or regretted the fact that he'd gotten caught.

"Don't," she said, a reckless anger rushing through her veins and helping her to block out the sight of him lying in the bed hooked up to all sorts of tubes and wires. "Don't lie to me, either. Geri and I have been through all of this. I know she's the one who took off after the girl, even after you told her it was likely a setup. I know she ignored your warning to stay where she was and ran into the street."

"You can't prove that," he said, maddeningly calm. "It's nothing but my word against hers."

Anger was a truly reckless emotion, she discovered. And she was frighteningly angry. "Geri said she had a clear shot at the suspect who shot you, but she didn't take it. She said she couldn't quite make herself take out what looked like a fifteen-year-old boy."

"Are you telling me you could have? Are you saying you would have done anything differently that night?"

"I wasn't there," she argued. "It doesn't matter what I would have done."

"It matters if you're going to sit in judgment of her. You have to ask yourself what would a reasonable person have done in that situation? What would you have done?"

"How can you defend her like this? You nearly died, Dan."

"I didn't die," he pointed out, as if that was all that mattered.

Jamie was fuming. "You didn't die?" she repeated incredulously. "What the hell is that supposed to mean? No harm done? That you don't hold her responsible for what happened—"

"I don't," he insisted.

"So the agency shouldn't either?" Jamie continued. "You think this is just about you? About nothing except how you feel? Or what you've lost?"

"I'm the one lying in this bed," he pointed out. "I'm the one who can't move a muscle from here down."

He touched his hand to his hipbone and made a sweeping downward motion. Jamie felt cold and weak and dizzy, all at once. She must have made some sound, something that drew his gaze to her. She felt her eyes flood with moisture, felt unable to hide anything from him then.

She hadn't asked what, if anything, he felt. Because she didn't think she was ready to hear his answer. But it had been more than forty-eight hours since the doctors dug the bone fragments out of his spine. The swelling would have disappeared by now.

He still couldn't feel anything, and he'd chosen to just blurt it out to her. Deliberately, she reminded herself, cruelly. She'd never known him to be cruel. Cynical, sarcastic, chauvinistic, self-confident to a fault, but not cruel. Jamie leaned back in her chair, finding herself in need of its support, feeling utterly weary and inadequate to the task she'd been given.

"Go ahead," she invited, weary of sparring with him with words. "Get it out. Say whatever you want to say."

He swore viciously, succinctly, then looked away. "I blame myself for this as much as I blame Geri, and, yes, I think my opinion should carry some weight. Lay off Geri. She's saved my butt more than once, and I don't want her hung out to dry over this."

"Dan..." she began. "You don't understand. This isn't just about what happened to you."

"What do you think it's about? *Us?*"

"No, I'm not talking about us."

"Jamie, there is no *us*. So don't sit there thinking we've lost anything or that Geri's to blame. Don't make this out to be some great tragedy, either, just because we never got to finish what we started."

She flinched. "I'll try to work on that," she said. "I'll try to learn not to give a damn about anybody. The way you do."

"What did you think was going to happen, Jamie?" he said wearily.

She closed her eyes tightly, trying to hold back the tears.

"We would've had sex, all right?" he blurted out. "Probably really good sex. For a while. But it wouldn't have lasted, and it wouldn't have meant anything. At least not to me. It never does to me."

"Are you trying to hurt me?" she asked, her voice quiet and throaty and much too weak. "Or to make me hate you? Because you should know that you're doing a really good job of it."

Satisfied, she saw that she'd finally managed to silence him, although it had come too late in this war of words to be considered a victory. She hated sinking to his level. But she was tired of being manipulated and insulted and hurt, and she struck back, going at him in the same way he'd come at her.

"Doc is dead," she said.

"What?"

"He's dead," she repeated, watching the emotions flicker across his face, reading them easily in the seconds it took for him to control his reaction.

It occurred to her that by springing the news on him like that, she'd done precisely what he'd always told her to do. She had knowledge he didn't possess, and she'd used it to learn what she needed to know, in spite of how he might feel.

And she'd accomplished one thing. She knew now he hadn't known about Doc.

"I'm sorry," she said sincerely. "I know the two of you were close."

He turned away from her then. She wouldn't have thought it possible, but his face turned even paler than it was before. She sat beside him without saying another word as the minutes ticked by.

Finally, he asked, "What happened?"

"Apparently one of the scientists we were guarding that night shot him."

"What?"

"A Dr. Alexander Hathaway, an American working for a government contractor. He was inside the lab that night. There were no signs of forced entry into the lab, his fingerprints on the door. He opened it from the inside and walked away. No one's seen him since then," she explained. "His fingerprints were on the gun used to kill Doc."

"So it was a setup."

She nodded.

"And we walked right into it."

"I know you and Geri both thought the shooters were

kids from one of the local gangs. But we think they must have been foreign agents, most likely affiliated with some terrorist group.''

''Why?''

''Apparently Hathaway's discovered some sort of terrorists' dream weapon. We don't know much more than that.''

''How the hell are we supposed to find him if we don't even know what he discovered?''

''We're not supposed to find him. The FBI and the CIA caught the case. Word at the office is that the president himself ordered us out of it, because he was so angry we lost Hathaway in the first place.''

Jamie waited, knowing it was a lot to take in all at once. She'd had four days, and she still could hardly believe all that had happened.

''So they're keeping this quiet?'' Dan asked. ''No APB? No local law enforcement? Just CIA and FBI?''

''Hathaway's on top of the FBI's most wanted list, but for killing a federal agent. There hasn't been any mention of top-secret research being missing, although I'm sure the whole thing will come out if Hathaway isn't found quickly. I don't know what kind of progress has been made, but whatever Hathaway was working on has the Pentagon scared to death.''

''I didn't know,'' Dan said. ''I had no idea…''

''I know.'' Jamie picked up the tape recorder one last time and clicked it on. ''I just need to clarify a few things. When you left the front doors of the warehouse, you radioed Doc first?''

''Yes.''

''It was his voice that answered? You're sure?''

''Yes.''

''He never gave you any indication something was wrong?''

''No,'' he said, then paused to think. ''Wait, I did know

something was wrong. When I caught up with the girl, Geri had the guy who'd been holding the gun on the girl. We were in the alley. Too far back to see the front of the warehouse. I tried to reach Doc on the radio to tell him what happened, but he didn't answer.''

"What happened next?"

"I got shot."

"How long between the time you left the warehouse doors and the time you tried to raise Doc and he didn't answer?"

"Thirty seconds, maybe."

Jamie nodded, knowing what he was doing. Measuring the distance from memory, thinking of how fast he'd been running, of how much ground he could cover at various speeds. She'd run the distance herself the day before from the warehouse doors to the spot where he'd been found.

It would have taken split-second timing. Hathaway had to know they were coming for him. He had to be in communication with them, had to be ready to take Doc out as soon as his accomplices drew Geri and Dan away from the front of the warehouse, and then disappear.

But was thirty seconds enough time for someone to shoot Doc with a Colt .45, get to the alley, shoot Dan with a prototype gun, then shoot Geri seconds later? Which meant someone was mistaken—or still lying about something. One of them had to have lost their weapon before Dan was shot.

"One last thing," she said. "Your weapon? Think for me. Where was your weapon when you were hit?"

"At my back. Tucked into the waistband of my pants. I had my hand on the handle."

"You're sure."

"Jamie, no one's ever taken my own gun away from me."

That had been her first reaction when she heard the ballistics report. No one would get his weapon away from him. Still, if he had his when he was shot, if Geri had hers as she claimed, if Doc had been at his post inside and nothing out of the ordinary had happened thirty seconds before… It wasn't possible. Ballistics didn't lie.

In this case, the ballistic evidence said Dan and Geri had been shot with a 6 mm, a high-powered bullet used by the prototype weapons the agency was testing. They weren't available on the open market yet. No one else had them, except the manufacturer. Which mean someone was lying. If the weapons were ever located, technicians could fire the weapons and check for markings on the bullets, then use serial numbers to find out which agent's weapon was used in the shooting. But so far, they hadn't recovered the weapons.

Frustrated, Jamie clicked off the tape recorder for the last time.

"Dan, we'll have to go over this again," she cautioned.

"I know."

"Geri's in the next room," she said carefully. "She's been asking to see you. But I can't leave you and Geri alone until…"

He nodded, understanding.

It was basic procedure in investigating a crime. Separate the witnesses, the victims, the suspects, everyone, until all their statements had been taken. Memories were amazingly fluid, even when you didn't have to worry about people making up a story to protect themselves. She was taking a risk, letting Geri in. But she might learn everything she needed to know, as well.

If the situation were reversed, Dan wouldn't hesitate to bring the two of them together, if he thought he'd find out what he needed to know.

"Do you want to see her?" she offered.

"Yes."

Jamie pushed open the door, spoke briefly to the guard. A moment later, Geri, looking oddly vulnerable sitting there in a hospital gown and a robe with her right arm in a sling to immobilize the injury to her shoulder, was there. Jamie dismissed the nurse and pushed the wheelchair to the side of Dan's bed herself.

She took one quick glance at the two of them. Geri's face was anguished, guilt-ridden. And Dan's? Was that compassion she saw? Kindness? Understanding? Concern? He certainly hadn't shown any of those things for her today.

And then she simply couldn't watch any longer. Jamie walked to the door and turned her back on them, praying they would tell her what she needed to know so she could put this whole mess behind her.

Dan knew his partner well. She could be tough as nails when she put her mind to it. She didn't take crap from anyone, didn't lose her cool under pressure. She was a straightforward, strong, tough, extremely capable woman, and he admired her for all those things. He had never seen her cry. He'd made as many mistakes as she had, and he wouldn't let her blame herself entirely for what happened.

"Buck up, soldier," he said.

Geri shook her head sadly. Her face was utterly pale, her eyes glistening with tears.

"Don't," he said softly. "Don't do this to yourself."

He watched as her normally rock-solid composure crumbled, as she fought a losing battle with her emotions. Obviously, kindness wasn't going to cut it here.

"God," he groaned softly, "if I'm doomed to spend the rest of my life surrounded by a bunch of weeping women who are going to fuss over me, or try to take care of me or—even worse—feel sorry for me, I swear I'll throw myself out of the first open window I can find."

From the corner of the room, he saw Jamie flinch. Geri

looked puzzled. There was a brief spark of anger, which he hoped would simmer and grow. But it died out as quickly as it appeared, and she looked hurt all over again.

"It's not going to work, Dan."

He shrugged easily and worked up an uneasy grin. "I had to give it my best try."

Geri nodded, still fighting tears.

He might have to watch her cry, too, because he hadn't let himself look at anything but her sad, pale face. Because he didn't want to see her in that wheelchair, didn't want to think of what his life would be like in one of those.

He most definitely didn't want to think about Doc.

Or Jamie.

So, what was left? He decided to take care of his partner.

"It's as much my fault as yours," he explained.

"No," she insisted.

"Come on, Geri. You know me. If I thought this was your fault, I'd be yelling right now. I'd bring down the plaster on these walls, and your ears would be burning. I am not a nice man or an easy one to work with, and you know that better than anyone."

She shook her head again. Tears slipped from beneath her tightly closed lashes. She bent her head until it rested against the mattress, the top of her head against his right side. Dan knew that because his eyes told him, not his body. It was unnerving to realize he didn't feel the top of her head pressing at his side.

"I'm sorry," Geri whispered. "Dan…I'm so sorry."

Her shoulders started to shake, and Dan made an instinctive move to sit up and take her in his arms, forgetting for another split second that his body no longer responded the way it always had. He swore softly, put his hand on Geri's head to let her know it was okay. She could stay here like this if she needed to. He would do his best to comfort her, as he hadn't allowed himself to comfort the woman standing near the door with her back to him.

God, Jamie, he thought, not letting himself glance in her direction. *Just go away.*

It had been a fantasy, after all. Him and Jamie, saying those things to her, kissing her as if he could devour her whole, thinking they could have a future together. He wouldn't let her sit by his side and try to smile and pretend it didn't matter if he couldn't stand up. If he couldn't draw her to him deep in the night, pull her body beneath his and slip inside of her and make love to her, like a man.

It had been a flat-out lie when he told her making love to her wouldn't have meant anything to him. There'd been a time when he *hoped* it wouldn't. But a man didn't spend years wanting a woman who meant nothing to him, and now he saw that he'd waited until it was simply too late, until he had nothing to offer her but a monumental struggle with no guarantee he'd ever be the man he used to be.

He thought again of that first night he spent in this room, groggy, half of him numb, half of him hurting like hell, lying in the dark, close to going stark-raving mad until he opened his eyes and saw her sitting by his side and holding his hand tightly in hers. She looked like an angel that night. Like a little slice of heaven. Like a savior.

Save me, Jamie, he thought. *Take me away from here. Make it all fade away.*

But he couldn't ask that of her. He wouldn't put her through the struggle that lay ahead of him.

Chapter 6

A month later, Jamie walked into Dan's room late one night and found it empty. Her heart lurched sickeningly for a moment, even as her head told her he was fine, that he was getting stronger every day.

She, on the other hand, still woke up in a cold sweat, dreaming of those nightmarish days after the shooting. It didn't help that she still had to see him from time to time because of her job. Not that he was being uncooperative or unkind, as he had been that day in his hospital room. He'd kept things strictly businesslike between them, being distant, calm, quiet, answering her questions, but nothing more.

Perhaps she should be grateful for his indifference, but after weeks of it, she'd found indifference could hurt just as well.

Turning away from the empty room, Jamie went to the nursing station, where she found a familiar face, a forty-something nurse with kind eyes.

"Hi, Annie. How's your favorite patient?"

"Going stir-crazy," she complained. "Making all of us crazy, as well."

"He's not in his room."

"I know. He likes to be alone, and that's a difficult thing when you're stuck in a hospital. He's been roaming the halls for the past week trying to find some peace and quiet. I finally thought of sneaking him into the next wing. It's being renovated, so no one's there at night after the construction crews leave. Most of the rooms are finished now, and one of them's a solarium. I took him down there an hour ago and promised to leave him alone."

"Oh." Jamie hesitated.

"Come on." Annie took her by the arm. "I wouldn't dare barge in on him now, but if you're willing to risk it, I'll show you where he is."

They walked past a construction zone barricade, down a deserted corridor. Jamie said, "He'll be leaving soon, won't he?"

Annie nodded, stopped herself before adding anything more.

Weeks ago, Dan had ordered his doctors to stop talking to anyone about his condition—something Jamie found particularly hurtful. She couldn't make herself stop worrying about him.

Her pride hadn't let her come right out and ask him how he was doing. She could tell just from looking at him that he was almost well. She supposed he'd be leaving the hospital soon, and she knew he was in physical therapy, because she arrived one day while he was there and had to wait until he was finished to talk to him. A few people had mentioned his name in connection with a nearby government rehabilitation facility where Geri was already located, working to regain full use of her right arm and shoulder. Jamie suspected Dan would be going there soon, and she might never see him again, if he didn't come back to the agency.

She found the door at the end of the deserted hallway, pushed it open to a small, darkened room filled with couches and chairs and plants. The far wall and half the ceiling was made entirely of glass, and during the day she supposed it gave the patients the impression of being outdoors. But it was late now, and the sky was black. Thunder rumbled ominously. Lightning flashed in the distance. It had been raining on the other side of town, where she'd come from, and it looked like the rain was following her.

Jamie shivered, both from the thought of the coming storm and from the look in Dan's eyes when he turned his head and saw her. She expected to find him in the wheelchair, something she dreaded. But the chair was empty, parked beside the sofa. He was sitting on a sofa with his arm stretched along the back of one of the cushions, looking so wonderfully normal, impossibly handsome and strong.

"Hi," she said tentatively.

"Hi." He watched her with an unnerving stare. "More questions?"

"A few."

His shoulders rose and fell with a long, slow breath, and he nodded toward the chair beside him. "Have a seat."

Jamie draped her coat over the chair and dared to take a seat on the far end of the sofa on which he was sitting. A crack of thunder startled her. She flinched at the sound. The air-conditioning kicked on a moment later, and she shivered.

"Cold outside?" he asked.

"A little." Jamie said. "I need to go over some things with you. About the Section 123 report. Tanner's after me to wrap it up, and I still have a few inconsistencies between your version of what happened and Geri's."

Like whose weapon he was shot with and which one of them decided first to leave their post to try to save the girl.

With a wry smile, Dan said, "There's nothing else I can tell you, Jamie."

"Of course not." Which meant he was protecting his partner, to the bitter end, despite what it cost him. She folded her arms in front of her, ran one hand up and down the opposite arm in a vain attempt to warm herself, and tried to make sure he understood how this was going to play out. "You know we're going to hang somebody out to dry on this?"

He nodded.

"Tanner claims it's the way of the world. We lost Hathaway and his work. We lost Doc, and someone has to pay for that."

Dan nodded. "That's the way it works."

"I don't think this was your fault," she insisted. "I think you were in a lousy situation, and you made a split-second decision, one I'm glad I didn't have to make."

Dan bypassed everything but the bottom line. "Blame me, Jamie," he said softly.

"I can't do that."

"Why not?" He leaned farther back against the sofa cushions as if it meant nothing to him.

"I don't think it's your fault."

"You're missing the point. Someone's going down for this, and the list of possibilities isn't that long. It's not going to be Doc," he insisted.

"No," she agreed.

"Geri's a good agent. She can still be a good agent, and I want her to have that chance. Which leaves me."

"But what about your career?"

"I'm not coming back, Jamie," he said easily. "So it doesn't mean a damn thing to me if my name shows up on that report as the reason why the whole operation went sour.''

''Dan—''

''Listen to me. It's not like I'm making a huge sacrifice here. My career's over. Do you understand what I'm telling you? I'm never going to be mobile enough to be a field agent again.''

She turned her head away, closed her eyes and fought against a tightening in her throat that threatened to choke her, fought to hold back a fast, hot rush of tears, as she imagined the worst.

That he wouldn't walk again?

He hadn't said that exactly. She fought to find reassurance in the fact that he hadn't come right out and said he wouldn't walk again. He said he wouldn't be mobile enough to be a field agent. That could mean anything. That he could walk but not run. That he could run but not climb a mountain or hack his way through a jungle, if need be.

She pulled herself together enough to face him. He was wearing that same expression he had when she'd been trying to get him to admit it was Geri's fault, not his, that the operation at the warehouse had gone bad. The one that said Jamie could do her damnedest; he wasn't talking.

Exasperated, she stood up to leave. ''I can't put my name on a report full of lies. I won't.''

''Think about it, Jamie. Nothing you say in that report is going to change anything for Doc or for me.''

''I can't do it,'' she repeated.

From outside came a streak of light, then the booming sound of thunder. Already on-edge, she gasped, her self-control a tenuous thing.

Dan reached for her hand. Surprised, she let him pull her down to sit beside him, felt his hand on her shoulder, his touch gentle and reassuring and so wonderfully warm.

"Let it go, Jamie," he urged. "Put it behind you, and move on."

He was confusing her terribly now. He never touched her. He wasn't nice to her, either. And while she would like nothing more than to sit here, savoring his sweetly satisfying touch, she knew he was telling her to forget much more than the report or the shooting. He wanted her to forget about him as well, but she hadn't found a way to do that.

Maybe if he'd never held her in his arms. Maybe if she didn't still dream about that quick, hard embrace in the hallway, about steamy, sweet kisses in the dark, she could. But she knew. She remembered.

Without warning, another crack of thunder sounded, and she flinched, his hand tightening on her shoulder, then kneading at the tension there.

"I've never seen you jump at the sound of thunder," he said.

"I'm tired," she claimed. "Jumpy. It's been a bad day. Bad week. Bad month. Tanner wants my report. He's been pushing the whole time."

"He's under a lot of pressure right now, and he's passing it down the line to you."

"I know, but I still have all of these questions, pieces that don't fit together the way they should. Did you know we hardly looked in the district for the two suspects and the girl you and Geri described? Doesn't that seem odd to you? Both of you said they looked like they came straight out of the gangs, and we've hardly looked for them here."

"I thought everybody agreed they were pros. Looking like gang kids let them move in and out of that neighborhood without drawing attention to themselves."

"I know. But shouldn't we at least look? Shouldn't we try to find someone who saw them? Or heard something that night?"

"Jamie, the agency doesn't have the case."

"I know. But our people are the ones who got shot."

"Let the CIA and the FBI handle it," Dan said.

"They're looking for Hathaway. Not the people who shot you."

"It's all connected. Find Hathaway, and you'll find out who shot Geri and me."

"I know that, too. But none of it explains why no one's working the case from this end. Why not try to find the people who shot you and let them lead us to Hathaway?"

"How do you know no one's looking?"

"Because I've been down there. I've asked," she said.

Dan was scowling at her. "Tell me you didn't go down there by yourself."

She ignored the question. What she did was no business of his.

"No one's been down there in weeks," she said. "Hardly anyone's asked questions there. Or searched around Burns Avenue. Think about it, Dan. That warehouse is minutes from the FBI and the CIA's headquarters. The task force has sent agents all over the country, all over the world, looking for Hathaway, but they haven't checked an area minutes away. Doesn't that seem strange to you?"

"There must be an explanation. Probably that the FBI and the CIA have information they haven't shared with us," he concluded. "Or Tanner knows things he's been ordered not to tell us. It happens, Jamie."

She sighed, wondering if she was wrong about this, wondering why she couldn't ignore that nagging little voice inside that told her something didn't add up.

"What did Tanner say about working it from this end?" Dan asked.

"That we screwed up and lost the case." She shrugged. "That if we want a chance to get the case back, we've got to be team players right now and stay out of it. That hopefully, once everybody calms down and we give the big boys someone to blame, we'll be brought back onto the case."

"He's probably right."

She stared at him. "Don't ask me to believe you'd back off and leave it alone if this was your assignment. I know you wouldn't."

"Okay, I probably wouldn't. But could you just stay the hell away from Burns Avenue?."

"Why?" she asked.

"Because it's dangerous."

She laughed. "This is a dangerous job. You know that."

And as soon as the words were out, she wanted to call them back. But it was too late. Was it too late for them as well? Was there nothing she could say to him? Nothing she could do?

"Dan," she tried. "I'm sorry."

He brushed off the comment, as if it was of no consequence at all. He leaned his head against the back of the sofa cushion and stared at the blackened sky overhead. Jamie checked her watch, amazed. She'd been here for nearly ten minutes, and he hadn't once tried to get rid of her. That had to be a record.

She took a minute to study the man beside her. He was wearing a pair of gray sweatpants and a Marine Corps T-shirt. His hair, which he normally kept very short, looked almost shaggy, curling a little on top and in back where it barely brushed against the collar of his shirt.

He'd been cooped up inside for a month, so his skin was paler than normal, and he'd lost some weight. But he would never be considered scrawny. Maybe it was just seeing him out of his hospital bed, sitting on a sofa, looking so normal, but she kept thinking that any minute he was going to get up and walk across the room. It was hard to believe he couldn't, that maybe he never would.

"You look good," she confessed. Gorgeous, she could have added. Sexy. Healthy.

He stared at her for a minute, then looked toward the windows again. "I'm getting out of here soon," he said offhandedly.

"I heard. Rehab?"

"Yeah."

"For what? A few weeks? Months?"

"Months."

Which meant that they could help him? Or that they were going to teach him how to deal with life in a wheelchair? She wanted to ask. Damn him for not telling her, for leaving it to her to ask.

She knew a little of what he was facing, wondered if he'd go through it alone, as he seemed to go through everything else in life.

"Have you ever known anyone who's been in extensive rehab?" she asked.

"Nothing like what I'm facing. Why?"

"One of my brothers blew out his knee a few years ago."

"Football?" he guessed. "Basketball?"

"No. He's a pilot. He bailed out of his plane a little too low to the ground, and his parachute didn't have time to open fully."

Dan smiled and shook his head. "Tell me something. Is there anyone in your family with a healthy respect for danger?"

"Someone from my family has served in every war this country ever fought. So yes, we're familiar with the concept of danger," she said, ready to defend her family to anyone. "My brother happened to be with the U.N. Peacekeeping Force in Bosnia when his plane was shot down. He was trying to keep it from crashing into a civilian area when he bailed out too late and ruined his knee."

"I'm sorry," he said.

"My youngest brother's a test pilot. He wants to take the space shuttle for a spin one day. And my other brother never made it home from the Gulf War."

Jamie froze, unable to believe she'd just blurted it out like that. She never told anyone that. It was too painful, even years later. But Rich had been on her mind lately, another thing dredged up by the shooting at the warehouse.

She shivered. She'd loved him so much. He was someone who put his life on the line day after day, and she'd lost him. Surely something like that would make a smart woman think twice about falling in love with a man who took risks every day of his life, and she liked to think of herself as a very smart woman.

"Jamie." Dan's hand closed tightly over hers. "You're freezing. Come here."

He tugged on her hand, and she knew she shouldn't let herself get any closer to him, knew it would only hurt more when it came time to leave. What did he mean by touching her this way, anyway?

"I'm all right," she insisted, thinking for once about self-preservation and her battered pride.

"No, you're not."

He tugged harder on her hand, more insistent this time. Her throat tight, her eyes burning, she let him bring her against him. Curled into his side, she put her head against his chest and sighed wearily. His arms, strong and sure, came around her, enfolding her in a wealth of warmth and comfort, a luxury beyond belief.

"I'm sorry," she said miserably, hating the idea of him seeing her fall apart.

"And I'm a jerk," he said bluntly.

But his arms tightened around her, and she felt the side of his face pressed against the top of her head. She snuggled against the hard muscles of his chest, feeling it rise and fall with each breath he took, hearing his heart thundering beneath her ear. It was amazing to have him sitting here holding her in the dark. No arguments. No sarcasm. Nothing but soothing warmth and strong arms anchoring her to him.

It was so nice, so unexpected.

She told herself she should move away from him, that she should forget about him. She was still furious at him, after all. She still wanted to smack his smugly handsome face for claiming there was nothing between them, except for the fact that he was willing to have sex with her, casually and briefly and with no strings attached.

She wanted to believe it was a blatant lie, too. Because somewhere deep inside her heart was a little spark of hope that she and Dan were meant to be together. No matter what he did or what he said, that little bit of hope simply wouldn't die. It meant he crept into her thoughts at all hours of the day, no matter how often she resolved to forget all about him. It meant she lay in bed at night dreaming of a single kiss from what seemed like a lifetime ago.

Those same feelings made it nearly impossible, when she finally stopped trembling and she wasn't so very cold, to ease away from him, retreating to her corner of the sofa. Dan stared at her with those wonderful dark eyes of his. She couldn't tell if he was relieved or if he regretted letting her go.

"Tell me about your brother," he said finally.

Surprised, she considered the request. "I don't know if I can talk about Rich."

"Then tell me about the one who jumps out of planes too low to the ground."

"Sean." She concentrated until she could see her oldest brother's face from happier times, when all of them had been home and safe. "He's always had a basic misunderstanding of the concept of gravity."

Dan laughed softly. Sean would like him, she decided. Her whole family would like him. Even more, they'd respect him and understand him. She wondered if they could show him he didn't have to be so alone in the world.

"Let me guess," he said. "Sean was one of those little boys who always wanted to fly?"

"He did fly. Off the roof, more than once. Off the top of the bleachers at the high school football field. Out of trees. Anything. The third time he broke his arm, one of the doctors told my parents they should consider getting him psychiatric help. They finally gave in and let him have flying lessons instead, and he hasn't broken his arm since. Just nearly ruined his knee. He's at the Pentagon now, a desk jockey if you believe what he says."

"You don't?"

"I believe him about as much as he believes me when I say I work for a division of the Commerce Department," she said.

"I see." He smiled.

Jamie nodded. "We have an unspoken agreement in the family these days. We strictly adhere to the military's Don't Ask, Don't Tell policy. I don't ask Sean if he really sits behind a desk all day at the Pentagon, and he doesn't tell me what he really does, although I'm sure it's more hands-on than he admits. I suspect he's with the JSOC."

That was the Joint Special Operations Command, a unit inside the Pentagon that controlled the military's top-secret counter-terrorism units, such as Delta Force and Seal Team 6, units with missions not unlike Division One's. If she knew Sean, his neck was on the line every day.

"You worry about him?" Dan asked.

"Of course I do."

"So it was you and three brothers?"

She nodded.

"You're the youngest, right?"

"Maybe," she hedged.

"Pampered and indulged from the day you were born?"

"With a general for a father? I marched the straight and narrow."

"Sure you did."

"I was saluting his photograph before I could walk. His version of a bedtime story was a tale about his days in Korea or Vietnam."

"You must have lived all over the place."

"We did. It was hard in a lot of ways, but it made us that much closer, too. No matter where we went we always had each other."

She looked at Dan, thinking of what she knew about his family. His brother had been here briefly after the shooting, but Jamie hadn't seen him. Obviously, they weren't close. His mother was dead, and his personnel records didn't have the name of his father. He'd been divorced for years. As far as she knew, a few of his friends from various branches of the service had dropped by to visit him here, but that was it. It was as solitary a life as she could imagine.

She wondered if it made him happy to live this way, if anyone could be happy being so alone in the world. And then she thought of what he was facing.

"You threw me offtrack," she said. "We were talking about you and rehab."

He gave her another one of those indulgent half smiles. "What about me and rehab?"

"Sean spent a month in a rehab place in Maryland after he wrecked his knee. There were people from all branches of the service there. Real tough guys and they all agreed that fighting to get back on their feet and back to active duty after a severe injury was the hardest thing they ever tried to do."

He cocked an eyebrow at her. "And I thought it was going to be a picnic."

She glared. "Is it just me? Or do you get a perverse pleasure from irritating any woman who gets too close for comfort?"

A slow, sexy smile spread across his face, this one genuine. She'd bet money on it.

"I think I'll take the Fifth on that," he said.

Jamie knew it was time to back off, but she couldn't resist making him one last offer.

If she was feeling a little more confident where he was concerned, she would have told him she was a very strong woman, that it was all right for him to lean on her a little. Of course, he'd probably never leaned on anyone in his entire life, especially not a woman. Still, she had to try.

"You know," she said as casually as she could, "You may actually find yourself needing a friend in the next few months. You could call me."

"Jamie—" he began, turning away, shutting her out.

Too far, she realized. Too fast.

It was like handling a witness who thought he'd be taking his life in his hands if he talked. Push too far, too fast, and he'd immediately back off.

Jamie decided her time was up. If she didn't go now, he'd throw her out or pick a fight to get her to go, which would ruin what had been a pleasant few moments with him. She got to her feet, reached for her coat.

"No strings," she promised. "No great expectations. And I promise not to sit by your bed and weep." He'd been talking to Geri when he said he would truly hate being surrounded by a bunch of weeping women, but Jamie knew he meant her to hear it, too. He despised any and all displays of sympathy, and he obviously wasn't ready to accept an offer of friendship and support.

"Jamie, I'm sorry," he said sincerely. "I should never have said that."

"No." She tried to shrug off the old hurt. "It was the

truth. It would have made you crazy to have anyone do that. Still, we could be friends. You could let me do that, at least. I really do want to help, if you'll let me.''

''Why?'' he asked. ''You don't owe me anything.''

She didn't remind him that he'd made it clear on two separate occasions that he didn't want her anywhere near him. Nor did she mention that she'd sworn a half-dozen times that she was going to forget him, that she'd cried her last tear for Dan Reese. Still, they had a history together that went back years, and she was grateful to him for a lot of things.

''I owe you a lot,'' she said. ''You've seen me through the worst things I've ever faced on the job.''

''Jamie, we haven't worked together in a very long time.''

''I'm talking about everything you taught me. Everything you drilled into my head,'' she explained. ''It's like I'm carrying a little bit of you around inside me. When everything gets crazy, and I can't think for myself, when everything's happening too fast and there's nothing but instinct to go on, I hear your voice. You've kept me alive more times than you can imagine. So, yes, I do owe you.''

A little embarrassed by the admission, she took her time about looking at him, found an expression on his face she couldn't begin to decipher.

Looking oddly off-balance, he said, ''I didn't realize.''

''Well, now you do.'' She shrugged uncomfortably, tried to smile, and told herself to get out of the room. ''Before you misconstrue everything I just said, I'm not offering to help because I owe you. I'm offering because I want to. Because—'' She fell silent, saving herself just in time. ''I'd better get out of here,'' she said, turning to leave.

It was the smart thing to do. Because if she stayed, if

she let herself finish what she'd started to say, she'd tell him everything.

I'm offering because of all these foolish dreams I have about the two of us. Because I'm afraid so easily I could fall in love with you.

Chapter 7

She'd taken three steps when she heard him say, "Jamie?"

Turning back, she said, "Hmm?"

He caught her hand in his, for just a moment, squeezing it before releasing it. "Be careful."

There was something in the way he said it that made it feel like goodbye, the kind of goodbye people said when they weren't going to see each other for a long time. It worried her, had her thinking he was up to something, something she wasn't going to like.

That odd tenderness in his voice, the brief touch of his hand, gave her the courage to take the next step. She leaned over him, one hand braced against his shoulder, and touched her mouth to his in a brief, soft kiss.

"I will. I'll be careful," she promised. "And I'll miss you."

He made a strangled sound of protest as she pulled away, and his eyes were burning with an intensity she'd never

seen in him before. She thought he was going to let her
walk away this time. But his hand, lightning-fast, found the
back of her neck and pulled her mouth back down to his.

"You just couldn't let it alone, could you?" he muttered.

Thrown off-balance, Jamie fell heavily against him. He
groaned. She worried that she'd hurt him, but he never took
his lips from hers, kissing her greedily. She jumped a little
when she felt his hand slip beneath the hem of her skirt
and slide along her thigh, the heat searing its way through
the thin silk stockings she wore.

"Come here," he muttered against her mouth.

She let him pull one of her legs across both of his and
tuck her knees into the sofa cushions on either side of him.
His hands slid higher, brushing the material of her skirt
aside, pulling her to him. He wasn't satisfied until he had
her straddling his thighs.

She gasped as she sank down on his lap, feeling a deli-
cious array of muscle and man beneath her, panicking for
just a moment when she realized the intimacy of their po-
sitions. She could feel the heat radiating off his body, felt
an answering warmth flooding her own.

He kissed as he did everything—with a passionate intensity, a brash confidence—and it shouldn't come as any surprise if he made love just the same way. Jamie had only
the briefest flickering of doubt, mostly that she was way
out of her league with this man. But she didn't care. She
still wanted him, didn't make the first sound of protest
when his hands slid beneath her long, loose button-down
sweater that doubled as a jacket. He grumbled when he
encountered the material of her blouse. His hands retreated
to her waist, dug beneath the fabric and slid up once again.
With a contented sigh, he found bare skin this time.

She felt him smile against her lips as he used his hands
to pull her closer, until they might have been fused together, her breasts crushed against his chest. She wrapped

her arms around his neck, let her fingers slide through the thick, soft hair she'd always wanted to touch.

"Kiss me," he ordered, holding her effortlessly, playing her body with the skill and ease that could only come from experience, taking her so far, so fast she was ready right then to simply come apart in his arms.

It had never been like this before, never gotten so out of control so fast. Her body seemed to have a mind of its own, needing him, straining to get closer to him, wanting him so desperately.

She felt one of his hands slide between their bodies, felt his knuckles brush across her breast. It wasn't until she felt cool air against her skin, then the heat, the slight roughness of his hands, that she realized he'd unbuttoned her blouse. He groaned, frustrated again, when his fingers found the fabric of her bra. His hand withdrew, found the bottom of her blouse and tried to tunnel up that way instead. But her blouse was caught beneath the weapon she wore holstered beneath her left arm.

With a deftness she should have expected from him, he withdrew the weapon, then loosened her holster and slid a hand beneath her shirt and over the quivering skin of her belly. His other hand shifted against her back, and she felt the fabric of her bra give way, leaving no obstacles between them. One of his hands slipped beneath her bra, to cup her breast. "Mmm," he muttered.

Jamie could have wept from the sheer pleasure that went shooting through her as he simply took the weight of one of her breasts and held it in his hand. She felt him draw in a deep breath, felt his chest expand with the effort it took. If there was any justice in the world, he was every bit as aroused as she was. When she pressed her mouth to his, she felt him brush his thumb gently back and forth across her nipple, sending heat spiraling to the spot between her thighs. She couldn't breathe, couldn't wait, couldn't do anything but beg.

"Dan, please."

"Please...what?"

"Kiss me."

"Here?" He brushed his thumb past her nipple once again.

"Yes," she begged.

He arched her backward, holding her with an arm at her waist. His lips landed first at the side of her neck and slid downward, trailing fire as they went and leaving her shivering as he made a warm, wet path with his mouth to her shoulder, over her collarbone and down. His hand still held her breast, pushing it up to meet his waiting mouth. He nosed the fabric of her blouse out of his way, and his mouth, warm and moist, opened, drawing her nipple inside, sucking on it, laving it with his tongue.

She shuddered, able to do nothing more than cling to him and let him do what he would, her only worry that he would stop. The feelings were so powerful, so intense. If she'd known it could be like this....

He fussed over her breasts, first one and then the other, as if he meant to devour her whole. When his hands cupped her hips and he shifted her even closer, she realized there was nothing but a few bits of cloth between them. Jamie wriggled her hips impatiently, seeking some relief from the throbbing emptiness in her body, found the proof that he was indeed every bit as aroused as she was, and any embarrassment she felt was forgotten.

His hands were beneath her skirt once again, sliding higher and higher, finding a thin strip of bare skin between the top of her stockings and the edge of her panties. She heard an odd hitch in his breath.

"What are you wearing?"

"Stockings."

"Where's the rest of them?"

She smiled. "That's all there is."

He still looked puzzled. She decided to let him find out for himself. Closing her eyes, she let her head fall to his shoulder as his hands traced the top edge of her thigh-high stockings.

He swore as his fingers skimmed the ring of material and bare skin all around her thigh, pausing between her legs, coming tantalizingly close to finding out just how aroused she was. If he so much as touched her there, he'd push her right over the edge.

Maybe he knew that, because she felt him shudder. His hands slid beneath her panties, cupping her hips and pulling her ever closer. She let her thighs spread wider, arched her back and her body came down hard on top of his, heat to reckless, relentless heat.

She would have done anything he asked then, would have given him anything just to have him end this, to have him fill all the empty places inside her. His fingers were digging into the soft flesh of her fanny, pulling and easing her back, again and again, showing her what he wanted from her, making her ache.

"Dan," she said, her voice pure need now. She was going to explode.

Then she felt it, felt the hair on the back of her neck tingling. The air in the room changed inexplicably, became oddly thick and heavy. Dangerous. For some reason, she suddenly knew she should watch her back.

Dan froze, his hands holding her still. Her instincts were screaming by then; she'd been an agent too long to ignore them. He felt it, too. She saw it in his eyes a split second before he shoved her to the left, until she was facedown and pressed against the sofa cushions. He fell to the side as well, landing heavily half on top of her, knocking the breath out of her, but moving unmistakably to shield her with his body. Overhead, the glass skylights and windows rattled ominously.

Then there was a brilliant flash of light that illuminated the entire room. Jamie heard faint crackling, popping sounds and then the explosion. Repercussions from the blast moved through the building like a wave, shaking the floor beneath her as the room went pitch-black and absolutely silent, except for the mingled sounds of their quick, shallow breaths.

She tensed as she heard another explosion split the sky in two, then realized the building had lost power when she heard the emergency generators kick in and noticed the red Emergency Exit signs were illuminated once again.

Those were the only lights in the room. She glanced back toward the windows and realized the entire area was dark and finally quiet.

The odd air of expectancy had dissipated, and she took stock of her surroundings. Dan had his arm around her shoulders, held her head down as well, and their legs were still tangled together, their bodies intimately entwined. Both of them were still breathing heavily, still heavily aroused. He eased himself off her and to the side, used the arm he had around her back to turn her onto her side and toward him.

In the dark, she felt rather than saw the smile on his face, then heard him laughing softly. She hid her face against his neck and shoulder, feeling more than a little embarrassed. In another minute, another second, he would have been inside her. The only thing that stopped them was the reflexes that had them both diving for cover, from what she thought must have been lightning hitting a transformer nearby and setting off an explosion inside it.

"So," he said, "have you ever been with a man who literally made the Earth move for you?"

She blushed furiously. He was still laughing softly when

he brought his face down to hers and took her mouth in a soft, slow, steamy kiss. She shivered and wrapped her arms around him tightly, because it felt so good. Because she knew somehow they weren't going to finish what they started and she wasn't ready to let him go.

When he broke the kiss, he pushed her face against his shoulder again and held her firmly with a hand tangled in her hair. Her pulse was still pounding. She could feel the blood rushing through her veins in a hard, heavy throb; every nerve ending in her body was on alert and begging for his touch.

He held her until their breathing slowed, until the fever-pitch of arousal had dimmed to a dull ache. His lips trailed soft kisses down the side of her face, stopping just short of taking her mouth again.

Jamie wanted him so badly. The only redeeming factor to the whole thing was that she was still in his arms. She wouldn't leave willingly this time. She put her hand to the side of his face, against a jaw that was rough and abrasive against her palm, and pulled his stubborn mouth back to hers. He groaned, but gave her a searing kiss in return.

"I've dreamed about you," she confessed. "About this."

"Jamie," he groaned. "We can't."

"Why not? And don't even think about trying to convince me you don't want me," she warned. "I'll call you a damned liar."

"I'm sorry," he said sincerely.

"You should be," she shot back, thinking of how very much he'd hurt her with what he said that day.

She wasn't ready to address what she thought was an equally ridiculous claim of his—that it wouldn't mean anything to him if they did make love. For the moment, it was enough to let him hold her some more.

Wrapping those gloriously strong arms around her, fitting

their bodies together as best he could, he used his hand to rub at the knot of tension in her lower back. The other brushed her hair back from her face. He kissed her softly, his touch soothing and comforting.

She snuggled against him, reveling in a tenderness he'd never shown her before and in the newfound ease between them. "I thought the building was going to come down around us," she said, her voice muffled against his chest. "You think a transformer blew?"

He nodded. "Bet every soldier in this building took a dive when it exploded."

She went to sit up, but one of her legs was caught beneath his, which were lying at an awkward angle. "I'm stuck."

"Give me a minute."

He braced one hand on the back of the sofa, the other on the cushion and with effort hoisted himself into a sitting position once again. She watched grim-faced as he used one hand to reposition his legs. It was too late by the time she looked up and realized he'd been watching her, as well.

"You forgot?" he asked.

Jamie nodded, trying to wipe all expression from her face, shivering once again.

"Me, too," he admitted

She remembered, too, that he had major surgery a few weeks before, that she'd been literally sitting on top of him moments before. But she didn't ask if he was all right, because she knew he'd hate that.

Her heart rate kicked into high speed as he reached for her again. The back of his hands brushed against her breasts, and she realized he was merely dressing her. He hooked her bra, rebuttoned her blouse. He dug down between the cushions of the sofa and pulled out her gun, tucked that into her shoulder holster and pulled her sweater back into place.

There was another flash of light behind her, and even though she was braced for the thunder that time, she still jumped a little when it came. She jumped again when his fingertips brushed across her forehead, smoothing back her hair and tucking it behind her ear.

"Shh," he said in a soothing voice, letting his hand linger, his fingers spread wide and threading through her hair, his palm against her cheek. "You're trembling again. Is it London? Did the blast remind you—"

"No." In London, she'd been on the ground, a curious ringing the only sound in her ears, her body being pelted by debris before she realized how close she'd come to being blown to bits.

"Tell me," he insisted.

"It's the storm. Ever since the night you got shot... It stormed the whole night. I stood in the doorway to my patio watching it, heard something that sounded like a Huey taking off around three in the morning, and I swear it had to be the one that brought you here. I just stood there listening to it, and when Josh came to the door, I knew. I knew it was you."

Dan caught her hand in his and held it.

"And the next three nights," she said, "when you were unconscious and fighting off the infection and shock, it stormed the whole damned time."

Now, if there was thunder and lightning during the night, she woke up screaming, reliving the whole nightmare.

"So," she said, forcing a smile. "Now you know. I'm like a little kid who's afraid of the thunder."

"Things will calm down," he said. "They'll get back to normal. I know sometimes it seems like it won't. But it will."

"Maybe. But I'm not going to forget this," she said firmly, daring him to tell her he'd forget her. "I'm through letting you push me away."

"Jamie," he groaned.

"I want to be with you. You want to be with me," she said, trying to keep it simple, when what she wanted was so much more complicated. "We're both adults. We're free to do as we please. So what's the problem?"

"It wouldn't be fair to you."

"Why?"

"Get real. I can't even stand up."

"Not now. That doesn't mean you never will."

He frowned, getting that look in his eyes that said she was seriously annoying him. "There are no guarantees I ever will."

"I don't recall asking for a guarantee about anything. I just want to be with you."

"Jamie, I can't even make love to you the way I want to."

She glared at him, getting seriously annoyed herself. "You're trying to tell me you were somehow disappointed by what just happened here?"

"No."

"It didn't feel good enough? It wasn't exciting enough?"

"No."

"Or there's something so much more satisfying we could do, if only your legs worked the way they used to? You have the nerve to think that matters to me? To think it's more important to me than the two of us finally being together?"

"No," he shouted. "I'm telling you it matters to me."

Damn. She'd been so sure he was finally through fighting her.

"Why?" she whispered.

"I don't know how long I'm going to be in rehab. I don't know whether I'll walk out or crawl. I can't make any

promises about how ugly my whole attitude's going to be when this is finished, and I won't put you through that.''

"You couldn't get away from me now if you tried," she boasted. "You're going to be moving a little slowly for a while, remember?''

Dan swore. "You've got your whole life ahead of you. You're strong and whole, and you haven't been sucked into this whole business the way I have. You can still get out, still have a life that doesn't involve chasing after the scum of the earth and risking your neck and seldom being in the same city for more than a month at a time. You deserve—''

"Don't you dare presume to tell me what *I* want or what *I* need. Don't treat me like a little girl and tell me you know what's best for me.''

He backed off physically, retreated emotionally behind a cool, distant stare. "All right," he said. "I won't.''

"Dan," she pleaded, recognizing the determined look in his eyes. "Don't do this. Don't shut me out.''

"Jamie, I don't have anything to give you right now. I don't know if I ever will.''

"And if you did? What would happen if you did?''

"I don't know.''

Fuming, she vowed, "I won't give up on you.''

"And I won't give in. Not on this.''

She was angry enough not to try to see him again for five days, and she hoped he spent the entire time having the same terribly erotic dream that she was—the one where they finally finished what they'd started in the solarium in the middle of the blackout.

But she was irritated with herself to find five days was all she could take. He hadn't called, of course. He never would. Damned stubborn man that he was.

When Jamie walked down the hall and into his room,

prepared for a nasty fight, she found the room empty. When she walked into the solarium, it was empty as well.

She rushed back to the nurses' station, found a woman she'd never seen before on duty. "Dan Reese?" she said, trying to sound calm. "Do you know where he is?"

"Let me check for you." She tapped a few keys on her computer. "Mr. Reese…here we go. He was discharged. Last week."

Discharged? Without a word to her?

Jamie thanked the nurse, told herself she was in a panic over nothing. She knew Dan was going into rehab. She walked outside, pulled out her cell phone and keyed in the number for the rehab hospital where Geri had been transferred. The person who answered the phone said they had no patient by the name of Dan Reese.

She called Division One, talked to three different people, none of whom knew where Dan was.

Moving more quickly now, her sense of unease growing every moment, she went back into the hospital, flashed a lot of ID around, and with considerable effort persuaded one of the nurses to tell her which doctor had signed Dan's discharge papers. It was Dr. Richardson. She'd dealt with him before, and he remembered her.

Jamie trailed him through the hospital and ambushed him in the hall. "Dan?" she said. "Where did he go?"

"I don't know, Ms. Douglass."

"What do you mean you don't know?"

"I mean I don't know."

"I don't understand. How can you not know?"

"He's an adult. I'm just his doctor. I can make recommendations about how long he should stay here and where he should go for treatment when he leaves. But ultimately, those decisions are his to make."

"You didn't want to release him?"

"No. I would have preferred to have him here another

week or so, but he didn't want to stay and we're not running a jail here.''

"But he's going to be okay? I mean...he's able to be out of the hospital now? Medically..."

"He still needs medical care. But at this point in his treatment, there are other places where he can get that care.''

"I...I have to find him."

The doctor sighed. "Ms. Douglass, he left here with a complete copy of his medical records in his hands. He wouldn't let us arrange to transport him to wherever he was going, wouldn't let me send his medical records directly to his new doctor. He didn't want me to consult with that doctor by phone or letter or any other means of communication. For some reason, he wanted a clean break from this place.''

"All right, but—"

The doctor's expression changed, that look of professional detachment gone, a compassionate man in his place. She'd broken through the reserve, and she could tell the doctor knew exactly what she was leaving unsaid.

"Ms. Douglass, he doesn't want anyone to know where he is. He was very clear about that.''

Not just anyone, she thought.

Her.

Damn him.

He didn't want *her* to know where he was.

Chapter 8

Six weeks later, Jamie met her mother for a quick breakfast before work. They ordered, found a seat, but before Jamie had taken the first sip of her coffee, her mother got to the heart of the matter.

"Well? What did he do to you now?" Mary Ann Douglass asked.

"Nothing," Jamie said.

She loved her mother very much and worked hard to shield her from the dangers involved with her job, but Jamie told her a great deal about the people with whom she worked. The name Dan Reese was a familiar one to her mother especially after he was hurt, in an accident, she claimed. A month ago, Jamie had tearfully confessed the more personal nature of their relationship, including the way Dan had pushed her out of his life. Now, she had to pay the price for her confession—keeping her mother up-to-date on what was happening between them.

"You did find him?"

"With enough time, I could find the man in the moon," Jamie bragged. "He knew I'd find him eventually."

"And?"

"He's at this ritzy rehabilitation facility in suburban Maryland, about ninety minutes away." It had taken her three weeks to track him down, and by then she was furious. "I couldn't even bawl him out over the phone. He left instructions with the switchboard not to put any calls through to his room. At least, not any of my calls."

"You didn't let it go at that?" her mother guessed.

"No, I didn't." One thoroughly humiliating day, she'd gone to see him. "There's a huge, brick wall around the place, a guard gate at the entrance, a private security force on site. Apparently, they cater to celebrities, politicians and foreign diplomats, and they have a drug and alcohol treatment program, too. Some of the people who check in are quite serious about maintaining their privacy."

"My daughter couldn't get inside the gate?"

"I tried," Jamie said evasively.

In truth, she'd been mad enough, and determined enough, that she'd flashed a government ID and tried to brazen her way through the guards, who informed her she couldn't go in without a court order or an arrest warrant, no matter what kind of government ID she produced. And Jamie had an amazing array of government IDs that she'd used to bluff her way into vast numbers of places.

"That man was unforgivably rude to you, and at the very least, he owes you an explanation," her mother decreed.

"I considered scaling the walls or checking in as a patient, but I found I do have some pride left where he's concerned." Who knew how long that would hold out, but for now, she'd managed to resist the urge to see him at any cost. "He doesn't want to see me, Mom. I don't know how much clearer he could make it."

"Then the man is a fool."

Jamie smiled, feeling better and thinking she'd send her mother to chew Dan out on her behalf. "He's so stubborn."

"Every man I've ever known is stubborn. You just have to explain to them the error of their ways. Eventually, the smart ones get it."

Jamie laughed out loud then. "I knew I could count on you to make me feel better."

Mary Anne Douglass got up and moved around the table to give her daughter a hug. Jamie felt tears stinging her eyes, and knew her mother saw them, too, when she pulled away.

"I keep thinking of Sean and what he went through, and then I imagine Dan going through that all by himself. I don't know what to do," Jamie confessed. "He's sure I'm better off without him because of what's happened to him, and he's not even willing to consider how I feel about it. He's made his decision, and he thinks he knows what's best for me. I think he's being noble, in some twisted sort of way."

"Oh, honey. All men have their faults. And there's nothing wrong with having an old-fashioned man who wants to take care of you and protect you. It can be annoying at times, but kind of sweet at others. You're strong enough that you're not going to let any man walk all over you. But you said he's spent his whole life alone, except for a marriage that didn't last long and ended badly." Her mother sighed. "How old is he?"

"Thirty-nine."

Her mother nodded. "Men tend to get set in their ways. If he's never let anyone get that close to him, I don't think he's going to change now. He may not be *able* to change, even if he wants to. But I do know one thing for certain—you can't change him. Love him, if you can't help yourself, but don't ever let yourself think you can change him into the man you want him to be."

"I don't want to change who he is. I just want him to let me be a part of his life. He needs me now, Mom. I know he does. This has got to be the hardest thing he's ever gone through."

"I'm sure it is," her mother agreed. "But think about what you've just said. This is the hardest thing he's ever had to face, and he's doing it all by himself. He knows you're here, Jamie. He knows you want to see him, and he won't let you. What does that tell you?"

"Well, that he's been alone too long—that things get bad, and he puts up those walls of his and doesn't let anyone near him."

"I'm sure that's all true," her mother said, as gently as possible. "But there's more to it than that. I think it says he doesn't know *how* to let anyone into his life. I know that's not what you want to hear, and I'm sorry. But you have to consider the fact that he may never be able to let you or anyone else truly be a part of his life."

Jamie turned her head away, not wanting her mother to see how deeply hurt she was, not wanting to think Dan still could hurt her this much.

"I don't know how to stop caring about him," she said miserably. She had a feeling things were going to get worse before they got better.

An hour later, Jamie strolled inside the staid, utterly respectable-looking four-story brick office building in Georgetown where she reported for work when she wasn't off on some mission.

On the fourth floor, she walked through a door discreetly labeled Linguistic Services, Inc., a company loosely affiliated with the Commerce Department. The outer office did indeed house a small business offering the services of experts who wrote and spoke more than a dozen foreign languages and hired themselves out, either to high-ranking diplomats and government officials doing business in the capital or to Americans with interests abroad. Jamie spoke four languages fluently, and if pressed, could communicate on a rudimentary level in two more, which gave her more than adequate cover for the job she was supposed to have.

She entered a door to the right, marked Private, waited at a second set of doors to punch a code into the numbered keypad, which opened a ten-inch square panel in the wall. She placed her hand against the pressure pad, which scanned her palm, then beeped twice as a reinforced door slid open.

In the next room, she pulled out her ID for the security guard, who punched a code at her desk that brought up a retina scan at the third and final security door.

Inside, Jamie headed for Tanner's office. A former CIA operative who got his start in the military, Tanner was a real up-and-comer, a go-getter, and he was probably close to firing Jamie because she still hadn't given him her Section 123 report. But Tanner, she found, was tied up. His secretary, Amanda, promised to try to work Jamie in if he got a break.

Closing her own office door behind her, Jamie sat down at her desk and thought about what she was going to do. Tanner had accused her of letting her personal feelings for the agents involved cloud her judgment on the issue, and she couldn't argue that point with him.

Much as she tried, it was impossible to keep her personal feelings out of this. Obviously, Dan was lying to protect Geri. She was the one who disregarded orders and took off after the girl, and that decision led to a chain of events of disastrous proportions.

As for the fact that they were shot with one of the prototype weapons, she thought it must have been Doc's. Dan must have been mistaken, either in thinking it was Doc's voice he'd heard on the radio or in thinking he talked to

him only thirty seconds before he was shot. Either more time had elapsed, which would have given someone time to shoot Doc, grab his weapon and use it on Dan and Geri, or he simply believed it was Doc who responded to his call on the radio. It had been storming that night. They had been fighting static and interference from the storm, and they didn't exchange more than five words the last time they spoke. Under those circumstances, how could he possibly be certain he was talking to Doc? Jamie didn't think he could.

She was up and pacing around her office at that point. All she had to do was write down the facts, substitute a few out-and-out lies and give it to Tanner. It was what he and Dan both wanted—for her to lay the blame squarely on Dan's shoulders, and be done with it.

Maybe that was the problem—she didn't want to be done with it. She still wanted to find the people who shot Dan and Geri. She was still angry and frustrated and hurt, and had no way to work through those feelings or to let them go.

She was seated at her desk again a moment later, when Geri Sinclair burst in. Geri had been back in the office on restricted duty for two weeks. Jamie wondered if she'd talked to Dan or seen him, but she hadn't found a way to ask.

Normally the epitome of calm, Geri slapped some papers down on the desk, leaned across it and demanded, "How could you do this?"

"Do what?" Jamie asked.

"Recommend that Dan be reprimanded in connection with the shooting and Hathaway's escape?"

"What?"

Jamie snatched up the papers, unable to believe what she was seeing. It was labeled a Section 123 report, marked Confidential, supposedly written by her with copies sent to a half-dozen people. Flipping to the back, she was even more surprised to find an excellent likeness of her own signature on the final page.

"Where did you get this?" Jamie asked.

"Tanner and Mitchell went over the findings with me this morning. You knew they would. You knew Dan would see this, too. I can't believe you placed the blame for this whole disaster squarely on him."

Jamie started to explain that she hadn't, that for reasons she couldn't understand, someone had written the report and forged her signature. But that was too incredible to believe. It wasn't just a serious breach of department procedure, it was also offensive and hurtful to her personally, but she wasn't ready to blurt all this out to Geri. Jamie had to think first, had to find out who'd done this and why.

"I told you what happened out there. I told you the truth," Geri said. "Don't you understand? It wasn't him. It was me."

"I heard—"

"I thought you cared about him," Geri said. "Even if you don't, I thought you were honest, at the very least."

"I talked to Dan about this," she said, carefully reining in her temper. "I would have thought you had, too."

"What does that mean?"

"Ask him," Jamie suggested. She should have left it right there, but couldn't resist adding the rest, to find out if he'd been in contact with Geri this whole time. "Assuming you know where he is. Assuming he'll speak to you."

Geri stood back and studied her, thoroughly and dispassionately. "He didn't tell you where he went when he left the hospital?"

Jamie couldn't admit to Geri that he hadn't. She was furious with herself for saying as much as she had. But she had her answer. Geri obviously did know where he was. He hadn't cut everyone out of his life.

"Why did you do this to him?" Geri said finally.

"I didn't do anything to him," she insisted. "This is what he wanted."

"What?"

"You should know. After all, he did it for you."

The instant the words were out of Jamie's mouth, she regretted saying them. She certainly took no pleasure in seeing the stunned expression that spread across Geri's face.

If Dan wanted her, that was his choice. Jamie would hold her head up high and find a way to wish them well.

"I'm sorry," she said, ashamed of herself for how poorly she'd handled this conversation. "I assumed you knew what he was doing."

Geri shook her head, and rubbed absently at the muscle in her right arm, the one that had been damaged in the shooting. She looked a bit like she had that night in the emergency room when she found out Doc was dead. Jamie wondered just how many lives had been torn apart by that one, awful night.

"I'm sorry," she said again.

Geri picked up the report and held it in front of her. "It isn't true. Dan didn't... You know it isn't true."

Jamie did know, just as she knew she hadn't written that report.

After Geri left, Jamie leaned back in her chair and tried to think about what do to next. If she could, she would have talked through the entire mess with Dan, because she trusted his take on things more than anybody else's. But he'd made that impossible, damn him.

If she couldn't talk to Dan, she'd go to Josh. He appeared to be a lightweight, a too-pretty man who just played at life, who flitted from one woman to the next and never took anything seriously. Jamie had believed all of those things when they started working together. But she knew better now. She also trusted him.

Jamie got up to find him. As she walked into the hallway, she came face-to-face with Amanda.

"Tanner has a break in his schedule," Amanda said. "He's waiting for you right now."

Feeling decidedly uneasy about facing him this moment, she muttered her thanks and followed Amanda down the hall. When she entered Tanner's office, he was sitting behind his desk, his attention focused on his computer screen. He motioned for her to wait a moment, and she did, getting angrier and more nervous every minute.

Finally, he turned to her and said curtly, "Is there a problem?"

Because he hadn't invited her to sit, she stood in front of his desk, feeling the urge to snap to attention, as she would have while a superior officer chewed her out in military school, something she greatly resented at the moment.

"I understand I've finished my work on the Section 123 report and submitted my findings," she said.

Tanner got to his feet, walked around behind her. She heard him close the door, none too gently.

"Yes," he said, from some point behind her. "You have."

"It has my signature on it," she complained.

"Yes, it does."

"How could you—"

"I've asked for it several times," he interrupted. "I've tried to be patient, while everyone from Mitchell on up has been on my back about this. It couldn't wait any longer. So I took care of it."

Took care of it? Jamie was livid. "You forged my signature on an official agency report, and I—"

"Careful, soldier," he cautioned, coming around her right side and glaring at her. "You might want to think carefully about who you're talking to right now. I know we don't often stand on ceremony around here, and maybe I've been lax, and let things get too informal. But I am still your superior, and you'd do well to remember that.''

"Yes, sir," she said firmly, holding her temper in check.

"I gave you an assignment," Tanner said. "Maybe one that was too much for you to handle, especially after I had to pull Carter away to handle something else. But I've been patient, I told you what was expected of you, and you chose to ignore all of that."

"What was expected of me?" she said, wanting to hear him say it. He expected her to lie.

Tanner sighed heavily and continued pacing back and forth behind her. "Allowing Hathaway to escape while in our custody was the worst error this agency has ever made. We're being scrutinized as never before, and I'm doing all I can to see that this agency survives. Do you understand that?"

"Yes, sir," she said.

"Good. Because I'm tired. I'm frustrated. I'm angry, and I don't have time for agents who can't follow a direct order," he barked. "You will do exactly as you're told, when you're told, and nothing else."

"Yes, sir."

"Jamie," he softened his tone just a bit, "as a section leader, there are things I often know that I can't tell you. There are things my superiors know that they can't tell me, and there are things that only the president and a handful of his top advisers know that the rest of us can only speculate on. But rest assured that the people at the top have the best information available to them as they make their decisions. Our job is to trust in the abilities of our superiors and to carry out their orders."

"Yes, sir."

"I know our agents have always been given a certain

amount of freedom when operating in the field. I know we've counted upon your good judgment and your initiative, that it's served this agency well. But I don't need that from you right now. Understood?''

"Yes, sir.''

"Now, I know this has been a difficult few months. I know we've all been working under a great deal of stress, and I'm willing to look the other way on some of the differences you and I have had since the shooting....''

"Differences?'' she said. A polite euphemism, if she'd ever heard one. He'd submitted a Section 123 report he'd written under her name, with her forged signature attached to it.

"We had to give up someone,'' he said sternly. "Dan was the senior agent. Geri's much less experienced than he is. He admits he knew she was likely to go after that girl, that he feels he should have done more to stop her. Barring that, his first responsibility is to the agency, to the mission he'd been given. He should never have left the warehouse that night. And everything went to hell from that point on.''

"So, what about Geri?''

"She'll be reprimanded, but allowed to continue with her regular duties as soon as she's physically able.''

"And Dan?''

"I talked with him a few days ago. This is what he wanted.'' Tanner eased back onto the front of his desk, relaxing for the first time. "Now, can I assume this is finished?''

Jamie had the feeling her career was hanging as precariously ever. Tanner probably wanted an apology, and she wasn't sure she could give him one. She was still too angry at the way this had been handled, at the fact that her name was on that report. Trying to sound properly contrite, without actually apologizing, she said, "It's been a difficult time.''

Tanner nodded. "If this has all been too much for you... If you feel you can't carry out your duties at the moment... Tell me now. If not, I want your word that you will do exactly as you're told from here on out. No questions asked. Understood?"

"Yes, sir," she said.

It was clearly a warning, one she had to consider carefully.

First, she needed to see what was in that report. How hard could that be? After all, supposedly she wrote it.

Two hours later, she had the report in her hand. Jamie took it and left the building, walking off the worst of the tension inside her. Three miles later, she sat down outside to read the report and got angry all over again. Not that the report held any great surprises or that it was so different from what she would have written herself—if she'd agreed to go along with the version of events Dan and Tanner wanted in the report.

Her anger came from the way Tanner had taken the matter out of her hands, in the fact that the report held her signature, and in believing she was the only one who truly wanted to find the men who shot Dan and Geri. Somehow that had gotten lost in the government's frenzy to find Alex Hathaway, especially once his fingerprints were found on the gun used to kill Doc.

But two other government agents had also been shot that night, and the people responsible for it had never been found. That aspect of things had been pushed onto the back burner somehow, and Jamie was having trouble accepting it. She understood the theory—that whoever had come to get Hathaway out of the country was responsible, that they were likely long gone, and that Hathaway's work was of vital importance and must be found. But Dan was in a wheelchair. Their lives had been torn apart, and the people responsible for it were still out there. If they were ever found, it would only be because someone found Alex Hathaway and, in the process, also found the shooters outside the warehouse that night.

Jamie couldn't accept that, either.

The case haunted her. So did the place. She'd been down there wandering around again the day before. There had to be something more she could do. And she kept thinking about the missing weapons, Dan's, Geri's and Doc's. They'd found the Colt used to kill Doc a few blocks from the warehouse, and she could accept the idea that in his haste to get out of the area, Hathaway might have dropped that weapon. She could accept that after shooting all three agents, someone did a quick search of their bodies, disarmed them and took their weapons with them.

But where were those weapons now? Still in the hands of the men who shot Dan and Geri? And if anyone used them to commit a crime, the six-millimeter bullets were sure to raise red flags with the investigating officers. Jamie wondered if anyone had spotted either the weapons or the bullets.

She could put in a formal request for information from the agency to the FBI, which kept a number of databases available to state and local law enforcement agencies across the country. But if Tanner saw the request, he'd know what she was doing—deliberately disobeying the order he'd just given her.

There had to be another way to get into the FBI databases. And then she remembered Amanda's fiancé…Rob Jansen. He was a computer expert; he helped maintain those databases. And he knew her. She decided it was time to ask for a favor.

Later that afternoon Jamie was feeling better. She'd made the decision to follow her instincts and keep digging for information on the shooting. She met Rob Jansen in person, explained the information she needed and gave him a vague explanation of why she didn't want to go through official channels to get it. He knew it was information she could easily have gotten access to by making a formal request through Division One, but he agreed to check the databases himself. That way there would be no official record that she'd requested the information, and no one but Rob and Jamie would know if they'd found anything.

She'd also have the satisfaction of knowing that at least she'd checked. Hopefully, Tanner would never find out.

That taken care of, she had to turn to the business at hand. She and Josh were attending a party at the French embassy that night. They were back on the assignment they'd been working on when the explosion in London temporarily put the job on hold. In honor of the occasion, she was dressed to kill, both literally and figuratively. But she and Josh were meeting at the agency first.

There was a stiletto strapped to the inside of her left thigh and a tiny but deadly .22 in her little black evening bag. The dress left no options for hiding a gun on her body. It was mostly strategically placed black sequins held together by a bit of flesh-colored mesh—nothing she would have selected herself, but she had to admit it was effective. In this dress, high heels, sheer black stockings and several thousand dollars in jewelry wrapped around her wrist and her neck, she could catch the eye of any man she wanted—including a certain reclusive Frenchman who was suspected of funneling sophisticated explosives from one of his legitimate businesses in the United States into the U.K.

Strolling through the office, she found Josh flirting with one of the secretaries. As always, he managed to look elegantly handsome, not a wrinkle to be seen in that wickedly expensive tux of his, not a blond hair out of place, and he was beaming at her.

"Wow," he said appreciatively, holding out a hand to her, then guiding her into a slow circle in front of him. "The poor fools at the party tonight will be babbling incoherently, and we'll never get a decent voiceprint on them."

Jamie smiled. She was familiar with the full force of Joshua Carter's smile and the smoldering look in his eyes. They'd impersonated a married couple—or lovers—on assignment often enough. But while she valued Josh's friendship and respected his abilities as an agent, she was curiously immune to his charms.

"Hit the dimmer switch, Josh, at least until we get to the embassy."

"Humor me. I'm on a mission." He winked at her, hooked his arm around her waist and pulled her off to the side where there was an open space.

"A mission?"

He pulled her into his arms, pressed his cheek to hers and started humming. "Dance with me," he ordered.

"I'm warning you, Josh," she said with exaggerated sweetness. "If this is a ploy to make some woman jealous…"

"Nope." He grinned, dipped his head and nuzzled her neck.

It tickled, and she laughed. Then he twirled her around and caught her close again.

"Josh," she warned.

"Come on," he whispered into her ear. "We're doing a mike check."

"We just did that in the lab."

"While you were dancing?"

"No, not while I was dancing," she said, confident that the new, ultrasensitive recording equipment built into the beads of her dress and into her earrings had been checked under a variety of conditions. "What are you up to?"

"In a minute," he insisted, pulling her even closer. "Could you look like you're enjoying this a little?"

Jamie sighed and gave in, taking a turn around the room with him. Then, impatient, she stepped out of Josh's arms. Turning to go to her office, she dragged him along with her. Once inside, she said, "Okay, what are you up to?"

"Dan's here."

"Oh." It was all she could manage, the last thing she'd expected him to say.

"He's been glaring at me ever since I walked into the office, and it gave me an idea." Josh smiled wickedly. "I thought we could give him something to think about."

She leaned back against the wall and took a deep breath, thinking this probably wasn't the wisest thing Josh could have done, but it probably wouldn't matter to Dan anyway.

"Did he see us?"

Josh nodded. "Looked like he could cheerfully slit my throat. Hell, what am I saying? He could really hurt me. If he comes after me, tell him to be careful of my pretty face, okay?"

"Don't worry," she reassured him. "You had it right the first time. Dan would go for your throat. Assuming he'd care if you and I were involved."

"He cares."

"He certainly has a funny way of showing it," she said, trembling.

Josh pulled her to him, held her for a minute, no pretense to the embrace this time. "You going to be okay?"

"I..." She gave up, let every doubt she had show. "I have to forget about him."

Josh laughed. "You've been doing a lousy job of it. I think you need to talk to him."

"I'm really mad at him," she admitted.

"Fine." He stepped back, grinned wickedly and pushed her toward the door. "Tell him all about it. He deserves to hear it."

Chapter 9

At first, she was nothing but a flash of light, a glint of gently swaying color glimpsed from the corner of his eye. Turning his head, Dan saw her as he'd never seen her before.

Jet-black hair and ivory skin wrapped in swaying, sparkling black beads. His hands faltered on the rim of the wheels of his wheelchair and a choking sound came from his throat. The dress... It made him think of a magazine layout of a well-known actress in a painted-on dress, a clever optical illusion of a woman who appeared to be clothed but wasn't.

But Jamie was dressed, he told himself. There must be fabric under there somewhere. The black beads had to be attached to something other than whispery soft, sweet skin.

But from this distance, it looked as if someone had draped a layer of strategically placed beads over her naked body.

Damn.

He'd always known she was beautiful. Even sweating, her face flushed, her body dusty and muddy, even exhausted and angry, yelling at him, crying over him…she was beautiful.

But he'd never seen her like this.

She took his breath away, had him feeling like an adolescent boy again with sweaty palms and a perpetual hard-on.

She did that to him, too. Especially after that night in the solarium.

He'd wondered if she hated him for the way he'd disappeared, if she had indeed moved on with her life. He couldn't blame her if she had, but it was only going to be a little bit longer, he kept telling himself. He'd waited this long, come this far in rehab. He could wait a few more days to talk to her—to explain.

He hadn't expected to run into Jamie today. He'd met with Tanner and was on his way out the door when he heard Jamie laughing, a muffled sexy sound that had heat curling inside his belly, making him warm all over. It sent him after one more glimpse of her before he left.

Then he saw shimmering black beads gliding down the hallway, and bare, ivory-pale arms twined around the shoulders of the man in a black tuxedo. The man was smiling as he dropped his mouth to the side of her delectable neck. She laughed again, as they danced. As the man twirled her around, his face came into view.

Josh.

Of course, it would be Josh.

Dan shoved the chair forward, down the hall and through the doorway of the deserted conference room, knowing he'd be smart to try to calm down.

It was hard to push a wheelchair when his hands were clenched into fists and when he really wanted to slam one of his fists into the wall.

No, he reconsidered. Not into the wall. A face. A mouth too pretty to be a man's. He'd ram that satisfied little sigh right down Joshua Carter's throat.

It didn't help in the least that Dan had no right to care whether Jamie was sleeping with Josh, whether he'd pushed her right into Josh's arms. Dan still wanted to strangle the man. Right after he ripped Jamie out of his arms.

From the chair? he reminded himself. It would be a neat trick to do either one of those things from the wheelchair.

Of course, long odds had never dissuaded him from going after anything he wanted. And he wanted Jamie.

He wheeled around and went to find her. When he didn't spot her after making the rounds of the office, he slipped into her office. The light over her desk was on. So was her computer. She'd be back, and he could wait.

Dan finally had accepted the fact that he was obsessed with Jamie, that he wanted her in every way possible for a man to want a woman, that he couldn't keep his hands off her when she was near him. All she'd done that day in the solarium was lean over and give him a quick kiss goodbye, and he'd hauled her up against him, had his hands all over her, had her nearly undressed in seconds. He'd been so crazy for her he'd forgotten that his legs didn't work the way they used to. He hadn't remembered until he found himself sprawled on top of her and had been hardly able to move.

It had been the stuff of his nightmares. When he'd been in the hospital and his mind drifted unerringly back to her and he remembered the way she tasted that night at the warehouse, remembered the feel of her body caught between his and the wall, and he wanted her despite all the reasons he couldn't have her, he made himself think of making love to her without his legs. He pictured himself lying flat on his back in a bed, pictured her pretty body sitting on top of his, moving slowly but urgently against him, and he imagined himself just lying there helplessly, motionless beneath her.

That image had been humiliating enough to make him push her away from him in the hospital.

But then she'd taken that image away that night in the solarium by so willingly spreading those sleek thighs of hers and settling her body against his. By letting him push her clothes out of the way and pressing her breasts against his chest. By kissing him as hungrily as he kissed her and rocking her body against his, as if she ached for him every bit as much as he ached for her.

She'd shown him that making love to her would be anything but humiliating. It would be urgent and edgy and utterly satisfying. Together, they could find a way. He knew it in his heart. But his pride got in the way and he left the hospital without telling Jamie where he was going.

Yet the idea of being with her had flirted around the edges of Dan's mind. Life with Jamie… What would that be like?

He'd had to remind himself that very little had actually happened between them. They'd worked together. They'd bickered a bit here and there. They'd made one date they never kept. And they'd nearly made love. Put that way, it seemed ridiculous that his feelings for her could be this strong. But there it was, staring him in the face. Now that he'd seen her after so many weeks, he couldn't fight his need for her any longer, and he couldn't stay away.

So he sat there in the corner of her office, cursing himself for what he'd done to her already and trying to figure out how to make it up to her.

Finally, she walked into her office and shut the door behind her.

He remained motionless in his spot in the corner as she pulled a .22 from the tiny purse she carried, loaded it, checked the safety and put it away.

Then she put one foot, in its black, high-heeled sandal, on the low table in the corner. When her dress, slit up one side, fell open at midthigh, his mouth went dry. Her hands reached for a thin, deadly stiletto strapped high on her thigh. She pulled the knife, flicked open the blade, examined it in the light, then froze.

She knew she wasn't alone.

"Expecting trouble?" he asked casually.

Slowly, she straightened and turned to face him. Dan noted a dangerous glint in her eyes as she walked toward him. She was breathing rapidly, the seemingly nonexistent material of the dress straining across her breasts, as she brandished the weapon in her right hand.

"You should be more careful," she cautioned. "After all, I'm armed and quite possibly dangerous."

"I'll keep that in mind," he said, fighting a grin. God, it was good to see her. "Are you planning to use that on me?"

"Well," she considered. "I guess that depends on what you have to say for yourself."

At the moment, it was all he could do to think clearly, knowing that not five minutes ago another man had his hands and his mouth all over her. He wanted to obliterate any trace of Joshua Carter's touch, wanted his own hands in her hair, and his taste on her lips, her neck and her cheek.

But there were some things he needed to tell her, some things he owed her. Gritting his teeth, he forced himself to admit, "I missed you."

Her chin came up defiantly. "Really?"

"Yes."

That only served to infuriate her even more. He saw fire flashing in her eyes, saw a grim look of determination there as well.

"Is that supposed to be an apology?" she demanded.

"Well—"

"Or an explanation? For letting me walk back into that hospital six weeks ago and find out you'd left without a word to me? For refusing to even pick up the phone and talk to me when I called?"

"Jamie—"

"I've never seen you run and hide from anyone. Or anything. I didn't think you had a cowardly bone in your body."

Ouch.

He deserved it, he told himself. He'd hurt her. Again.

Still...*a coward.* No one had ever called him a coward.

"What do you want me to say?" he asked. "That I'm sorry? I am."

She came to stand in front of him, too close to him. He could smell her perfume. Or whatever subtle scent she drenched her body in. He shifted uncomfortably in the chair, feeling cornered and not liking it a bit.

"Funny," she said, "You don't look sorry."

"Jamie..." he began.

She braced her hands on either side of the low arms on his chair. He leaned back as far as he could, but still, he felt heat and anger radiating from her body. He saw perfectly formed breasts and through the slit up the side of her dress, a smooth, silky thigh. Her scent washed over him, overwhelming him. Her breath skimmed across his mouth, giving him just a hint of the taste of her, making him want desperately.

All he had to do was reach out and take her.

He didn't care anymore that she'd been with Josh only moments before. She was with him now, and he wanted to keep her here, wanted to pull her across his lap and palm her hips and pull her to him, because he was every bit as aroused as he had been that day in the solarium. And he hadn't even touched her yet. He hadn't planned on letting himself touch her at all.

She leaned closer still, until her lips were aligned with his, until he wasn't sure if she was going to smack him or kiss him. He deserved the first, yearned for the second.

"I know," she whispered seductively, an angry woman scorned, "you told me once that it wouldn't matter to you if you and I did make love. You said it wouldn't last, either. I just didn't believe you."

"Jamie—"

"But don't worry." She straightened, gave him a cold, almost regal stare. "The last six weeks convinced me. I won't make the mistake again of thinking you give a damn about me."

She turned to walk away, but he caught her, held her with a hard grip on her arm until finally she faced him once again. But how could he beg her to forgive him for what from her point of view had to seem unforgivable?

"Jamie—don't go."

"This is what you wanted," she reminded him.

"No, it's not what I wanted," he said.

"Oh, I forgot," she said, livid now. "It's what you decided was best for both of us. As if the decision had nothing to do with me. Or anything I may have felt for you."

"You're right," he admitted. "That's what I did."

She folded her arms across her chest and glared at him. "Is *that* supposed to be an apology?"

Dan fought the urge to grin and to tell her she looked absolutely beautiful tonight. He knew just enough about women to realize he had only one option here—a full confession and a plea for mercy—something he'd never been willing to do for any woman before. But he had been a jerk, and he'd been absolutely miserable without her.

"I thought I might be able to negotiate with you," he tried instead.

"Negotiate?"

He nodded. "I'm prepared to make a full confession. In

exchange for that, I thought you might consider going easy on me? After all, I'm a man, and my species is notoriously inept and insensitive when it comes to dealing with women.''

''Inept and insensitive?'' she repeated incredulously. ''And I'm supposed to let you get away with it? Because I'm a woman and *my* species can forgive anything?''

He laughed, because he thought he was making progress with her and because it felt so good just to argue with her. ''Some women can,'' he admitted.

She shook her head and muttered something that didn't sound very forgiving.

''Jamie.'' Dan reached out and took her hand, curling his fingers around the back of hers, grateful when she didn't pull away. ''I'm sorry, babe. I'm lousy at this, and I just can't seem to stop hurting you. I swear it's the last thing on earth I want to do.''

All the fight seemed to go out of her. Her shoulders relaxed a bit. Her chin came down. Her eyes glittered with moisture, and her voice shook. ''Okay, *that* was something remotely resembling an apology. It needs work, but...''

''Maybe I'm not hopeless?''

''I'm not sure. You've obviously been indulged for too long by women with half a brain and a thing for arrogant—''

''Come on.''

''Stubborn—''

''Jamie.''

''Insensitive—''

He laughed again.

''Jerks,'' she finished.

''Maybe you could take me on as a project. Reform me. For the good of womankind,'' he offered, forgetting all the promises he'd made to himself about not touching her.

Tugging on her hand until she bent over him, he took

her mouth hungrily, the too brief touch only serving to make him want her more. "If it helps, I've been miserable the last few weeks. And not just because rehab is hell," he admitted.

"I might find some satisfaction in knowing you've been miserable."

He winced theatrically, ready to grovel some more. "Maybe we could discuss this outside the office? Preferably when you're not armed to the teeth?"

"Talk about what?" she said carefully.

"You and me."

She went still, staring at him, measuring, assessing, probably trying to figure out if she could trust him again. "Dan, I'm stubborn, but I'm not foolish. I don't make a habit of chasing after men who don't want anything to do with me, and I don't like playing games."

"I'm stubborn, too, and I can be incredibly foolish at times. No more games, Jamie. Promise."

"Well," she admitted reluctantly, "I suppose we could talk."

"You're a generous woman," he said.

"Yes, I am."

He laughed again, then glanced at the clock that read half-past seven, then looked back at her in that killer dress. "I take it you have to be somewhere tonight."

She looked at the clock as well. "Oh. Yes. Josh and I are going to a party at the French embassy, and I don't have much time."

"Okay." He dropped her hand.

"So, are you still at the rehab facility or have you…" Her voice trailed off awkwardly and for the first time, she let herself take a good, long look at his body in the chair.

He found himself holding his breath, braced for what he might find in her eyes. Seeing nothing but determination and a calm, steady gaze, he could breathe again.

"I have another couple of weeks there. Maybe a month. I haven't given up yet," he said carefully, measuring her reaction and wanting to make all sorts of rash promises about what he intended to accomplish before he came back for her. "Please, Jamie. Don't you give up on me, either."

"I won't. At least not until you've had a chance to explain yourself."

She leaned over and kissed him softly, sweetly. Dan felt heat unfurl inside his body, flaring up and burning steadily, seeping into every inch of his body. He pressed his hand against the side of her face, bringing her mouth back to his. Her lips parted easily. Her breath hitched, and he let himself savor the taste of her, the small intimacy of being inside her this way, even as he cursed the awkwardness of trying to kiss her while sitting in the damned chair.

Still, he went right on kissing her, needing her, knowing he'd take the memory of this back with him and it would help him through the long, lonely nights and frustrating days ahead, as the memory of her had done all along, ever since he woke up in the hospital three months ago. Even if she'd never known it.

"I missed you, too," she admitted as she broke off the kiss and stood up.

He watched, drinking in the sight of her, knowing he'd take this image of her back with him, that she was going to get him through the battle that still lay ahead. Dan smiled up at her, staring until soft color filled her cheeks and she walked around behind him. He started to turn around, because he wanted to look at her some more. But then he felt her come to stand right behind him, her hands settling on his shoulders, gently kneading the muscles there.

"God, you are like some kind of poison to me," she confessed.

"That bad, huh?"

"Obviously. I didn't kick you out," she complained. "If

I had any sense at all, I'd kick you out of my office. I wouldn't listen to anything you had to say, and I'd tell myself I'd suffered enough because of you.''

Dan would have been worried, if she hadn't been touching him as she spoke. "Believe me," he said. "You've tormented me the entire time I've been gone."

"I doubt we're talking about the same thing."

"You don't think you've messed with my mind? Or that you've gotten inside my head?" He laughed. "You honestly believe it's just about sex, Jamie?"

He held her by her arm and twisted around in the chair until he could see her.

"If it was just about sex, I wouldn't have stopped that day in the solarium. The damned building could have come down around us, and it wouldn't have mattered to me. We would have finished what we started. You understand that, don't you?"

"I—"

"Don't mistake me. I want you. Even though I know I shouldn't, I still want you." He let his eyes rake over her body in one long, slow, blatantly assessing look. "But this thing between us is much more complicated than that." She came tantalizingly closer, her hands settling onto his shoulders again, working in earnest over the strained muscles there. It felt so good to have her touch him that way.

"Jamie—I'm sorry about disappearing," he said. "I know there's nothing I can say to make up for what I did, but…I'm sorry, babe. It's practically a reflex to me, to push people away. Although I'm not usually so callous about it." But he found he was scared half to death of her, of the way he needed her in his life.

She said nothing, her hands now lying still on his shoulders.

"It's not you," he tried to reassure her. "It's just the

way I am. You know that, don't you? You know it wasn't you?"

"I wasn't sure," she said hesitantly.

Damn. Her words cut right into him. He'd hurt her terribly. And he thought he should come clean about everything, to give her fair warning, at least.

"Jamie, there haven't been a lot of women in my life in the last few years. None that meant anything to me, anyway." He hesitated. It had been a long time since he talked about this to anyone. "You should know...I was married once. A long time ago."

"I know that."

"And I wasn't what you'd call stellar husband material."

"Oh, I never would have guessed that."

She laughed, softly, sadly, and slid her fingers into his hair.

"I should try to explain it to you. I owe you that much at least." He sighed. "You remind me of her."

Jamie stiffened. "How?"

"She was so young. She didn't have a cynical bone in her body. When I met her, she was so happy. She always had a smile on her face. She could make me laugh when no one else could, and I took that innocent young woman and drained every bit of happiness right out of her. By the time she left me, she was a totally different person. I did that to her. I hurt her. I ruined everything for her."

"How?"

"She hated being a soldier's wife. Hated the long separations, the danger, hated what I was like right after I came home."

"You were a soldier when she met you, weren't you?"

"Yes."

"Did you change so much after the two of you were married?"

"I don't know," he said.

"Or did she think she was going to change you?"

"She wanted me out of the military."

"And you didn't get out."

"I wouldn't," he admitted. "She wasn't... The job..."

"Meant more to you than she did?"

He nodded. It had come down to that. He hadn't loved her that much, had never loved anyone or anything that much. He wasn't sure he was capable of such an emotion, but he was a stand-out at regrets.

"She wanted a husband who would be there for her. Babies— I made her miserable," he confessed. "And I don't ever want to do that to a woman again. I don't want to do that to you."

"And you're certain that any kind of relationship we might have would leave me miserable in the end?"

"I don't know, babe." He leaned back against her. Jamie's arms tightened around him.

"I just wanted you to know what it was like between me and her," he said.

"Okay."

"And Jamie? If there comes a time when this is too much...." He looked down at the wheelchair. "If it gets too hard... I want you to know that you don't owe me anything, all right? You can just turn around and walk away. Promise me you will."

"No."

"Jamie—" Her arms fell away. She backed away from him as well, and when he turned to face her, he could tell he'd said something very, very wrong. "What?"

"You don't understand anything, do you?"

"Maybe I don't."

"Dan, if I could forget about you... If I could just turn around and walk away, believe me, I would have done it by now."

He let the words sink in, found them profoundly satisfying. She couldn't forget about him, either. No matter how hard she tried.

He felt like a fool for waiting this long to see her again. Maybe he didn't deserve her, but he was going to do his best to give her whatever she wanted from him, whatever she needed.

"Jamie, I—"

The intercom unit on her phone sounded. A voice said, "Ms. Douglass?"

Jamie closed her eyes tightly. "Yes."

"Final mission briefing in five minutes."

"I'll be right there," she said, moving behind her desk and pressing a button to break the connection.

Dan wished he could get up and go to her. He wished he could take her in his arms and hold her tightly. He wished he knew exactly what to say to her and how to make things right. Now that he'd seen her again, he didn't want to leave her.

She looked as if the whole scene had thrown her totally off-balance. She ran a hand through her hair, pushing back a few strands that had escaped from behind her ears. Then she stood behind her desk, leafing through some papers, finally finding what she wanted.

"Dan?"

"Hmm?"

She held up a stack of papers. "Tanner gave you the Section 123 report?"

"Yes."

"Did you read it?"

"I skimmed it." He hadn't been interested in giving it a careful read. That damned report wouldn't change anything. He knew what he'd done. He knew he felt guilty about it, that he always would. Especially because of Doc.

"Would you look at it again? Carefully?" Jamie asked. "I need to talk through it with somebody."

"If you're worried about what it says about me…"

"It's more than that," she insisted.

"Okay," he said, wondering exactly what was wrong. "I'll read it."

"Thanks." She looked at the clock once more, picked up the tiny, glittering black bag she'd stowed her gun in, then grabbed the stiletto. "I really have to go."

"Can I call you tonight?"

"It's probably going to be late before I make it home tonight. Midnight, at least."

Which he took to mean that she'd be there alone, waiting to talk to him. He had a sudden image of her curled up in a rumpled bed, her dark hair fanned out against the pillow, creamy skin waiting for him beneath the covers.

This could prove to be a very interesting conversation.

"That's all right," he said. "I'm up late."

"Okay," she said.

He caught her hand as she walked past him, tugged her down for a frustratingly brief kiss. "Be careful."

"I will," she promised.

And then he sat there and watched as she walked into the hallway. Joshua Carter appeared, beaming at her, and Dan watched as they walked away together.

Chapter 10

She wasn't home at midnight. He knew, because he called. She wasn't home at twelve-fifteen, either. Or twelve-thirty.

He had no idea what she and Josh were supposed to be doing at the French embassy, but he was certain it had the potential to turn dangerous.

By twelve forty-five, he was thinking of bribing one of the orderlies to drive him to Georgetown, where she lived. By one o'clock, he would have been pacing if he'd been able to stand on his own for any length of time.

And finally, at a few minutes past one, she called him.

"Hi," she said, sounding sleepy and relaxed. And happy.

Happy to be talking to him? He could certainly hope so. He felt ridiculously better just to hear her voice.

"Hi," he said. He really wanted to say something like, "You're late," but knew he didn't have the right.

"I'm sorry. I was out later than I thought. Did I wake you?"

As if he could have gone to sleep wondering where she was and whether she was safe.

"No," he said. Then he heard a slow, sleepy sigh and a few other sounds he couldn't identify. "What are you doing?"

"Nothing."

"Jamie?" She must have pressed her hand over the mouthpiece of the phone, because he didn't hear anything for a moment.

"I don't want to tell you, all right?"

"No, it's not. What's wrong?"

"I'm just feeling a little self-conscious."

"Why?"

"Because I was hoping to get through this conversation without you figuring out what else I'm doing right now."

"This is starting to get interesting," he said.

She groaned.

"I know what I'd like you to be doing," he offered, ready to seduce her with words, if nothing else.

"And that would be?"

"I'll give you a hint. It involves a bed—yours. You'd be lying down on it. I'm still trying to decide what you'd wear. Something soft. Not satin. It would be too cold against your skin. Something warm. Touchable. Something short."

"I have soft, short things I wear to bed."

It was his turn to groan.

She laughed. Beautifully. Softly. The sound brought every nerve ending in his body roaring to life. Then he heard water, the gentle, rippling sound of water moving against a surface, and he groaned.

"You're in the bathtub?"

This was better than he imagined. No, worse. His body reminded him once again of just how long it had been since he'd taken a woman to bed with him, how long he'd likely have to wait before he had her with him in a bed.

"Dan," she protested.

"You are. You're in the tub." He swore, picturing an expanse of pale, ivory-colored skin and dark clouds of hair. And soft candlelight. If he ever saw her in the tub, he'd want the light to come from candles. She'd put something in the tub, that stuff she wore to smell so good. Bath salts, probably. They would make the water a little cloudy. Along with the rippling of the water so her image would be slightly distorted, letting him see her but not really see her.

Dan could hardly believe it. She was talking to him on the phone from her bathtub. *Naked.* The temperature in his room rose instantly. He was starting to sweat, could barely breathe.

"Do you have any idea what you're doing to me?" he asked.

"I told you I didn't want you to know. I was just tired and all wound up, but I wanted to talk to you. And a bath always helps me to relax."

"I'm not relaxed," he complained, feeling the heat settle low in his belly, feeling a slow, hard throbbing of his pulse.

"Sorry." She laughed again.

"No. You're not. You're enjoying this, and I'm…"

"What?" she asked innocently.

"What do you think?"

"Is there anything I can do?"

Dan groaned and cursed and smiled in rapid succession. "You're killing me, babe."

"Really?"

"You little witch. You know you are."

He heard another ripple of water, was crazy enough to let himself imagine what she might have been doing to make that sound. He was going to get her into that bathtub again, when he was there. He'd look his fill. Wash every inch of her. And then get into the tub with her.

Damn.

He wanted her now, had done nothing but dream of her

and want her and make love to her in his mind for weeks on end. He'd become obsessed with her to the point that there was nothing else inside his head except walking again and having her. Somehow, the two had become inexplicably intertwined. He would walk again. He would go to her. He'd have her.

She was going to be his reward.

Just a few more weeks, he told himself. He could wait a few more weeks. As far as he knew, no man had ever died from wanting a woman.

"So," he said, "have you forgiven me yet? Or do I need to grovel some more?"

"You don't grovel well at all, you know."

"Well, it's not something I normally do."

"Oh, that's right. You've been indulged to this point."

He tried to concentrate on the conversation, but it wasn't working. He could still hear the soft movements of her body in the water, could so clearly imagine rivulets of water running down her sleek, sexy body. He couldn't go on like this.

"Do me a favor, Jamie. Indulge me this one time. Go put on some clothes, and I'll call you back."

"Dan—"

"I'll beg, okay? Whatever it takes. Just get dressed. I can't have a conversation with you while you're naked."

"Dan—"

"I'm not kidding. Get dressed."

Jamie heard the click of the phone, and then nothing. He'd hung up on her.

She smiled, put down the phone and leaned back until her head was resting against the rim of the tub. He meant it. She was making him crazy, and she found the whole idea incredibly satisfying. After all, he'd made her crazy for years. And she wasn't getting out of the tub right away. Let the man suffer a little more.

When the phone rang a moment later, she brought it slowly to her ear and left her head where it was, leaning against the back of the tub, feeling happier and more relaxed than she'd been in months.

"Hi," she said softly.

Silence greeted her and then a rather formal, "Ms. Douglass?"

She sat up quickly, splashing water everywhere and nearly dropping the phone. She didn't recognize the voice on the other end of the phone. "Yes?"

"This is Detective Russell, D.C. police."

"Yes?"

"I'm sorry to call so late. I thought I had your office number."

"It's all right. I was awake." She jumped out of the tub and grabbed for a towel. "What can I do for you, Detective?"

"I put in a request for information with the FBI a few days ago about an odd-sized slug we found in the wall of a liquor store after an armed robbery, and a Mr. Jansen at the FBI asked me to call you. I work the night shift, so I tend to make calls either late at night or very early in the morning."

"It's no problem," she reassured the detective, trying to think like an agent, not like a naked woman who'd been caught in her tub. "This bullet...you haven't been able to identify it?"

"No, ma'am," he drawled. "It's smaller than anything I'm used to seeing, obviously made of something capable of piercing body armor. I'd hate to be out on the streets with these all over the place."

"I'd like very much to see it," she said.

"Name the day."

"What time does your shift end?"

"If I'm lucky, 7:00 a.m."

She frowned at the clock, then decided she didn't need sleep. Not if he had evidence. "I'll meet you in the morning. At your precinct house."

She thanked him, toweled off quickly and was riffling through her underwear drawer in search of a short, soft cotton nightgown when the phone rang again. This time she recognized the gruff, impatient voice.

"So," he growled, "I'm not the only man you converse with from your bathtub?"

"What?"

"Your messaging service," he reminded her. "It was kind enough to tell me you were on the phone at the moment, before it offered to take my message."

"Oh?" Her phone had a vast array of special features, including a messaging service that picked up when she was on another call and told the second caller precisely that.

"So, I'm not the only man who gets to talk to you while you're naked?"

"Not tonight," she deadpanned.

Dan swore.

"It was a cop."

"I don't care what he does for a living."

"It was work," she explained, hoping he was jealous. After all, the man had put her through hell. He deserved to suffer.

"Did you tell him you were naked?"

"Come to think of it…I don't think I mentioned it. We had other things to talk about. Like getting together first thing in the morning."

He swore again.

She just laughed at him.

"Is this the part," he growled, "where you tell me it's none of my business who you talk to at one o'clock in the morning? Or the part where I get slammed for not being the kind of man who wouldn't mind if someone else is after you, too?''

"Take your pick," she offered.

"Jamie—"

"I told you. He's a cop. He has an interesting bullet to show me."

"Okay."

"Maybe a six-millimeter."

"Really?"

"I thought that might get your attention." She gave up on finding a nightgown, just stretched out on the bed and pulled the covers over her. "I had a friend at the FBI watching for queries about unidentifiable bullets. I may have gotten lucky."

"Where was this one found?"

"They dug it out of a wall at a liquor store in the District after a robbery five days ago."

Dan whistled. "Good work."

"Well, we don't have a match yet. Just something a ballistics person hasn't been able to identify."

"You're going to take a look at it in the morning?"

"Yes. It's the first thing I've seen that looks remotely like a lead in this case."

"I should let you get some sleep," he offered.

"Mmm."

"Did you make it to bed?"

"Uh-huh."

"Want to tell me about your nightgown?"

She wondered if it was possible to blush all over, marveled at the tone of the whole conversation. He obviously wanted her to know he wanted her. And that he wanted to finish what they had started that night, which now seemed so long ago.

"I'm not wearing anything at all," she said boldly.

"Jamie," he protested.

"What?"

"I'm stuck in this place for at least a few more weeks. Maybe a month."

"They won't let you out?"

He groaned. "It's not exactly a prison. I could leave any time I wanted, but I need to be here right now. Rehab isn't a nine-to-five, Monday-through-Friday kind of thing."

"Oh," she said carefully, forced to think again of the physical limitations he might be facing when he was finished.

But it didn't matter, she told herself. Dan would still be Dan, and she'd still care about him. Oh, she was nervous about the struggles they would face, but she wanted him— any way she could get him.

"I thought about what you said this afternoon," she said. "About…your injuries. I want you to know that whatever happens, I can handle it. We both can."

"Baby, I never wanted you to have to handle it."

"Well, I never wanted you to have to handle this, either, but you don't exactly have a choice. Neither do I."

"You don't even know how much control of my legs I'm going to get back. I don't know that myself right now. I'm not sure how I'm going to get through this."

"But you will. You have the strongest will of any man I've ever known. Whatever happens, you'll deal with it. And so will I."

"The chair—"

"Hasn't changed the way I feel about you." She sighed, searching for anything she could say or do to convince him. "What if I was the one in the chair? Would it change what you felt for me?"

"Jamie—"

"Would it? Would you turn around and walk away from me?"

"No," he said.

"Then how can it be so hard for you to believe me when I say it doesn't change the way I feel about you? And don't even begin to insult me again the way you did today by telling me to just turn around and walk away."

"I meant it," he said.

"Which makes it even worse," she complained. "You wouldn't walk away from me, Dan."

"No, I won't."

She waited, and he said nothing, although she thought she'd made some headway with him. "I want to see you," she said again.

"I'll be there. In a couple of weeks."

"And in the meantime, I'll come to you."

"Please don't."

"Why not?"

"Because I don't want you here."

"Oh," she said, wincing at the hurt that came along with his words, at the idea of battles still to be fought.

"This is something I need to get through by myself."

"No, it's most definitely not the kind of thing you get through on your own."

"Jamie, please. Give me a couple of weeks. The worst of this will be over, and we'll be together."

"Until things get tough again?"

"What?"

"We'll be together until something bad happens. Until some problem crops up, and you disappear on me?"

"You think I'd walk away from you when you needed me?"

"No, I think you'd walk away when *you* needed *me*. I know it. You've already done it once, and that matters a great deal to me."

She started to shake, feeling scared and alone, thinking again of her mother's warning. She couldn't change him.

He couldn't give her something he simply didn't have to give.

But damn it, she'd been so hopeful that this time it would work. But if he never let her truly be a part of his life, if he kept things separated into neat little compartments, some of which she could be a part of, and some she couldn't, how would she handle that? How could she overcome it?

"You can't give me a little bit of yourself and hold back the rest," she said, her voice breaking.

"Jamie," he said, sounding so very sad.

"Think about it, Dan. Think very carefully. I can take the wheelchair. But I can't handle the walls you're determined to put between us."

"I don't know what to tell you," he admitted finally. "I've been this way for a long time. I don't know how to be any other way."

"Tell me you'll try. Tell me you'll talk to me about what you're going through there and how it makes you feel. Lean on me a little. Tell me you'll think about letting me come see you."

"I'll talk to you," he said quickly. "Every night when you climb into bed. You can tell me about your day, and I'll tell you about mine, while I lie here and go half-crazy imagining what it would be like if I was there with you."

"You don't have to imagine," she insisted. "You *could* be here with me if you weren't so damned stubborn."

He swore. "You don't fight fair, babe."

"You taught me not to."

"Jamie—"

"You can't fight me and yourself. I don't think you'll be able to stay away from me," she argued. "I think you're tired of being alone. And I'm right here waiting for you. All you have to do is come to me."

"It's not that simple," he claimed.

"It's every bit as simple as that. Come to me, and I'll

show you." Then she thought of one more argument. "If you won't do it for yourself, do it for me," she said. "Maybe you don't need me now, but I need you. I have a bad feeling about this whole mess with the shooting. I'm not sure what I should do next, and I need you. I'm worried this thing's going to burst wide-open and once it does, I don't know what's going to happen."

"Then back off. Now. While you still can. I can be there in two weeks, Jamie."

"I can't wait that long."

"Then at least stick close to Josh. This is no time to be running around on your own."

"Josh is busy."

"Doing what?"

"I'm not sure. Tanner pulled him off the Section 123 review weeks ago. He's been quiet about it, and I haven't pushed him to tell me what he's been doing."

"Back off, Jamie."

"Come and help me," she countered.

"God, you are the most stubborn woman I've ever met."

"And you're an incredibly exasperating man. Arrogant, stubborn, irritating. I must be crazy, but I just can't forget about you, no matter how mad you make me."

"I guess that means we were meant for each other," he said.

"You *guess?*" she exclaimed in mock outrage.

"We can't even have a conversation without arguing."

"That's because you're still fighting it."

"It?"

"Us," she explained. "Give it up, Dan. Give in to it."

"I want to," he confessed. "God, I want to. Good night, babe. I'll talk to you tomorrow."

She was still smiling as she hung up the phone, because she felt hopeful once again, and she didn't think she'd have long to wait before he showed up at her door.

Chapter 11

She wasn't home the following night when he called, and he didn't like it one bit.

Dan had pushed himself to the limit that day, because he was sick and tired of hospitals and doctors and therapists. He was impatient to get on with the rest of his life, impatient to get to her. He also had a nagging feeling that she was right about the shooting at the warehouse—that something really odd was going on, and she was caught in the middle of it. He worried about what she was going to do.

She wasn't a reckless person, and she was very well trained; he'd made sure of that. But he'd feel a lot better if he was beside her. No one would work harder than he would to keep her safe.

He almost decided to say to hell with his intentions—which were to go to her on his own two feet. Because she'd made it clear that he could come to her right now, and she would welcome him.

So it was nothing but stubborn pride that was keeping

him away from her now. That, and knowing he was so close to getting back on his feet. His leg muscles were strong enough now to hold his weight for short periods of time, but nerve damage that hadn't healed and likely never would had left him unable to control some of the muscles in his legs—particularly the left leg. The best he could do at present was shuffle along with the help of a cane. Maybe one day he could walk without it. Maybe not. It was still too soon to tell.

Truthfully, it was bothering him less and less every day. He'd accepted the fact that he wasn't going back to the job he once held. He'd find something else to do eventually. With the money he had in the bank, he could take his time about deciding on a new career.

For now, he intended to concentrate on Jamie. On making her smile, making her laugh, getting her used to the idea that she was his. Primitive as it sounded, he wanted to own her, body and soul, putting the stamp of his touch and the feel of his body on her, like a brand she could never erase. He intended to make her his. In every way that mattered.

If he pushed, in two weeks or so, he could walk out of here. There'd still be work to do for his legs, but he would do it as an outpatient and spend his nights with her.

Dan glanced at the clock, getting edgier as the minutes slid past and he still didn't know where she was. When she said she needed him there, his first thought was that she was merely trying to make him *feel* that she needed him, simply because she wanted him to be with her.

But maybe her worry was genuine. Maybe there were things she hadn't told him, things that could lead her into real danger. If she was in trouble, he'd be there for her. His only misgivings were not knowing how effective he could be right now in covering her back.

Of course, he couldn't ask her any those things, because she still wasn't home.

Dan called Jamie's number every fifteen minutes for the next hour, and by one o'clock in the morning, he'd gone a little crazy. She wasn't there, but it didn't necessarily mean she was in trouble, he told himself. She could simply have been called away on assignment, so quickly she hadn't had time to call him. It was possible. Unlikely, he thought, but possible. At one-thirty, he decided to call the agency, just in case something had happened to her.

He dialed the number with a hand that wasn't quite steady. Curiously, Tanner's secretary was there. He told her he was looking for Jamie. Amanda said a priority briefing was in progress at the office. Jamie should have been there, but wasn't. She hadn't answered her phone all afternoon or evening. She hadn't responded to a priority page, either.

Dan kept asking questions. Someone from the agency had been trying to reach Jamie for two and a half hours with no response, which was troubling. Nobody ignored a page about a priority briefing.

So where was she?

Dan gritted his teeth and asked about Joshua Carter, who was in the briefing. Amanda promised to ask him to call Dan when the briefing ended. He was about to hang up when she asked him to wait a moment—the meeting had just broken up and Tanner wanted to speak to him.

"I wanted you to know," Tanner said, when he came on the line a few moments later, "that the CIA and the FBI haven't gotten anywhere in finding Hathaway. They've given up on keeping this thing under wraps and are going public with a full-court press. We're back in it, and I wish you could be here and be a part of this."

Dan thought it over. The man had shot and killed Doc. Whoever helped Hathaway escape had left Dan struggling to walk again, left him starting over at thirty-nine without a clue as to what he'd do with his life. Dan wanted the man caught, and it seemed odd not to be a part of that effort. But it didn't bother him as much as he expected it would. At the moment, all he wanted to do was find Jamie.

"I think I'll leave the bad guys to you," he said.

"Sorry it has to be that way."

"Yeah," Dan said. "Listen, I've been trying to get hold of Jamie, but I'm not having any luck. Amanda said she couldn't reach her, either. Do you have any idea where she is?"

"Hang on," Tanner said cryptically. He put Dan on hold, picked up the phone a few minutes later. "Sorry, I didn't want to have this conversation in the hallway. Jamie and I had a little disagreement this morning, and I suspect she's decided to take a few days off to think some things through."

That was odd, Dan thought, especially if the agency had finally been brought back into the search for Hathaway.

"You had a disagreement?" Dan said carefully.

"The lady's stubborn as hell," Tanner complained.

Dan laughed. "Tell me something I don't know."

"I'll admit it's not all her. Things have been nuts around here. Everybody's tense, and I'm getting squeezed from both ends. You have no idea of the pressure that's being put on everyone to get Hathaway back. I know it's been hard on all our agents, too. But I've got to have some cooperation, and I'm through asking nicely for it."

Dan couldn't imagine Tanner asking nicely for anything, but he got the picture.

"You can't tell the woman anything," Tanner complained. "She's had her own ideas about this investigation from the beginning. I've tried to give her some time and some room, and I respect her judgment. But I have priorities of my own, and I'm shorthanded with you out and Doc gone. I can't have Jamie running around doing whatever she thinks is most important and ignoring what the people chewing on my butt want done.''

"She's hardheaded," Dan agreed. "Do you have any idea where she is?''

"Cooling down, I hope. I threatened to suspend her yesterday if she tried to countermand one more order I gave her.''

"Oh.'' She hadn't told Dan that.

"Yeah. She came in here this morning telling me it's time to canvass the northwest quarter—all because a cop dug a bullet out of a liquor store wall, and no one's been able to identify it yet.''

"Is it a six-millimeter?''

"I don't know. The D.C. police have it, and we're trying to get it released to us so our ballistics people can check it,'' Tanner said. "Even if it is a six-millimeter, what's it going to tell us? That someone dumped one of the weapons as they headed out of town, and some punk found one and used it to hold up a liquor store.''

Dan had to agree. That was probably what they'd find.

"So where did you and Jamie leave it?''

"I told her I thought we were going to be brought in on the search for Hathaway, that if she was going to be a part of it, I'd expect her full cooperation. That meant giving her full attention to whatever assignment I gave her. Let's just say she was less than enthusiastic about doing things my way. She claimed she might need some time off to get her head together, but I suspect you and I both know what that means.''

Dan swore. "She's going to nose around down there by herself.''

"I've warned her," Tanner said. "If I find out she's done that, I'm going to lose every bit of the manners my mother worked so hard to teach me. So I hope she's just cooling off somewhere right now.''

"Do me a favor," Dan said. "If you find the lady, have her call me. We have some things to discuss."

"Sure thing."

"Thanks," Dan said, hanging up the phone.

He tried Jamie again and still got no answer at her apartment. It was nearly two o'clock, and his stomach was in knots. He tried to talk himself out of a full-blown, gut-wrenching certainty that something was very wrong. She could have gotten caught up in something related to work, could have been oblivious to the fact that it was late, he told himself.

But she'd have her pager. The page would have taken priority over everything else. She wouldn't have ignored a priority page unless something was terribly wrong.

Dan's phone rang. He snatched it up and said, "Jamie?"

"No," said a smugly amused voice. "Josh."

Dan had no time, no patience for niceties, as he demanded, "Do you know where she is?"

"I know where she should be—right here. But she's not."

"She was paged about the briefing. She didn't respond," Dan said. "She and I were supposed to talk tonight, and she hasn't called. She isn't answering her phone at home, either."

"You think she's in trouble?"

"Yeah."

"Well, hell," Josh said. "I don't need to sleep tonight. Do you?"

"No," Dan said. There was no way he would be able to sleep tonight.

"Where do you want to start looking? Her apartment?"

"Fine. It's going to take me an hour and a half or so to get there."

"I'll ask some questions around the office," Josh offered. "Maybe somebody saw her today."

Dan hung up the phone, reached for his clothes and dressed hurriedly, his mind going back to those first, few hazy recollections of awakening in the hospital after his shooting. He'd known that everything had changed. He'd felt the unfamiliar stirrings of panic, then he'd felt amazed that anyone's world could shift so irrevocably in the blink of an eye. He'd kept thinking that all he needed to do was to go back in time, just the space of a day, and somehow stop it from happening. But he couldn't. It was too late, and he knew it the instant he woke up.

He felt the same way now. He wanted to go back to the previous night. To imagine her lying naked in the tub. To hear her say she'd be there at her apartment waiting for him. And that all he had to do was come to her. He'd heard her say she was afraid something was going to happen, that she needed him with her. He'd heard himself stubbornly, stupidly saying he needed another two weeks at the rehab hospital.

What a fool he'd been to ever take such a risk with her safety.

Dan bribed one of the security guards who was going off duty to drive him to Georgetown.

At the door to her apartment, he found his heart thundering, found himself almost dizzy at the thought of what he might find inside. Praying he was wrong, he lifted his hand and knocked, just in case she'd arrived in the ten minutes that had elapsed since he last tried to call her on his cell phone. The last thing he expected was to have the door swing open and find Josh standing there.

"I have a key," he explained.

Dan scowled, but said nothing. *Josh* had a key.

"She got annoyed after the first time I broke in here," Josh explained. "So she gave me one."

"You make a habit of breaking into her apartment?" Dan said as he wheeled himself inside.

"Not anymore," Josh said.

Dan didn't ask. It wasn't the time. He just wanted to know where Jamie was. "Did you find anything?"

"I just got here. No signs of a struggle. Her car's gone. Her purse and her keys, too. So's her gun. There's a message on her answering machine from her parents, saying they arrived safely in Rome, and about twenty-four hangups. Those would be you?"

Twenty-four, huh? He was in bad shape.

Dan glanced over at Josh, who was obviously enjoying some aspect of this evening, and scowled.

Josh nodded to the hallway on the right. "Why don't you check the bedroom? I'll go through this room and the kitchen."

Dan turned right, not wanting to know why Joshua Carter knew where her bedroom was. He found the room empty, the floral-patterned comforter in a tangle in the middle of the double bed. He went to the side of the bed, ran his hands over the ivory-colored sheets and for a minute pictured her here in this room, in this bed. It was a quietly pretty room, the furniture sturdy, heavy and obviously old, the wood a polished mahogany. He could have seen her here, last night, if he hadn't been so damned stubborn. He could have woken up in this bed beside her this morning.

Forcing himself to take care of the business at hand, he looked through her closet and her dresser drawers. Everything was neat and clean, giving no indication she might have packed her things and taken off, or that she'd left hurriedly.

He had trouble maneuvering in the bathroom. The space was simply too narrow. So he carefully got to his feet and found handholds to brace himself as he looked through the room.

It smelled of her in here, something light and sweet and utterly enticing. In a small wicker basket in the back corner of the tub, he found small, lavender-colored packets of bath salts. Picking one up, he inhaled deeply, the scent slaying him. Like a man obsessed, he shoved the packet of bath salts into his shirt pocket, despite the fact that the scent would make him crazy.

He was sitting on the rim of the bathtub when he looked up and found Josh standing in the doorway, eyeing him and the empty wheelchair curiously.

"Find anything?" Dan asked, standing and bracing himself with a hand against the wall as he made his way back to the chair.

"No," Josh said, watching. "Does she know you can do that?"

"No."

Josh cocked an eyebrow. "I wouldn't want to be you when you try to explain why you've kept this little secret from her."

Dan glared at him. "I'd be happy for the chance to give her an explanation. *If* we could find her."

Josh nodded. "She left a message on my answering machine at home. Told me she needed to talk to me tonight, that she'd call back later. The message came in at 2:38 this afternoon. She didn't call back. Three people who were at the briefing tonight remembered seeing her at the office around midmorning, but no one knows where she was for the rest of the day."

"What about relatives?"

"She has one brother stationed in Texas right now, and another one who works at the Pentagon, but he travels a good bit. I haven't called him yet. But if we do call him and nothing's wrong, we'll never hear the end of it from her. I think her family tends to be a bit overprotective."

"Friends? Neighbors?"

"I don't know anyone else to call," Josh said.

"Did she tell you about the six-millimeter slug?"

"No."

Dan filled him in on that. "This morning she was planning to meet the cop who was working the burglary case. Why aren't you working this with her?"

"Because I'm supposed to be doing something else, too," Josh said cryptically.

Dan let it go. He didn't care what Josh was doing. He just had to find Jamie. They decided to call the police. They weren't as forthcoming at 4:00 a.m. over the phone as they might have been during the day to a request in person for information about a shooting at a liquor store and the name of the cop working the case. Dan and Josh got six different friends and acquaintances out of bed before they had the cop's name and found him coming off duty at 7:00 a.m. in a precinct that contained the warehouse where Dan was shot.

Detective Russell had seen Jamie the previous morning, had walked her through the liquor store that had been robbed, supposedly by local teenage hoods with an unidentified weapon. From the description of the suspects, they could have been the same as from the warehouse shooting. Of course, so could a few thousand other teenage hoods in the district. Still, the fact that they were so close to the warehouse, coupled with the odd-sized slug found in the liquor store wall, made the whole thing too much of a coincidence to dismiss.

"She wouldn't let this go," Dan told Josh as the two of them stood on the sidewalk outside the liquor store.

"I know. But why the hell wouldn't she call one of us?"

Dan closed his eyes and cursed himself and his own stupidity, his foolish pride that kept him away from her thirty-six hours ago when she'd asked for his help, six weeks ago when he'd cut her out of his life, years ago when he first chose to deny everything he felt for her.

He couldn't lose her now.

"She told me Wednesday night that she was worried, that she thought this thing was going to blow wide-open," Dan admitted.

"It doesn't make any sense," Josh said. "The whole thing never has."

"We took a wrong turn," Dan said. "We assumed we'd been set up by professionals who came in, got Hathaway out and left the country. We've been looking everywhere but here. Because we were sure we weren't dealing with exactly what they looked like—a couple of gang kids."

Grim-faced, Josh nodded.

"Let's start over and assume that they were from one of the local gangs, that they're right here somewhere. That they waltzed into something they didn't understand, and now a government agent is dead and they're nervous. Jamie's down here asking questions about the gun. What are they going to do?"

"Follow her," Josh suggested. "Maybe grab her off the streets and ask her some questions of their own?"

Or worse? Dan thought. If she didn't answer their questions? If they didn't like the answers she gave them? If they got the information they needed and had no further use for her?

He couldn't let himself think about that; not if he was going to think clearly enough to find her. He checked his watch, saw that it was almost noon now. No one had seen or heard from her in nearly twenty-four hours.

He thought of the amount of ground they needed to cover, of all the resources the agency had. "Are we going to do this ourselves?" he asked Josh. "Or do we have to bring some people in on this?"

"You want to keep it quiet?" Josh asked. "Why?"

Dan told him Jamie had argued with Tanner, had been threatened with a suspension if she didn't drop it. He didn't think he was overreacting to the situation; he truly believed she was in danger. But if they were wrong and they went to the agency for help and she had disobeyed a direct order by simply being here and asking questions, they could get her suspended.

"That's the reason you don't want to go to anybody at the agency?" Josh inquired carefully.

"What other reason could there be?"

Josh said nothing.

Dan, who'd been running on sheer nerves all night and all day, had simply been pushed too far. "If you know something that could help us find her, and you're not telling me, I swear to God, I'll—"

"Okay," Josh cut him off. "I think we should wait before we go to the agency for help on this—because I'm not sure who we can trust."

Dan let the full implications of that sink in, felt his anxiety level soaring to new heights and his anger growing to a reckless, dangerous level. "You think someone inside this agency was working with Hathaway?"

"I'm not sure. I don't think we should take the chance by bringing anyone else in on this just yet."

"She's been gone for nearly a day now." He felt sickened by the direction his own thoughts were taking, but forced himself to continue. "She could be dead by now. Or dying while we stand here arguing on the street. If you know something..."

"I'd tell you. For Jamie's sake, I would. But right now, I've got nothing but suspicions."

"Your own?"

"Tanner's. He's had me looking into the possibility that someone in Division One was involved."

"Who?"

"If he has a name, he hasn't given it to me. He's just worried that Hathaway would need help getting out. He'd been under guard for months. Security was going to get

tighter still when he was moved out of D.C. If he made
arrangements to sell his formula, it's not hard to imagine
the buyers looking for a little inside help to get Hathaway
away from us.''

"Does Jamie know any of this?''

"No.''

"I can't believe this,'' Dan said. "One of our own people... Do you believe it?''

"I don't want to. But we can't ignore the possibility.''

"Okay,'' Dan said. "We'll find her ourselves.''

By midnight, they had questioned enough reluctant witnesses in the area to know that Jamie had been there the
previous afternoon. Slowly, they were piecing together the
route she'd taken, moving west from the liquor store toward
the warehouse.

Dan knew they had to be close to finding her. He could
feel it. He could sense that she needed him, that he had to
find her right away. He'd never worked this way before,
this urgently, this intensely, never had this much at stake
before.

By the time the sun was coming up, they'd narrowed
their search to a series of abandoned buildings in a one-
block area. Two people admitted hearing shouts and
screams coming from somewhere on that block earlier in
the day. Someone else reported seeing people keeping
watch outside a couple of different buildings. They had a
frustratingly unremarkable description of a car seen in the
area, a beige or dirty white Honda, several years old, with
oversized tires and a muffler problem, but no one had seen
it for twenty-four hours or so.

Dan and Josh grimly debated the wisdom of searching
inside the buildings on their own versus the risks they'd
take by going to the agency for help. They decided to press

on, with the help of Detective Russell and some of his colleagues.

Ten minutes later, they started kicking in doors. They'd go building by building, if they had to. She was here, and they were going to find her. They were starting on the third building when a car suddenly accelerated out of an adjacent alley. It was a dirty white Honda.

"That's it!" Dan shouted.

Russell got on his radio, calling for anyone in the area to assist them in stopping the car. The license plate was caked over with mud, the numbers indistinguishable, but they had it in sight. Seconds later, they could hear sirens headed their way.

Dan drew his weapon, ready to shoot out the tires if necessary. He wasn't going to let this car disappear. He was taking aim when the car swerved to the right to avoid a car making a turn in the intersection. The Honda ended up on the sidewalk.

It never came to a complete stop, just skidded sideways and slowed down. Dan watched in amazement as one of the car's doors opened, then in horror as someone was shoved out of the car. The body went flying through the air like a rag doll, landing hard on the pavement, remaining there, motionless and deathly still.

The car tore off, tires screeching. Other cars were still coming through the intersection, and the body was still lying on the side of the road.

He couldn't tell if she'd been hit by one of the passing cars or not. But he saw a thick mass of dark hair that fell almost to her shoulders, saw skin that gleamed white in the near darkness, and he knew.

It was Jamie.

Chapter 12

It seemed to take him forever to get to her. All around him there was chaos, people shouting and screaming and cars with their horns blaring, zipping all around. Cops were arriving, too, in response to the radio plea.

Dan was oblivious to everything but her. He had to get to her. It couldn't be too late.

He had a good bit of advanced training in first aid in trauma cases, so he knew what he had to do. Still, he had to fight not to scoop her up into his arms the minute he got close enough to touch her.

Sitting on the street by her side, he pushed the hair back from her face. Finding her mouth and her nose, he leaned close to reassure himself that she was indeed breathing. Rapidly and shallowly, but she was breathing.

His fingers trembling, he felt for a pulse in her neck. It took agonizingly long seconds before he was sure he'd found a pulse.

Josh was kneeling at her other side. "Is she alive?"

"Yeah. She's breathing, and she has a heartbeat."

"We radioed for an ambulance," he said.

Dan nodded.

Reaching out to touch her cheek, Josh said, "I'm going to go after the car."

Dan backed away for a second, trying to think like a medic instead of a man. She was lying crumpled against the unforgiving pavement, half on her side, half on her stomach. Her clothes were dark, the sky just beginning to be light; it wasn't easy to see. He looked her over quickly, checking for bleeding, finding it, but in no great quantities.

He was running his hands over her arms, checking for broken bones, when he found the rope. It was tied tightly around her wrists.

Stunned, so angry he was shaking, he pulled a knife out of his pocket and cut the bindings, then gently separated her hands. They felt like ice, and he used his own hands to warm them, to try to get the circulation going again. He knew what it was like to be tied up; her entire arms would ache, and so would her shoulders, maybe her back, depending on how long she'd been this way and how tightly her wrists were bound together.

Her ankles were bound together as well, and after checking again for broken bones in her legs, he freed her ankles and worked over her feet. Then he checked her ribs and her back. No broken bones. She didn't move an inch as he ran his hands over her body, didn't make a sound. Her head was tilted at an angle that worried him.

He wanted to check the rest of her for bleeding, wanted to see how badly she'd hurt her head when she was thrown out of the car. The way she had fallen was oddly reminiscent of the way the girl was that night at the warehouse. He wanted to hold Jamie close and warm her with his body, reassure her with his touch.

But he was afraid to move her.

"Oh, God," he groaned. What had those people done to her?

He leaned over her again, looking at what he could see of her face. The entire side visible to him was swollen and bruised. Someone had hit her. More than once. He nearly lost it when he saw a thin stream of blood coming from her nose and her mouth. It could be a sign of internal bleeding.

There was blood on the pavement underneath her face as well. Enough to worry him, but not enough to make him take the chance of rolling her over without the proper equipment to stabilize her head, neck and back. It took tremendous willpower, but he left her in that position, as he'd found her. He did cover her with his coat, and with another one offered by a uniformed officer who'd come to stand beside him to direct traffic.

"Ambulance is only a few blocks away now," the officer reassured him.

Dan could hear the sirens. He checked her again. She was breathing, her heart was beating. And he was with her. He wouldn't leave her again. He would never let himself be away from her again when she needed him, when she was afraid. It had been a long, long time since he'd begged for anything, since he'd prayed. But he did that now.

He remembered how strong and steady her gaze had been when he'd awakened in the hospital after the shooting, remembered her telling him with absolute certainty that no matter what was wrong with him, she could handle it. If he never walked again, it wouldn't make a difference in the way she felt about him.

At the time, he thought she was talking nonsense, making a lot of promises she hadn't thought through simply because she believed he needed to hear the words.

But now he understood.

He just wanted her to get through this, to live, and he

wanted to be by her side, to have her in his life. Whatever those bastards had done to her, whatever lasting damage they might have inflicted, he would still need her, in the same way he needed to breathe. He couldn't imagine ever leaving her, no matter what.

He understood now what he'd put her through in the last few months. This was how she felt when he'd been shot. This was what it was like to be able to do nothing more than watch and wait and make rash promises to God, if only He would grant you the one thing you needed most. To let the person who'd come to mean more to you than anything live.

It was agony. It was maddening and frustrating, the kind of thing that made a strong man realize how very weak he truly was. The sheer power of his feelings for her left him stunned and shaken. The thought that her life now hung in the balance, and there was nothing he could do, that it was totally out of his hands now, was nearly enough to make him crazy.

"Oh, God," he prayed, leaning over her, letting his hands feather through a few strands of her hair, kissing the side of her bruised face.

He rode with her in the ambulance, and he proved himself useful as they quickly assessed her condition and stabilized her head, neck and back in preparation for the journey to the hospital.

Dan sat by her side holding a bag of IV fluids that slowly dripped into her arm and watching the readout on the cardiac monitor. Her heartbeat was fast, and her blood pressure alarmingly low, as was her body temperature.

It had been cold overnight, he remembered. What had Jamie been doing when it had turned so cold, he wondered? Where had she been? What had they been doing to her?

He peered between the orange, rectangular braces on either side of her head, looked down into her pale, lifeless and bruised face and felt a murderous rage coming over him. With grim intent, the paramedic sitting at her other side was monitoring her vital signs. Her breathing turned even more shallow, her heart rate sped up, her blood pressure dropped. She was in a dangerous downward spiral.

"Talk to her," the man suggested.

Dan's hand settled against the top of her head, slowly stroking her hair. He kissed her forehead, put his lips against the right side of her face as close as he could get to her ear, and called her name.

"Jamie— Come on, babe. I finally came to my senses. I'm here now, and you promised you'd be waiting for me."

She didn't stir. He told her all about rehab, all the things she'd wanted to know that he'd refused to share with her, but he got no response. The ambulance went bouncing over a bump in the road, jarring the entire vehicle, and she finally reacted—grimacing in pain.

"Jamie," he said urgently. "Come on. Talk to me."

Her eyelids flickered open, her gaze unfocused, her pupils dilated. She looked up at him as if she had no idea who he was.

"Jamie? It's me. I'm right here beside you."

"Dan?" She mouthed the word.

"That's right." He forced a smile. "I'm here."

Her eyelids slid down. She mumbled something he couldn't make out.

"What?"

"Don't tell," she whispered.

He went still. "Don't tell? Who, babe?"

"Anyone."

"Jamie?" he whispered more urgently than before. "You don't want me to call anyone? Your parents? Your brothers?"

"No."

"The agency?" he tried. "You don't want anyone from the agency to know you're here? Or what's happened?"

"No," she said faintly, sounding worried. And scared.

He went still at her words, the implication clear. It meant someone from the agency was involved.

Did she know that for sure, or did she merely suspect it? What had those bastards told her? Did she think they were going to come after her in the hospital?

Dan hoped to hell someone did try to get to her. He wouldn't let anyone touch her, but he'd at least know who was responsible for hurting her this way. Then he'd have someone to punish, would be able to unleash that cold-blooded, murderous anger rushing through him.

"I'll take care of it, babe," he promised.

She drifted back into unconsciousness, and he sat beside her. His hand stroked her hair, his face next to hers, so he could hear every breath she took and reassure himself that she was truly alive, that she was safe and by his side. But there were so many ways in which a woman could be hurt. Squeezing his eyes shut, he broke out into a cold sweat at the ugly images flashing through his head.

When he was finally able to, he forced himself to take another long look at her. Her shirt had been ripped open at the neck to make room for the cardiac monitors attached to her chest. Through the opening, he saw bruised, discolored flesh. And he remembered cuts, scrapes, the beginnings of bruises on the rest of her body, now covered with a thick, thermal blanket.

Dan knew she was strong and fast, an incredibly capable and courageous woman. But there'd always been something so delicate about her. He'd seen her traipse through the mud and the swamp, seen her sweating and ready to fall over from fatigue, seen her burning with the fire of anger, hurt in that devastatingly quiet way of hers when he'd said something designed to push her away.

But he'd never seen her like this. Never seen her fearful and disoriented and so weak it scared him. This was what he'd wanted to protect her from. When he'd ridden her so hard through her Intermediaries, he honestly hadn't wanted her to make it through the program. Because he never wanted her to go through anything like this.

Close calls were a part of the job. A bullet here and there. A knife. A fall. A fist. Usually there were weeks of preparation, an adrenaline rush that came hard and fast, that carried you through until the job was done. At times, there were a few dizzying moments of terror when things went wrong.

But this... There were rope burns on her wrists and her ankles. Those bastards had her for a day and a half. They'd held her prisoner. Tied her hands and feet together. Beaten her.

He felt sick inside and bitterly angry with himself for not being able to prevent it from happening. And he would make them pay.

Jamie thought she must have split her skull in two. The noises were assaulting her, the light blinding her. She moaned, broke out in a cold sweat and started to shake.

Someone held her hand, she realized, the touch blessedly warm and reassuring. "Shh," a voice said, a soft, female voice. "You're safe now. We're gonna take good care of you."

"Who?" she whispered. "Where?"

"You're in the emergency room at St. Mary Margaret's."

St. Mary Margaret's?

It was too close. She breathed in deeply, flinched at the resulting pain in her side, wondered how she'd gotten away. Or if they'd simply left her for dead. She couldn't imagine they'd given her up willingly.

And then she remembered—the car. They'd shoved her out of the car in a desperate effort to slow down the people chasing them.

Oh, God, the car.

The kindly nurse squeezed her hand more tightly. "It's all right. I'll stay with you. Or I'll call someone for you, if you like. Who can I call?"

Dan, she thought. She could have sworn she'd heard his voice, sounding rough and strained and insistent, as she was drifting in and out of consciousness. But he was in Maryland, an hour and a half away. She panicked, thinking of what could happen to her in an hour and a half, and she knew what she had to do.

"Josh," she told the nurse, having to concentrate hard to come up with his cell phone number and beeper number.

It would have to be Josh. He lived nearby. The agency offices weren't far, either. If the nurse could find him, he could be here in minutes.

"Okay, I'll be right back," the nurse said.

Dan was sitting in a chair against the wall opposite the treatment room Jamie was in when the nurse walked out. Awkwardly, he got to his feet. Leaning heavily on a black cane, he walked slowly across the hall. He stopped the nurse by putting his hand on her arm.

"How is she?" he demanded.

The nurse took one look at the way he was leaning on that cane and tried to help him back to the chair. "And what did you do to yourself?"

"It doesn't matter," he said impatiently. "The woman in there. How is she?"

"And who are you?"

"Dan Reese," he said simply.

"Her husband?"

"No. She's not married."

"Next of kin?"

"No. Her parents are out of the country, and her brothers...I don't know where her brothers are. I rode here with her in the ambulance. I'm..." He couldn't put into words what he was to her, what he felt for her, settled for simply saying, "I have to know how she is."

"We're still assessing her condition."

Dan could have put his fist through the wall. "Is she going to make it?"

"Right now, she's extremely weak, her vital signs aren't good and we're still checking for internal injuries."

He absorbed all of that, piece by piece, willing himself to be calm, to try to act halfway civilized and not like some madman. Drawing on hard-won patience, Dan said, "I need to see her."

The nurse looked him in the eye and said, "I'm sorry. She's asked me to call someone else."

The words cut deep. He winced, then realized the implication of what he'd been told. "She's conscious?"

"Right now, she's drifting in and out."

"I need to see her," he repeated.

"Look, I—"

"Ask her," he insisted. "My name is Dan. She'll see me."

"All right." The nurse's eyes flashed a warning. "Wait right here."

Dan turned around and leaned heavily against the wall. She'd been conscious, he reminded himself. And coherent enough to give the nurse a name and phone number.

Not his.

He wouldn't think about that now.

Restlessly, he pushed a hand through his hair and closed his eyes.

Oh, God, Jamie.

The nurse came back quickly. "She'll see you."

He turned, ready to push his way into the room, but the nurse blocked his way. "We need to come to an understanding. Someone's been using her for a punching bag."

"I know," he said. The woman was still glaring at him. Finally, he realized why and said, "It wasn't me."

"All right," she said, as if she didn't believe a word he said.

"Do you think I'd be half out of my mind worrying about her, if I was the one who did this to her?"

"I wouldn't think so. But I've seen it happen. Ten years in the ER, and you've seen just about everything."

Through clenched teeth, Dan said, "I'm not going to hurt her."

"Not here, you're not. I won't have you upsetting her, either."

"Of course not."

"She looks bad," the nurse warned.

"I know."

"The doctors are still with her. They'll likely be in and out for hours. But she's scared, and if it makes her feel better to have you with her, they'll probably let you stay."

"I understand."

The nurse finally stepped aside. Dan pushed open the door and found himself reluctant to go any farther. He looked at the gurney in the midst of the room, saw her hair, a rich, black pool of color against the stark white of the sheet. Her cheek was bruised, one eye puffy, her lip swollen and split. The injuries seemed to stand out even more in the light. On her forehead, near her hairline, there was a big piece of white gauze, now stained red. Three people hovered around her, bent over her right leg, blocking his view of the lower half of her body.

Leaning heavily on the cane, remembering the things he'd gone through himself in a hospital not too far from this one, he felt sick inside, felt a rage start to burn low in his belly and spread throughout his entire being.

He didn't want her going through anything like that.

Dan moved slowly. He'd graduated to the cane only days ago, and it took a great deal of concentration and effort to move with so little support. All too easily, he could fall flat on his face. He schooled his features to wipe any traces of fear and outrage from his face. He was three steps away from her when her head turned slowly to the left and she saw him. "Dan."

She was breathless, her voice sounding so weak, it scared him all over again. He rushed the last three steps, something he couldn't afford to do. His cane clattered to the floor, the sound bringing all eyes in the room to him, something he would have found humiliating under any other circumstances. But today, he simply didn't care.

Jamie did. The stark clatter of the cane against the hard flooring startled her. She tensed, jerked a little, the abrupt movement hurting her.

The nurse pushed a stool to the side of the gurney. Grateful, he sank down onto the stool and bent over the battered, bruised face of the woman he feared he'd never see again.

"Sorry," he whispered, his hand stroking gently through her hair. "I'm still clumsy, still bumping into things and knocking them over."

She tried to smile again, her eyelids drifting downward. "You're not even here."

He had to bend even closer to catch the words. "I'm not?"

She shook her head and winced.

He spread his hand wide against the top of her head to halt the movement. "Be still, Jamie. It won't hurt as much if you stay still."

"Promise?" she said drowsily.

"Promise."

"I know you're not here," she insisted.

"Why?"

"You're walking."

Dan sighed. "That's debatable."

"You can't walk," she insisted.

He began to understand. He had a lot of explaining to do. "I'll tell you about it. I'll explain everything later. When you're better. Okay?"

A single tear seeped from the corner of her right eye, which was drooping shut. "Dan?"

"Yes, babe."

"Don't leave me."

"I won't, Jamie. For as long as you want me, I'll be right here."

He pressed his lips to her bruised face, kissed away her tears, then lowered his forehead to hers and let it rest against her soft skin. And when he wanted to shout and rant and rage at what had been done to her, he forced his voice to be quiet, to soothe and to try to calm, to reassure.

"Go to sleep, babe." He kissed her again, softly, this time pressing his lips against the corner of her bruised lips. "I'll be right here."

He sat by her side for the next few days. She was unconscious most of the time, exhaustion taking over and giving her body time to heal. She had hairline fractures in two ribs, extensive bruising to several others, a badly sprained ankle and a head injury that had given the doctors fits. It was a contusion, which meant the soft, sensitive tissues of the brain slammed violently against the inside of her skull, causing swelling. Dan knew at one point the doctors had considering drilling a hole in her skull to relieve the pressure. He was thankful it hadn't come to that.

Then he'd been torn, trying to decide whether it was more dangerous for her to stay here or be moved. The two men in the Honda had gotten away somehow, and they were still out there. Jamie had been afraid they would come after her, even here. She'd been afraid to let anyone from the agency know she was here, possibly for the same reason.

She ended up remaining in the hospital for another day and a half while the doctors closely monitored her head injury. Even then, they didn't want to let her go, despite the fact that her life might be in danger if she stayed. Dan and Josh had covered their tracks as best they could, through a network of old friends at the 911 emergency dispatch center, the ambulance service, the police force and at the hospital. Where they didn't have friends, they fabricated a story that they hoped was plausible. They tried to convince everyone Jamie was in the federal witness protection program, that the people who'd hurt her this way were still after her. Finally, because Dan had sworn to have a doctor on the premises day and night, and a nurse watching over her, they agreed to release her.

Dan was able to get in touch with an old friend of Doc's, someone Doc knew from Vietnam, who was flying a medevac helicopter for a hospital in the area. He took Jamie and Dan from the hospital in D.C. to the rehabilitation facility in Maryland where Dan had been staying.

It was more private than any hospital he knew, and it had on-site security and a medical staff on duty twenty-four hours a day. Dan hoped he was doing the right thing in taking her there.

He rode in the back of the helicopter beside her. Jamie slept most of the way, probably because of something the nurse shot into her IV a few minutes before they left the hospital.

It was almost noon by the time they arrived, later still when the doctor checked Jamie's condition. Dan got Jamie settled into one of the private cabins on the heavily wooded grounds of the hospital, built for people who no longer needed immediate hospital care but had to have access to the extensive rehabilitation facilities there.

Dan didn't plan to leave her side, but he had to sleep sometime, so he needed help with security, too. There were a half-dozen ex-military men among the private security team at the hospital, and Dan had enlisted the help of two of them. He set up his own security perimeter around the cabin, complete with trip wires and infrared sensors, and he was well armed.

That was it, he thought, making his way inside. He'd done all he knew he should do. Now they waited. Either Jamie knew who was responsible for this, and he and Josh would find that person, or that person would come after her.

Either way, Dan would be ready.

Jamie's head throbbed dully. Her chest hurt, too. Her entire body felt like one big bruise, heavy and stiff and sore. She was faintly hungry, would kill for a glass of water and she was afraid. Automatically, she reached for the gun she normally wore in a holster under her left arm.

It wasn't there.

Somewhere inside her head, the knowledge of what had happened was lurking, waiting for her to find it, to deal with it. Involuntarily, she shuddered, the slight movement painful and frightening.

She didn't want to remember. The temptation to close her eyes and drift back off into the fog was looking more attractive all the time. But she sensed a great deal of time had passed already while she was in never-never land.

Slowly, carefully, she looked all around the room, a small, simply furnished bedroom. She was certain she'd never been here before.

Turning her head, she felt the first flickering of awareness that she wasn't alone. She heard someone breathing. Turning farther to the right, she saw a hand—a man's hand, large and tanned, lying palm up, the fingers relaxed and open against the side of the bed in which she was lying.

She went utterly still, studying that hand.

Images were coming back to her. Hands that hurt. Hands curled into tight fists. Bare, bruised knuckles. The slap of an open palm. Pain.

Inside, she recoiled from the memories, from the images and the sounds, but she couldn't escape them. They were inside her own head, all around her.

That was why it hurt so bad when she moved.

The urge to get up and run was strong. But from the way her head had throbbed when she'd done nothing but turn to the right, she doubted she'd get very far.

Determined to know what she was facing, she looked to the right again, saw the hand, followed the length of a solid, muscular arm encased in a brown shirt, the sleeves rolled up nearly to the elbow. The arm was attached to broad shoulders, to the body of a man reclining in a big chair pulled to the side of her bed. His head was tilted back against the far side of the chair, her line of sight showing her a glimpse of brownish-blond hair that tended to curl at the ends and a jaw in desperate need of a shave.

"Dan," she said, her voice not much more than a rusty whisper.

He didn't stir.

She reached out to touch him, even as she prayed that he was real and not some image conjured up by her jumbled, aching head. He'd been a part of her dreams. He'd murmured reassuring words, held her hand and brushed away her tears, kissed her aching head. She had no idea how much of it had been real.

Whatever time had passed had left her with the sensation of sinking below the surface of water, the world fading away. Every now and then, she managed to get to the surface. She'd have a second or two in the real world, then she'd slip beneath the water again.

This time, she thought, reaching for him, this time it was real.

Her fingers settled against the warm, reassuringly solid flesh of his forearm. He was next to her. As far as she was concerned, there was no better place in the world to be.

She watched and waited, felt reassured simply by touching him. He shifted this way and that. Suddenly, he went absolutely still. She waited beside him, motionless. Nothing moved except his eyelids. He stared at her, warily. Maybe he didn't believe what he was seeing, just as she'd been scared to believe what her own eyes told her. Dan. Jamie tried to summon a smile for him. He shifted again in the chair, sitting up straight this time, still watching her in that intense, silent way of his.

"You're real," she said. "I didn't believe it until I touched you."

His smile was slow to come and a little sad. His hand cupped the side of her face, his fingers spread wide and slid into her hair, his thumb traced the line of her mouth. She leaned into the touch, welcoming it, savoring it. Her eyes flooded with tears. The sensations were so intense, so overwhelming. More than once, she'd believed she'd never see him again. Never touch him. Never hold him. Never, ever make love to him.

And here he was. It seemed like a miracle to her, like the answer to a prayer. She wasn't letting him go this time.

Her tears spilled over, rolling down the sides of her face. He was closer now, sitting on the bed next to her. He leaned over her, his hands on either side of her face.

"Oh, babe. Don't."

He kissed her tears away, his touch the gentlest she'd

ever known, curiously only making her tears fall faster. She couldn't help it.

"Everything's going to be all right," he said.

"I know."

Part of those tears were from sheer relief, part of them pure joy. After all, he was here.

He pulled away for a moment and looked at her, the intense expression on his face enough on its own to send her heart racing. She'd been right earlier. He desperately needed a shave, the shadow of his whiskers darkening his already tanned face. There were new fatigue lines at the corners of his eyes, dark, half-moon smudges beneath them. Wonderful as it was to see him, he looked exhausted. She wondered just how much time had passed, how much she'd missed.

He kissed her again. "Don't be scared. I'm right here."

"What day is it?"

"It's early Tuesday morning."

Tuesday. That couldn't be right. She'd seen him Wednesday. Talked to him on the phone that night. Gone to work Thursday morning. Unless she'd lost nearly a week. "Tuesday?"

He nodded.

She got scared again. "I don't..." she began, then the words just wouldn't come. "A week?"

"It's all right," he repeated, again and again, his lips against her ear, his body carefully surrounding hers without putting his weight on her.

"I'm all right," she said finally, pulling herself together by sheer force of will alone.

Dan didn't seem to believe her. He looked worried and so very sad. She thought again of the time she'd spent sitting by his side when he was in the hospital, thought about endless hours and agonizing waiting and terrible uncertainties. Long days, even longer nights. Bleak, uncompromising regrets that they'd wasted so much time, that they might never get their chance to be together. She studied his face carefully this time, decided he looked like a man who'd been to the verge of hell and back again, the trip taking its toll.

"I want to hold you," he said. "But I'm afraid I'll hurt you."

"Let's risk it," she said, needing to feel his arms around her.

He shifted around until he was lying on his side on the bed, then carefully fit his body against her side. He put his weight on his right elbow and leaned over her. Jamie pressed her face against the side of his neck and his shoulder, and his hand was in her hair, stroking and soothing once more.

"God, Jamie. I wasn't sure I'd ever see your face again. I've never been so scared before."

The words brought fresh tears to her eyes. She shifted carefully, trying to get closer to him, not caring if it did hurt. She needed him, pressed her hand flat against his chest, could feel his heart thumping away, could feel his chest rise and fall with each breath he took.

He was so big, so solid, so very much a man, and she wanted to do nothing more than put herself in his very capable hands and let him take care of her, which seemed decidedly odd for a woman who'd fought long and hard for her independence and had to convince everyone around her that she could take care of herself.

But she would leave the incongruities to be worked out another day, when every breath she took didn't hurt and her head wasn't throbbing, when she wasn't feeling so vulnerable and so needy. Right now, she just wanted him close to her, all around her.

She grabbed his shirt and held on to him, breathed in the scent of him and let the wonderful warmth of his body soak into her. They stayed that way for a long time. Finally, when she wasn't so shaky and her tears had stopped, her fears receded to a manageable level, she let him ease away from her a bit.

He gazed down at her, with a hard, possessive stare, then seemed to be assessing her condition very carefully. "How do you feel?"

"Like my entire body is one big bruise."

He grinned a little. "That's not far from the truth. How's your vision? Blurry?"

"No."

He held up his hand. "How many fingers?"

"Four."

"Good. What day is it?"

"You just told me. It's Tuesday."

"And you remembered. That's good, too." He turned all grim and serious again. "You scared me, babe."

"I scared myself."

"Do you remember what happened?" he said carefully.

She nodded, her mouth gone dry. Even if it had to be done, she dreaded telling him everything, dreaded making herself remember it enough to recount the tale for him.

"Tell me," he said. "You talked to the cop. Russell. He took you to the scene of the liquor store robbery."

"Yes." She closed her eyes, tried not to breathe too deeply, because that hurt, and launched into her story. "It was only about ten blocks from the warehouse, and I wanted to walk the route, to see what was between the two."

"By yourself?" he growled.

"It was daylight. There were people all around."

"Okay. I'm sorry. Tell me what happened, and I'll keep quiet."

"I thought I saw the girl. The one you and Geri saw get

beaten up that night. She was just walking down the street, and I followed her.''

Dan groaned.

''I know I shouldn't have. I know I should have taken someone down there with me. I was going to; I planned to come back that night. But I wanted to get oriented to the surroundings. And then I saw the girl. I couldn't just let her get away. I followed her into an alley, and the next thing I knew, five guys jumped me, and I couldn't fight off all five of them. They dragged me inside an old, abandoned building and tied me up.''

Dan swore. She flinched, closed her eyes, shuddered at the memories coming back more clearly now. They'd threatened her, tried to intimidate her, to get her to talk to them.

''They were asking me about the shooting at the warehouse. They wanted to know who got shot. Who got killed. Who you and Doc and Geri worked for. They thought you were FBI. And they wanted to know what was going on inside the warehouse.''

''You're telling me they didn't know? How could they be a part of it and not know?''

''I don't know. But I swear two of them and the girl were the same ones you and Geri described. And they seemed to be caught in the middle of something they didn't understand, something that has them scared and angry.''

''So why did they grab you?''

''Because I was asking questions about the shooting at the warehouse. Because they thought I had answers. Because they wanted to get someone's attention.''

''Whose?'' he growled.

''Whoever got them involved in this. They said they saw me with him, on a sidewalk somewhere. They thought if I wouldn't tell them what they needed to know, they could use me to send a message to him.''

"What's the message?"

"That they know who he is and where he works. That they could grab him, just as easily as they grabbed me. That if he tried to renege on their deal, he wouldn't get away from them in one piece."

"Who?" Dan said. "Who are they working for?"

"I don't know. They didn't use his name. They were getting frustrated because I wouldn't answer their questions, so I didn't think it was a good time to try to get them to answer mine. They just called him 'the man.'"

"So it could be anybody."

She nodded. "They asked a lot of questions about Hathaway."

"The FBI and the CIA went public with the search the day after you disappeared," he told her. "They put out his name, plastered his photograph all over the place. Apparently he's made some kind of advance in plastic explosives that has everybody scared out of their minds."

"These guys swore they didn't have anything to do with Hathaway's escape or with killing Doc. They seemed angry about the whole thing."

"Except that they were willing to shoot me and Geri."

"Yes, but they didn't expect to bring the FBI or the CIA or us down on them," she said. "Do you think it could be true that they didn't know? That someone we know was using them? Someone we work with who just needed help getting Hathaway out of there?"

"Tanner thinks it's possible. He's had Josh looking into it for the past few weeks."

Jamie took a minute to let that sink in. "I can't believe Josh didn't tell me."

"I don't think he's told anybody. The only reason he told me was because he didn't want us going to the agency for help in finding you. He wasn't sure who we could trust."

"You were looking for me?"

"God, yes," he groaned, bringing his face down to hers once again.

He kissed her softly, pressed his cheek against hers and rested there beside her. She let her hand slide into his hair, holding him against her, letting him chase away the horror of what she'd been through and the fear of what was to come.

"Where are we?" she asked.

"You wanted to visit me at my rehab hospital. This is it."

"This?"

"We're in one of the cabins on the property. I wanted to get you out of the hospital in D.C. as quickly as possible, but you were still in bad shape. This place has a fully equipped medical center. One of the doctors on staff used to be chief of the trauma unit at a big hospital in Chicago. He's been looking in on you. So's one of the nurses. And two of the security guards are ex-Marines. I cut a deal with them, and they're taking shifts watching the cabin. Josh and I rigged a security system, too."

She started to shake, thinking of the precautions they'd taken, the seriousness with which they viewed the situation.

"Hey," Dan said, looking down into her eyes. "No one's going to get to you here."

She nodded, hoping that was true, but if it was someone within their own agency, she knew the kind of resources that person would have when it came to finding people.

"Jamie, I'd kill them before I let them hurt you again."

She stared up at him. It was no idle threat. He meant it; he was more than capable of killing someone. "I know. I'm glad you're here."

"I'm going to take good care of you, babe." He kissed her again, softly, gently. "And I'm not letting you go this time."

Jamie meant to smile, meant to show him how happy that made her, but somehow she ended up crying instead, and he just held her, soothing her as best he could with his touch and the feel of his body next to hers.

Chapter 13

She slept again for hours, and Dan stayed beside her and held her. When she started to stir again, he called the doctor to check her over, then found himself banished from the room. When the doctor finally came out of the bedroom, he was smiling. In short, she was damned lucky, he said. Sore, weak, scared, but otherwise whole. He left a mild painkiller for her and prescribed more rest, but he reassured Dan that she was going to be fine.

Dan hadn't really believed it until she'd finally opened those pretty brown eyes of hers and talked to him in a way that made sense, and not in the incoherent ramblings of the first few days.

He was headed for the bedroom when Sheri, one of the nurses who'd been helping him look after Jamie, walked into the main room of the cabin.

"Can I see her now?" he asked.

"I'm not sure—" she began.

"What's wrong?"

"Nothing's wrong." She smiled reassuringly. "She insisted on getting cleaned up. She's soaking in the tub."

He frowned. "Do you think that's a good idea?"

"Well, it wasn't easy for her to get in there, but she seemed to think it was worth the trip." Sheri grinned. "Now, I've got to get home, and she's going to need some help getting back to the bed. Think you're up to it?"

He thought about Jamie, naked in the tub, thought about helping her out of there, getting her dried off, dressing her and putting her back to bed. Then he grinned, too.

Sheri did, too. "I know. Tough job, but somebody's got to do it. You got somebody to call if you need help?"

He nodded. "Thanks."

She winked at him. "Enjoy yourself."

Dan just stood there. Enjoy himself? He would love to. But his lady was sore and bruised and weak as a kitten. It was not the time for what he had in mind. Of course, there were a lot of things a man could do for a woman to help her feel better.

He grinned, thinking of a night that seemed so long ago when he'd been here and she'd been so very far away, soaking in her own tub. He'd gotten lots of ideas that night, and not all of them involved strenuous activity.

The lady deserved a little pampering, and he was certainly up to that.

Leaning on his cane, he walked into the bedroom, then to the bathroom door that was cracked open a couple of inches. "Jamie?" he said, his back to the door. "Are you okay?"

"Mmm." She sounded sleepy and utterly relaxed.

"Can I come in?"

"Well, someone will have to sooner or later. I'll never make it out of here without help."

"If that's an invitation, I accept."

"Wait," she stopped him. "Turn out the light first."

He reached in and flicked it off, heard the water lapping against the side of the tub and thought she must be hiding from him as best she could. He opened the door, and the windowless room was dim. She'd sunk down into the big tub so he saw nothing but her bent knees, her head and the enticing curves of her shoulders. The distortion of the rippling water, coupled with the darkness, left a lot to his imagination. But he had a very vivid imagination, and it hadn't been that dark when she'd been stretched across his lap that day in the solarium. He remembered everything about that day, just as he'd remember every detail of this one.

She was lying against the back of the tub, her head pillowed on a rolled-up towel, her eyes closed. Her dark hair was loose and wet along the ends. He would wash it for her, he decided, itching to feel the silky strands beneath his fingers.

"This is the first time I haven't felt like I was seeing everything through a fog," she said drowsily. "While I was out of it, I had the oddest dreams."

"Really?"

"Mmm. You were there. You were with me. In the ambulance? Or the emergency room?"

"I was there, babe," he began.

"You were walking…" And then she opened her eyes. He watched as she looked at him, at his feet planted firmly on the floor, at his legs, the cane, the way he leaned against the wall. By the time her gaze met his, he didn't know if she was going to yell at him or cry again.

He figured he had a fifty-fifty shot at either one at the moment.

She considered for another minute, a hurt, accusing look coming into her eyes. "You didn't even tell me?"

Ouch. A week ago, he wouldn't have felt so guilty about that. He would have justified it by saying it was his life, his body, and no one's business but his own. He would have told himself he'd been a loner his whole life, that spilling his guts to anyone didn't come easily to him, particularly to a woman.

But that was before he'd seen her thrown from a moving car. It was before he'd spent a hellish few days at the hospital waiting for information from a half-dozen different specialists about how she was, all the time fighting to make them understand he had a right to know. Because it was killing him to wait and to watch and to worry, to not know if she was going to be all right or when she was going to wake up.

He remembered the way he'd treated her after he was shot, remembered pushing her away with words designed to hurt her. He'd instructed his doctors not to talk to her or anyone else about his condition. He'd checked himself out of the hospital behind her back and disappeared, and he'd refused to talk to her or to see her for weeks on end.

If she'd done that to him, he'd have gone stark-raving mad, and he wouldn't have been quick to forgive her, either.

"I'm sorry," he said inadequately. "I didn't understand."

"Understand what?"

"What I was doing to you," he said carefully. "I didn't know how much I was hurting you by shutting you out of my life."

"I just…I can't believe you didn't tell me." She closed her eyes and turned her head away. "I'm starting to think my mother was right about you."

"I wasn't aware that your mother knew me."

"She knows enough about men to warn me that I'll never be able to change you into what I want you to be. Or what I need you to be. That I'm fooling myself if I think I can."

Dan froze. He didn't often miscalculate this badly.

Maybe he had thought this would be easy, that he would explain and beg her to forgive him, and she would, because she was incredibly generous and stubborn and for some reason she wanted him and had never quite given up on him. But maybe he was wrong. Maybe he'd abused her generosity and her trust once too often.

So he stood there leaning against the wall, feeling like he was choking, wondering what he could do, what he could say. He was truly sorry, but the words seemed too insignificant when weighed against what he'd done, the hurt he'd caused.

"Jamie..." he began, then thought of what she'd said.

I'll never be able to change you into what I want you to be. Or what I need you to be. I'm fooling myself if I think I can.

"What do you want me to be, Jamie? What do you need from me?" He'd give her anything within his power to give.

"I want into your life. Inside your head. I want you to stop keeping me at arm's length."

Dan closed his eyes. *That.*

He had a quick flashback to the final, bruising days of his marriage, to another woman he'd left hopelessly disappointed, one who wanted inside his little world herself.

He had to try to make Jamie understand it wasn't her. It had never been her. It was always him.

"Jamie—this is hard for me. I've never been able to let anyone inside my head. I've been a loner all my life—"

"I know, Dan. But I can't do this anymore."

"Jamie, please. Listen to me. I told you about my wife. I never really let her in. I disappointed her and drove her away instead, and there probably wasn't anyone in my life I'd been closer to than her. My father took off before I was born, and my mother—to put it mildly, she was cold-hearted, distant. Unfortunately she was too easily distracted from raising her kids or earning a living by a bottle of cheap booze or any man who came along.

"I've always taken care of myself, always kept to myself. Somehow it seemed safer, smarter that way. But, Jamie…you make me want to be different, and you've given me more chances than any man deserves."

Dan took a breath. She couldn't understand a fraction of what he felt for her, because he'd never shown her. He certainly hadn't told her.

And he wouldn't—he couldn't—lose her now.

Jamie just looked up at him. Tears were forming in her eyes.

Moving carefully, awkwardly, Dan lowered himself to the floor and sat down, putting his back to the wall so they were sitting side by side, nothing but the wall of the bathtub between them. It was a struggle for him to get into that position, something he normally wouldn't have let her see. But it was honesty time, and this was as honest as he could get. He was still a mess physically.

He'd be lucky if he ever got back to his feet from this position, but he didn't care. He needed to be close to her, and he thought he was making her uncomfortable by standing over her and by looking at her.

He thought again of what she'd asked of him. He thought of what he'd learned in the last few, harrowing days, of the way he'd changed.

"I saw you come flying out of that car," he said, plunging right into the worst of it, the blackest thoughts running through his head. "I saw your head connect with the pavement, saw you crumple like a rag doll. When I finally got to you, my hands were shaking so badly I couldn't tell if you had a pulse or not at first, and even after I found it, I couldn't quite make myself believe that you were still alive.

"I have never been that scared in my life. Not when that

kid shoved his gun in my face on the street outside the warehouse. Not when I was lying in the hospital that first night thinking I would go out of my mind if I had to live that way for the rest of my life. It didn't even come close.''

He stretched his arm out along the rim of the tub, reached for her hand, which she slipped inside his. He felt marginally better.

''They let me ride in the ambulance with you,'' he continued. ''But when we got to the hospital, and they rushed you inside that room and closed the doors in my face… I could barely breathe. I haven't prayed in years, Jamie, but I did that night.

''I started to think of what I must have put you through when I got shot. I thought of what it must have been like to be able to do nothing but stand outside the door and watch. I've never felt so helpless in all my life. I thought about all the time we'd wasted and how stupid I've been.

''Then the nurse finally came out, and she didn't want to tell me anything. She didn't want to let me inside the room where you were, and I swear, if she hadn't, I would have taken that place apart with my bare hands, piece by piece, until I got to you.

''She was asking me exactly who I was and was trying to figure out if I had a right to know how you were, and I was remembering the way I'd kept you in the dark the whole time I was in the hospital, then disappeared on you for six weeks. I couldn't…'' he sighed, the words stuck in his throat. ''I can't believe I was that cruel to you. I just…I didn't have any idea what I was putting you through.''

He squeezed her hand, grateful for that small contact with her. ''I'm so sorry, babe. I know that can't begin to make up for that. I know I always seem to be apologizing to you for something. Honest to God, I don't know what I ever did to deserve you. Jamie…please…''

His words trailed off. He felt curiously empty inside and

incredibly vulnerable. He'd never felt vulnerable to a woman before, and she hadn't said a word back to him.

"That's what's going on inside of me right now," he said. "That's as honest as I can be."

He turned his head to look at her, saw the sheen of tears on her face and reached over to wipe them away. She shivered, and he wasn't sure if she was upset or just cold, but he needed something to do, so he dipped two fingers into her bathwater, found it cool to the touch and reached for the knobs that controlled the water.

"Let me warm this up for you," he said, then remembered something.

From the pocket of his shirt, he pulled the bath salts. *Hers*. He opened the package and emptied it into the tub. She glanced warily at him. The fragrance that was so familiar to him—because it was hers—filled the room.

She noticed it as well. "Where did you get that packet of lavender bath salts?"

"I stole it from your bathroom."

"When were you in my bathroom?"

"A few days ago when Josh and I were trying to figure out where you were."

"You and Josh searched my apartment for me?"

"Yes."

He resisted the urge to add that Josh had a key. She knew Josh had a key. What he really wanted to know was *why* Josh had a key, but he wasn't going to ask. She was mad at him already, justifiably so, and he doubted she was going to volunteer any information about Joshua Carter and keys to her apartment.

"Do you want to know why I stole your bath salts?" he offered instead.

"You have a fetish for them?"

"Just yours," he admitted, cutting off the water and

reaching for a bar of soap in the soap dish in the far corner of the tub, thinking he simply had to touch her.

Maybe it was a cop-out, but there were all different aspects of intimacy, and he understood the physical ones quite well. He wanted to touch her, merely to put his hands on her. He needed to. It was one more way to cement the bond between them.

"I've been smelling that scent on your skin for years," he said, " and it drove me crazy. I knew it wasn't perfume, because it was all over you. Even in your hair. And I couldn't stop thinking of exactly how your entire body came to smell so good. I closed my eyes and thought about powder, one of those big, old-fashioned powder puffs, about you dabbing it all over your body. But that wouldn't explain the hair. Neither would perfumed lotion, although I could picture you smoothing that over your skin, too. And then I decided it had to be something you put in the bathwater. It was the only way to get that scent all over you."

She looked more than a little interested by the time he was done, seemed quite taken with what he was doing with his hands—rubbing at the soap until he worked up a lather.

He touched his hand to the top of her right knee. "Give me this leg, babe."

She lifted it a bit, and he did the rest, taking her foot between his hands and running his soapy hands over it, gently massaging as he worked his way from her toes to her ankle.

"Dan?"

"Hmm?"

"What are you doing?"

"Groveling," he said, getting turned on just by touching the sole of her foot. "Am I getting any better at it?"

"What?"

"At groveling? You said I was no good at it, so I thought I'd work on it. I thought I needed to."

"Really?"

"Yes. I've been an ass, more times than I care to remember where you're concerned, and I need to find a way to make amends."

"Well," she considered. "I've never had a man wash my feet for me before."

"I'm glad to hear it," he growled, hating the image that brought to mind, of her with any other man.

"It's an original approach."

"That's all? Original?"

She considered. "It feels good."

That didn't begin to describe what it was doing to him. He let his hands slide up from her ankles to her calf, lathering soap along her skin as he went, feeling her tense and go still as his hands slid higher.

"I intend to do a lot more than your feet, babe. If that's all right with you?"

"I don't—"

Her words gave way to a gasp as his soapy hands slid beneath the surface of the water, to midthigh. He wrapped both hands around her leg, gently massaging, forcing himself to hold back now, not letting those hands go any farther.

"I wanted to do this a week ago when we talked on the phone. I wanted to get out of my bed, find someone to drive me into D.C. and show up at your door. I wanted you in the tub waiting for me. And I intended to run my hands over every inch of your body, and then get in that tub with you. I've damned near lost my mind wanting you, waiting for you, arguing with myself that there had to be some way to forget about you, when I just couldn't bring myself to do that."

"Are you finished?"

His heart skipped a beat as he tried to figure out what she was talking about.

"Staying away from me?" she clarified.

"Babe, I've got my hands in your bathwater. I've accepted the fact that there is no way to forget about you, that I was a fool for fighting this for so long."

He found his bar of soap again, started lathering it between his hands and went to work on her other leg, giving it the same painstakingly slow treatment he gave the first one, thinking it was sheer heaven to touch her this way. Her thighs especially were slaying him. He remembered having his hands on them that night in the solarium, finding that strip of skin at the top of her thighs where the stockings ended. He remembered tracing his path around that strip of bare skin, slipping his hands beneath her panties and cupping her buttocks, guiding her to him, rocking his body against hers.

He started to sweat in the steamy, fragrant air of the bathroom, and he was painfully aroused and resigned to living with it for now.

He took her hand next, working his way up her arm, then doing the other. She was still reclining against the back of the tub, her eyes closed. She sighed from time to time, smiled a bit. He tried not to look down into the water, to the blurry image of her submerged body, because it was hard enough to touch her like this and still maintain some semblance of control.

He finished with her arms, then wondered at the wisdom of going any farther.

"What next?" she murmured lazily, smiling at him in a way that seemed to say he could do anything he wanted with her.

A muscle twitched in his jaw, which was every bit as tight and as hard as the rest of him. He thought of all the ways he could pleasure her. With his hands. With his mouth. With his tongue. Wondered if she could take that without him hurting her. Wondered if she wanted him a fraction as much as he wanted her.

She couldn't, he told himself. It didn't seem possible to want anyone this much, to need anyone so completely. And yet he did.

Backing off, thinking of her sore ribs and her head, he reevaluated his plan. "Your hair," he said. "We need to wash your hair somehow."

She slowly lowered herself farther into the water, her knees rising, her shoulders sinking. He could tell it hurt.

"Jamie, wait," he said. "I don't want to hurt you."

"I want to do this. I want to be clean. I want you to scrub every inch of my body, and take away…"

She stopped abruptly, and he thought of the one thing he hadn't asked any of the doctors, the one thing no one had mentioned to him. He simply hadn't possessed the courage to ask, hadn't been sure he wanted to face the answer.

But now… Now it was right there. He'd thought it was odd, knowing how weak she was, how sore she was, that she would want to take a bath. But maybe it wasn't so odd after all. Maybe she needed the cleansing, healing powers of the water. Maybe it was important enough that she could endure whatever discomfort it caused her, to be able to feel clean again.

When he looked back at her again, her gaze was steady, her voice matter-of-fact. "I don't think this is going to work unless you get in here with me."

He waited, thinking there was nothing he'd like better than to be there with her in his arms, her entire body pressed against his. He gave her time to think about it, time to change her mind. She didn't, just waited patiently for him to come to her.

His hands went to the buttons on his shirt, which he undid one by one. "I'll smell like a bouquet of flowers," he pointed out.

That won him a small smile. "It's a sacrifice, I know. But you're groveling, remember?"

"Mmm. I had no idea I'd have to resort to such extremes."

He shrugged out of the shirt, braced his hands on the side of the tub and the handrail along the bathroom wall and lifted himself, until he could sit on the lid of the commode, and from there, get to his feet. He was wearing a pair of sweatpants, because they were relatively easy to get in and out of. Relatively being the operative word. With her watching him, getting out of them seemed incredibly awkward to him.

He turned toward Jamie. He was through hiding what had been done to his body by that single bullet. He wouldn't call what he was doing walking. He hobbled along, using a different, less efficient set of muscles to propel his left leg forward. But he was on his feet and grateful for that.

He found her waiting for him, watching him. As he stood there, she reached for him, her hand coming to rest against the still-reddish ridge of the surgical scar along his side and his back.

He met her stare head-on, unflinchingly. No more hiding.

She smiled faintly, her hand skimming down his side, stopping again against the back of his right thigh. He sucked in a breath. Her hand slid along the muscle at the back of his thigh, exploring lazily, sensuously, until he thought he would go out of his mind.

"Jamie," he protested.

"Hmm?"

"This is not a good idea."

"Why? You had your hands all over me."

"I'm not sure how much more of this I can take."

Her thumb came around to the front of his thigh, rubbing at the tension in that muscle, sliding through the tightly curling hairs that covered his legs, teasing again. He had visions of that hand sliding higher, learning everything there was to know about his body. Or, if that wasn't possible today, stroking him to satisfaction.

It wasn't what he wanted for their first time. But he was starting to crave any bit of completion they could find together.

"Get in the tub," she ordered.

"Yes, ma'am," he drawled, winning another smile from her.

He studied his options for a moment. The tub was bigger than most. But either way, this was going to be a cozy fit. He wanted to have his hands free, to be able to reach as much of her as possible, and he wanted her to be as comfortable as possible, too.

"Can you slide forward a little?" he asked, sitting on the side of the tub, pivoting and using his hands, until he had a leg on either side of her and he could slide into the water behind her.

When he was leaning against the back of the tub, he put his hands on her shoulders and helped ease her down into the water until they got her hair wet. She sat up straight, her head tilted back just a bit, and he admired the delicate shape of her neck and her back as he worked the shampoo through her hair, careful to stay clear of the bruise on her temple.

"Mmm," she said. "That feels so good."

He helped her back down into the water again, worked the soap out of her hair, then eased her back against his chest, until she was sitting between his thighs. He had her head against his shoulder, both his arms around her, holding her gently. He was afraid she was still uncomfortable. But the way she sank back against him, so trustingly, so willingly, the way she let herself go limp in his arms and nuzzled her nose against the side of his neck told him that she wanted this as well. That she needed him.

He was going to give her whatever she wanted tonight.

He would indulge her, pamper her, spoil her. Whatever else happened between them, he intended to own her, body and soul. To brand her with his hands and his mouth and his entire body—as his.

She'd certainly left her brand on him. He would indeed smell like her, all over. It would likely make him crazy tomorrow, walking around smelling the scent of her on his skin, but it didn't matter. His senses were on overload already. How much worse could it get?

He was touching her completely now. Her legs pressed against the inside of his, her bottom snugly against his groin, his erection nestled against the fleshy part of her bottom he'd once held in his hands. Closing his eyes, he realized just this would have been enough for him. He'd wanted so long, wanted so intensely that he could just let go, right then, and at last ease the overwhelming tension building inside his body.

But he didn't, because this wasn't about what he wanted. This was about her and anything he could do to make her feel better, to take her mind off what she'd been through. He wanted her to know he was here for her, that he was going to take care of her, if she would just let him.

He slid his arms around her waist, keeping the touch deliberately light, seeking out the worst of the soreness along her ribs so he knew which places to avoid.

"Here?" he asked, finding a spot for his arm and hand. "Is this all right?"

"Uh-hm."

He just held her for a while, with her head on his shoulder, his mouth against her forehead, lining the side of her face with little, teasing kisses. Next he found the soap, lathered it in his hands, started at the tops of her shoulders then moved along her collarbone, to her neck. She arched her neck, her chin going up, her head leaning back against him.

It felt so very good to touch her. Her skin was luxuriously soft and smooth, like satin. He wanted to cover every last inch of her, to map her body by touch alone.

"I have never, in my entire life, wanted a woman as badly as I want you right now," he confessed, letting his slick, soapy hands find her breasts.

He took the weight of them in each of his hands, held them gently, felt her nipples pucker up and turn hard, for him. He teased them with the pads of his thumbs, told himself when he got her out of this bathtub, he would put his mouth on her breasts, tasting them, rolling her nipples around with his tongue. He could make her come just from that, just with his mouth and his hands.

She moaned, her head turning, her mouth seeking his. He shifted her carefully to one side, so he could fit his mouth to hers, kissing her deeply and as gently as he could. One of his hands was still on her breast, still holding it, memorizing the feel of it. The other slid lower along her belly, the delicate muscles contracting all along the path he took. He found a patch of curls that no doubt matched the raven strands of hair on her head, and his hand slid lower. Her thighs parted for him, and with one finger, he teased at the opening he found, as he kissed her desperately, greedily.

She moved her hips against his hand once, twice, learning the limits of what her body could take, tensing against the pain. He backed off instantly.

"I'm sorry, babe. I know you're not ready for this. I had no intention of taking things this far."

He removed his hand, letting it rest against the delicate soft skin of her belly.

"Don't stop," she said, taking his hand in hers and pushing it lower. "I'll be still, and it won't hurt. Really. Just don't stop."

"Jamie," he protested.

"Don't stop."

His hand slid deeper, teasing again, feeling her body open up to him. With two fingers, he pushed inside of her, imagining it wasn't his fingers slipping into her. It would be a seemingly impossibly tight fit. He worried that he would hurt her, that he was hurting her now. But she was so slick, her body heated to a feverish level. He stroked her smoothly, in and out, not letting his body pick up the erotic rhythm with an answering one of his own.

He stayed still, nothing moving except his hand and his mouth, and somehow she did the same, until he heard low, whimpering cries erupting in her throat, until she couldn't kiss him any longer, could only lie there weakly against him. He felt the muscles in her thighs clenching, tighter and tighter, knew what she wanted, what she needed, but somehow, she managed not to move and trusted him to give her what he could.

He stroked her, in and out, holding himself to an easy rhythm for fear of hurting her. And when she begged him, pleaded with him to end it, when he knew she was ready and that she couldn't take anymore, he did. Moving faster, pushing his fingers inside her one more time, he took her right over the edge. He felt all those delicate muscles deep inside her clenching around him, felt her entire body trembling, felt it go on and on, and let himself imagine the next time. He would be inside her, the next time.

Of course, this was certainly no hardship, to focus so fully on her and her response. He felt the climax ripple through her as he listened to the sounds she made, holding her as she lay heavily against him.

His own feelings sneaked up on him. His erection was cradled tightly against the sweet curves of her buttocks. He wanted to turn her around, and lift her on top of him. To have her sitting on his lap, her thighs spread apart, so he could slide deep inside her as she rode him, milking his body of every last ounce of pleasure.

Of course, he couldn't do any of those things, couldn't let himself so much as move. Then he found he didn't have to move at all. He was near the edge himself now. Maybe it had simply been too long and he wanted her too damned much. There would be a next time, he promised himself, and he would be inside her.

He groaned, tensed, went absolutely still, feeling like a kid who was all of sixteen and so eager he couldn't even control his own body. Jamie wriggled her bottom against him, and he used his hand to hold her steady.

"Be still," he said, his voice hard and tight.

She did it again, just pressed her bottom against his groin, the pressure absolutely exquisite. He was throbbing heavily; as close as they were, she had to feel it, too.

"Jamie, I swear, if you do that one more time, I'll…"

"What?" she said, sounding sleepy and satiated and seductive as hell. "What will you do?"

"You're a smart woman. Figure it out."

She laughed softly and carefully eased away from him. He should have been relieved, but found himself reluctant to let her go. Then he realized she wasn't moving away from him. She was trying to turn around—a neat trick given the confines of the tub and the extent of her injuries. "Wait a minute," he said, his hands at her hips, ready to help her, to guide her.

She turned to face him. Kneeling between his spread thighs, she smiled knowingly at him, and he knew he was in serious trouble. Through the dim light, he saw water running down her body. From the damp ends of her dark hair. Over the delicate bones of her collarbone. Down two delectable-looking breasts. He'd held them in his hands.

Kissed them through the thin fabric of her shirt and then through nothing at all. Had seen teasing glimpses of them as they broke the surface of the water when she'd been lying against him in the tub. But he'd never seen them like this, seen all of them, bare and beautifully rounded, dripping with moisture and her pale skin glistening in the dim light, her nipples taut and begging to be kissed.

"Oh, baby," he groaned, his chest heaving with the effort it took to breathe.

She smiled with that sleepy, sexy look of hers, the one that said she knew exactly what she was doing to him, that her power over him knew no limits, and he wondered how he'd ever managed to resist her all these years.

She leaned forward, her pretty breasts easing against his chest, her arms wrapped around his shoulders. He tilted his head back for her kiss, was careful to hold her loosely in his arms, his senses reeling. Her body was slick and damp and warm, feeling so delicate and soft as she pressed against him. He found the sexy curve of her neck and kissed it, nibbled a bit until she shivered and held him tighter.

This was better than that day in the solarium. So much better. The water was warm and the feel of it only added to the sensual pleasures between them. And this time she wasn't wearing anything at all.

He let his hands drift lower, cupping her buttocks, finding smooth skin and sleek muscles beneath them. He felt them flex and tighten with every little move she made, imagined holding her this way while she took him inside her on another day just like this one, when she was well. He would pull her tight against him, ease her away, set the rhythm he wanted, the one she needed. He would make her beg, make her cry, make her wait, taking her closer to the peak each time and then carefully backing away, until she was mindless with a desperate wanting for him.

"Help me," she said.

"Hmm?"

He felt her weight shift and then her knee was against one of his thighs, burrowing into the space between his thigh and the side of the tub. He shifted his leg to accommodate her, and only then did he realize what she was doing. She'd found that same position he'd guided her to that day in the solarium. She was sitting across his lap, facing him with her thighs spread wide, her weight on him, their bodies pressed intimately together.

It was just what he wanted, what he couldn't have, what she couldn't take today. His hands closed around her upper arms, holding her still. "We can't."

"I think we can," she insisted.

"I'll hurt you," he argued.

"Then we'll stop. But not until then."

It was not the kind of argument he'd ever had with a naked, willing woman, but one he was determined to win. "Babe, you don't have to do this. I'll be okay."

She played dirty, reaching between them and down into the water, her hands closing around him, her eyes opening wider with shock and he thought with pleasure. His body jerked in response, unbelievably seeming to harden even more at the gentle, insistent pressure of her hands.

He could let her do this, he decided, let her stroke him with those delicate hands of hers. It might kill him, but he wouldn't move a muscle. He'd watch desire turn her eyes smoky and dark, watch that satisfied smile spread across her pretty face, feel her hands stroking him. That would be more than enough.

He smiled back at her, relaxed a little, ready to stop fighting it and simply let himself go, as long as he could be still somehow. Oh, yeah. This would be more than enough, he realized. What he hadn't counted on was the way her thighs tensed, the way ever so slowly, she leaned the weight of her body against his, guiding him to the tight, wet opening of her body.

"No," he said, sounding like a drowning man, moving to stop her.

But it was too late. She smiled again, pressed down against him just a little, and he was right there, poised on the brink of being inside her. He felt heat, felt what seemed to be an impossibly narrow opening, felt that gentle pressure she was exerting which threatened to do away with every ounce of resistance he had.

"Jamie, don't do this. I told you I can wait."

"We've waited for years," she said. "Years. I don't want to wait another second."

He groaned, his instinct to protect, to worry about her needs first, to clamp down on his.

She sank lower, taking him inside, just the blunt tip. The way he felt tonight, he figured he had about a mile to go before he was fully inside her. But this was okay. Just this, he told himself. He could let her do just this. He could come just like this.

"Please," she begged. "I need you, too. I need to feel you inside me. All the way."

"I'll hurt you."

"You won't," she said, pressing down upon him again. "Help me, Dan. If you won't do this for yourself, do it for me. I want you so much. I need you."

Dan groaned. He couldn't fight that. How could any man in his position fight against a plea like that? His hands cupped her buttocks again, and she relaxed, letting him control the movement now, letting him take her weight in his hands.

It was doable, he decided. If she simply needed to feel him within the tight sheath of her body, he could give her that. He'd already decided he'd give her anything she wanted, anything he had to give. He could control himself somehow and give her this.

"Don't move a muscle," he warned. "And if this hurts you, you tell me. Right away."

Controlling her movement with his hands, he used the weight of her own body, let her sink down upon him, slowly easing his way inside. The pressure was exquisite, a thousand tiny muscles inside of her shivering and pulsing around him, working to accommodate his swollen length. She felt so tight, every sensation multiplied a hundredfold, a thousand. It made him wonder if every other woman had been nothing but a dream. If nothing before this had been real.

The pleasure was so intense, a tight, burning sensation that reached to the very core of him. He started to sweat with the effort it took not to give in to the demands of his body, to take her quickly, pressing deeply inside, withdrawing and thrusting in time to the beat of his heart, taking her with strength and power and almost no restraint.

Not tonight, he reminded himself.

He dug his fingers into her buttocks and eased her down a fraction of an inch more. She moaned sweetly, her head coming down to rest against his shoulder as she went limp in his arms, giving herself up to him.

She was going to kill him, he decided. This was going to kill him. He felt as if he'd run a marathon, climbed a mountain, jumped out of an airplane without a parachute. She was every bit as dangerous and enticing as any mission he'd ever been given. And she was his mission tonight. Pleasing her. Slipping inside her and making her come again and again, if that was what she wanted, what she needed.

She moaned.

"Tell me," he said, worried at the look of utter concentration on her face.

"I can't..."

"It hurts?"

"No, it's too much."

"Here?" Again, he used his hands to bring her down around him, taking a little bit more of him.

"Yes," she gasped. "I can't...."

But she could. He would show her. "Do you want me to stop?"

"No, but...."

"Then you do it," he said. "Whatever you want. Whatever you need. Take it."

She stared at him, surprised by the idea, excited by it, a little apprehensive. He wondered again if he was hurting her, was ready to put a stop to this whole thing, when she pressed her body onto his, sinking ever so slowly downward, finding a way somehow. "It feels so good," she whispered urgently.

His fingers tightened on her buttocks, his nails digging into them until he forced them to relax before he left marks of his own on her. He felt as if they had come thousands of miles, a journey measured in long, lonely years and endless denials of all that was between them, to reach this moment. Somehow he'd always known she was meant for him, even if he thought she deserved someone so different from him.

He considered telling her he loved her, because he was fairly certain he did. His only doubts were about his ability to feel that particular emotion, to recognize it for what it was. He'd never truly loved a woman before, had tried for a long time to convince himself he couldn't and that he was better for lack of loving anyone or having anyone's love in return.

But if he was capable of loving anyone, it would be her.

"Jamie," he whispered urgently, trying to say it all with just her name, somehow managing not to move at all though every nerve in his body was screaming at him to do so.

Her body still closed around him so tightly, clenching and pulsing and heating him through and through. And he loved being inside her, had loved so much the way she'd given herself to him, had cried out his name and collapsed in his arms.

"Dan," she said, begging now.

"It's all right," he soothed. Ready to guide her over the edge, he reached a hand between them, finding the place where her body gave way to his, feeling her spread open wide around him, tracing the opening with his thumb, finding the feeling so erotic.

She gasped. "Please."

"Shh. Leave this to me. Trust me. It'll be just like before. Just as good. Better, even. Because this time, I'll be inside you," he promised, stroking her softly, feeling her muscles clench around him.

"Now," she whispered. "Please. Now."

And then he couldn't wait any longer, either, stroking her with his thumb, finding that it was indeed enough just to hold her, to look at her, to be inside her.

"Feel it?" he urged. "Feel what you do to me. Feel how much I need you. How crazy you've made me."

And then he just let go of everything else. His erection was pulsing hot as he came for the first time in his life without moving a muscle. His body collapsed, his soul soared. There was indeed nothing in the world of any consequence except him and her and the magic they made together.

He closed his eyes, wanting to memorize the pressure of her body cradling him, the new slick heat between them, the deep shudders of satisfaction racing through him. Her body tensed, as his had. She rode him without moving a muscle, either. Clenched down hard, easing a bit, only to do it all over again.

It was exquisite, mind-altering, earth-shattering. It was everything he'd ever dreamed and more.

Jamie, he thought.

Finally.

When the roaring in his ears receded, he realized she was laughing softly, the sound incredibly sexy, as she lay heavily against him.

He pushed her head back, just enough to find her mouth. He kissed her softly, slowly, again and again until the ache and the tension eased, leaving him utterly drained, utterly exhausted and unbelievably satisfied, given the restrictions that had been placed on their lovemaking.

"Are you all right?" he asked when he could breathe again.

"Uh-huh."

"Lady, you are dangerous," he said.

"I didn't do anything," she reminded him. "I was just lying here having a bath."

He swore. "All you have to do is breathe, and I'm as hard as a rock."

"Really?"

"Yes. Really."

"And that's a problem?"

"It used to be." Now he planned on making it his pleasure. Watching her breathe. Watching her smile. Watching her come again and again.

He took her chin in his hand, tilted her face up to his, waited until her gaze met his. "You are so beautiful, babe," he said.

"Dan, the whole side of my face is one big bruise."

"I don't give a damn," he muttered. "You've always been beautiful to me. You always will be."

He let himself kiss her once, carefully, softly.

"I can't believe how much time I let us waste. I can't believe I managed to live without you this long, but that's over. You need to understand something. You're mine now. I won't let you go again."

He wanted to make sure she understood, wanted to hear her admit it.

"All I ever wanted," she whispered, "was to be with you."

And then she smiled up at him, kissing him this time, one of her hands sliding into his hair and pulling his face down to hers. He kissed her back, hungrily, greedily, thinking he could spend a lifetime pleasuring this woman. Learning all of her secrets, taking all of her fears away, standing between her and anyone else who dared lay a hand on her.

When this was all over and she was healed, he was going to take her far away from here. They were going to lock themselves away from the rest of the world and discover everything about each other. Every secret. Every yearning.

He could give her what she wanted, what she needed. It would be enough, he told himself, panicking a little at the thought of how very much he needed her in return.

Chapter 14

They lingered in the tub. Jamie was relaxed and tired and so wonderfully satisfied lying there in his arms. He'd soaped her body all over again, teasing her, soothing her, seemingly happy just to have his hands on her.

"Don't you dare go to sleep on me," he said.

"Why not?"

"Because somehow, we've got to get out of here. I need to get you back to bed."

She smiled lazily, ready to put aside for now all her lingering doubts about him, to give herself this day with him. "Really?"

"Yes. And don't get any ideas," he warned. "You're going to sleep. You're going to be sore enough from all this."

"I don't care. It was worth it."

"We'll see if you feel that way in a few hours," he said.

The truth was, no matter how gentle he'd been, she could already feel her body protesting. She knew getting out of

the bathtub and making her way back to bed wasn't going
to be any picnic. But she wouldn't have traded these moments with him for anything in this world, no matter what
the future held.

Moving carefully, slowly, with his help, she made it out
of the tub. Dan dried her off as if she were a child and
completely helpless. He gave her one of his T-shirts, one
that fell to midthigh on her, and nothing else to wear, grinning wickedly as he surveyed his handiwork after dressing
her, toweling her hair dry and combing it out. Leaning
heavily on him, while he leaned on his black cane, they
made it back to the bed. He pulled back the covers and
tucked her in, leaned over and gave her a gentle, lingering
kiss.

"Sleep with me," she said.

"I intend to."

She smiled, watching him make his way across the room.
He checked the view from all the windows, called someone—the guard, she assumed—and talked to him for a few
minutes. He picked up a gun, a nine-millimeter, placed it
on the bedside table within her reach, told her it was loaded
and ready.

"Want something to drink?" he asked, standing in front
of an open refrigerator. "Some juice?"

"Yes, please. And one of those wonderful little pills the
doctor left on top of the dresser."

"Wonderful little pills?"

"Mmm."

He brought her the glass, examined the bottle of pills,
shook one of them into her hand, and helped her sit up so
she could swallow the pill. Looking solemn and stern, he
said, "I did hurt you."

His concern was sweet, especially coming from such a
big, tough guy like him. "Dan, everything hurt before you

ever laid a hand on me. You just took it all away for a while.''

His frown eased a bit. He checked the locks on the doors, turned out lights, looked out the window one more time, then set the cane down on the nightstand and sat down on the side of the bed. She watched as he used his hand to guide his left leg onto the bed. She was lying flat on her back, and he rolled onto his side beside her, until their bodies were barely touching.

He stretched an arm across her stomach. His hand landed on the soft cotton of the T-shirt he'd given her to wear, and she smiled as she felt that hand burrow beneath the bottom of the fabric until his palm was pressed flat against her stomach, her skin quivering in response. Heat radiated outward from his hand, flooding through her.

She inched closer, seeking that wonderful heat, the solid, reassuring, exciting pressure of his body, and grinned. She had a cat, once, who'd nose his way into a favorite spot at her side. He'd slide into position beneath her hand and wait for her to stroke him while he purred.

She was very nearly purring, herself, because it was heavenly to share a bed with him. She nestled against him. His fingers spread wide, and he used his thumb to tease along the underside of her breast. Then she turned his head to hers and kissed him deeply.

''Stop that,'' he said.

''Why?''

She snuggled against him, feeling the tension coming into his body. He was thoroughly aroused. She felt him, hard and throbbing against her thigh, felt her whole body soften in response.

''We are not going to do this again,'' he insisted.

''But—''

''No way,'' he said. ''I already feel guilty over what happened in the tub. I'm not going to make it worse.''

She was going to suggest there was no reason for him to stay this way, that she would be more than happy to take care of him. "I could...I mean, we don't have to..."

"Jamie, it wouldn't do any good. I think as long as I'm stretched out on a bed with you and have my hands all over you, I'm going to be this way. No matter how many times we make love."

"Oh," she said, finding she liked that idea very, very much.

"Go to sleep," he told her. "And if you don't behave, I'll sleep on the sofa again. Or in that awful chair beside the bed."

"*Behave?*" she said.

"Yes, woman. Keep your hands and those sweet-tasting lips of yours to yourself."

"*Woman?*" she argued.

He laughed, kissed her forehead and whispered, "You need to rest, so your body can heal. And once you do, neither of us will be getting a lot of sleep."

"Promise?"

"Count on it, babe."

She leaned her head to the right, her lips finding his, kissing him softly and surely, marveling at the way she felt entitled to that kiss, at the idea of sleeping here in his bed all night long, waking beside him in the morning.

For a while, when those people had her, she believed she wouldn't get away, that they'd kill her without the slightest twinge of conscience. It made her think about what she'd done with her life thus far, about the things she'd regret if she didn't live to see another day.

She shivered involuntarily. Dan eased his body a little closer, put his head next to hers and whispered into her ear. "Hey? It's all right. You don't have to be afraid anymore."

"I was just thinking...."

"Jamie? Those men? What did they do to you, babe?"

"They pretended I was a punching bag, until they figured out I wasn't going to tell them what they wanted to know."

"And then what?"

"They yelled, smoked, drank, swore, argued about what they were going to do with me next. And then they pushed me into a car. A few blocks later, they...I don't know. Shoved me out?"

He swore. "Yeah. Right out the door. I mean before that. What did they do before?"

"I told you, they hit me."

"Okay," he said. "I thought... I was afraid they might have..."

She closed her eyes, shivered again, knew where this conversation was going. "No, they didn't."

He looked unconvinced. "When we were in the bathtub, and you said you wanted to be clean, that you wanted me to scrub every inch of your body and take away... something, I thought—"

"No," she insisted, not wanting to think how close it had come to that. She had wanted desperately to be in the water, because they'd left her feeling dirty somehow. And she'd wanted Dan, desperately, because she'd always wanted him, always needed him, never more than she had today.

"Don't lie to me," he cautioned.

"I'm not," she said carefully, because there was murder in his eyes. Because if he ever came face-to-face with the people who'd held her prisoner for those hellish hours, she wanted him to be able to think like an agent and not like a man who was consumed by anger and a need for revenge. Not that he wasn't already dangerously angry. She simply didn't want to add fuel to that fire.

"You're afraid," he said.

"Who wouldn't be under the circumstances? We've got a bunch of teenage gangsters who nearly shot and killed you, who may be working with someone we know. We don't know what we're facing, and we don't know where to turn for help, because we don't know who we can trust anymore. Aren't you afraid of all that?''

"No, I'm pissed that somebody hurt you this way, and I'm going to catch the little bastards who did it," he swore. "They're never going to hurt you again. No one is."

She smiled. It wasn't exactly a declaration of love, but she'd take it. He'd staked his claim earlier, after all. She was *his*. It sounded positively primitive, but it had still thrilled her on some elemental level, in a way that surely no independent woman should ever admit. The truth was, she wanted to be his, and his alone. She wanted him to belong to her as completely as she belonged to him. She wondered exactly what it meant to Dan Reese when he laid his claim to a woman. Was it something purely sexual? Could he be this tender? This solicitous? This attentive to all the women he took to his bed? This protective of them?

She'd always known he was charming, had never felt its full-blown effect directed at her. Oh, she was in trouble, she thought, her eyes drifting downward.

"It's been a long day, babe," he said. "Go to sleep."

She leaned into his side and tried to ignore every ache and pain in her body. She concentrated on the feel of his big, warm hand, fingers splayed, palm pressed flat against her belly. She listened to the sound of his breathing and let her mind drift, let the medication she'd taken dull the edge of the pain just enough to let her sleep.

She slept late the next morning, woke to find that her head didn't hurt at all. Her ribs were still sore, but not as bad as yesterday. Her ankle was tender, as well, but she managed to hobble to the bathroom on her own, brush her teeth, wash her face and get ready to face the day.

Dan had left her another T-shirt to wear and a pair of

his swimming trunks, probably because they had a draw-
string waist. She dressed, hobbled to the kitchen, found
juice and muffins. Hungry, she ate two of them.

There was a note from Dan, saying he had a session with
his therapist, that there was an ex-Marine named Walt outside watching the cabin, so she didn't have to worry.

She ended up back in the bed, feeling tired and achy but
better than the day before. Smiling lazily, she thought of
sleeping in his arms the night before, thought of whispered
conversations in the dark when he'd told her all the things
he wanted to do to her when she recovered from her injuries
and when this whole mess was over.

She must have dozed off, because the next thing she
knew, Dan was beside her. She turned instinctively into the
warmth and the mass of solid muscle at her side. He was
sitting up, his back leaning against the headboard. Her
hands slid around his waist, her head finding a pillow in
the flat expanse of his chest. She snuggled like a cat, rubbing her cheek against the soft flannel of his shirt, liking
that little hitch of his breath, rubbing her hands along the
powerful muscles at the top of his thighs.

"Mmm," she said. "Good morning."

"It's almost three o'clock, Jamie," he said, sounding
worried.

"Really?"

"Yes." His hand slid through her hair, pushing it back
from her face and tucking it behind her ear. "Are you still
hurting? Did you pop another one of those pills?"

"It's not as bad as it was yesterday, and no, I didn't take
anything. Why?"

"We did too much yesterday."

"Uh-uh."

"I *know* we did too much, but I was afraid I really hurt
you."

"Dan, I'm fine."

He kissed the top of her head, let his hand slide beneath the covers. She felt it, so warm, against her lower back. He started kneading at the muscles there, rubbing, helping her to relax even more. "How's that?"

"Wonderful. Don't stop."

He laughed. "Bossy little thing, aren't you? *Do this. Do that. Don't stop.*"

"Bossy? You think *I'm* bossy? You're impossible. Arrogant, overbearing, stubborn, frustrating." Jamie sighed, smiled. "You're lucky I put up with you."

The hand against her back stilled. He eased her away from him and slid down into the bed beside her, leaning over her, so she could see his face, could see dark eyes and soft lips, a determined jawline and short blondish hair she longed to touch.

"You're right," he said, his lips pressing softly against hers, his hand cupping the side of her face. "I am lucky you put up with me. I feel lucky just to have you here beside me. And I feel extremely lucky that you're going to forgive me for fighting against the idea of the two of us for so many years." He paused, smiled just a bit. "You are going to forgive me for that, aren't you?"

"Well, I suppose I could."

He grinned, and she realized just how devastating he could be when he unleashed all his charms. "I should have been with you, babe. All along. And for damned sure, I shouldn't have let you go after those men by yourself. I'm so sorry about that."

"I'm going to be all right," she reassured him.

He still looked worried, running his hands down her side, across her body, asking about certain injuries, fussing over her and soothing her with his touch. Finally, when he was satisfied she truly felt better, he turned his attention to other things.

"We need to talk about this. About us."

Still a little scared by the prospect, she leaned closer to him. "I thought we settled things yesterday."

"We settled the fact that together we're like dynamite and a lit match."

"Yes, we are." That summed it up nicely.

"And I don't think that's ever going to change."

"No?" she teased, trying and likely failing to make light of it.

She shivered, unable to help herself, thinking of the powerful way he'd claimed her as his. It had been overwhelming, earth-shattering, world-altering, at least to her.

She'd never been a woman to take a sexual involvement lightly. But this…this had been different. She would never forget him, never forget what it had felt like to be wrapped in his arms, naked, with her body straining to take all of him inside of her. She'd never forget the dangerous look in his eyes, the utter satisfaction and contentment she felt afterward when she lay there trembling against him.

But that was her. She had no idea what it meant to him.

Mind-altering sex was not the same thing as love. It wasn't commitment. It wasn't a relationship. Or a future.

"Years from now," he whispered, "I think you'll still be able to walk into a room and have me aching and ready in five seconds flat. You'll still fit like you were made to be in my arms, probably still make me crazy and still be trying to wrap me around your little finger."

"I will?" She was liking the sound of this more and more.

"Yes." He turned all serious again. "Jamie, I know I'm no bargain…"

"Mmm," she teased. "I remember. Frustrating, maddening, arrogant—"

He pressed two fingers against her lips. "I'm not talking about my sweet disposition. I'm talking about the way I'm hobbling around on this damned cane. It's not going to be as bad as it was yesterday, but I'm not sure how much better it's going to get, either. I can walk, maybe without the cane in time. But there's always going to be a limp. I won't be running any marathons.''

"It doesn't matter to me."

"Babe, I don't know how you can be sure about that right now, and that worries me."

"Dan, I swear to you, when I think of the kind of man I want to be with, I've never considered the fact that he could or couldn't run a marathon as a deciding factor. I don't know any woman who does."

He swore, looking thoroughly exasperated. "You know what I mean."

"You're telling me if I'm looking for a jogging partner, it won't be you. I can live with that. If you're telling me you won't be out in the field for the agency again because of certain physical limitations, don't expect me to be upset by that. The idea of you running around getting shot at doesn't exactly thrill me."

"Jamie, there's more to it than that, and you know it."

"Okay, let's think about this. I could probably find another man who isn't nearly as arrogant as you or as much of a chauvinist as you," she teased. "One who isn't as brave or as strong or as determined. I can't imagine he'd make me feel the way you do, can't imagine wanting another man as much as I want you." Jamie sighed. It was no good. She couldn't keep it light. She wanted him too much. "I've never admired another man as much as you. Never waited this long for one. I really don't go around throwing myself at men who aren't interested in me."

"Believe me, lack of interest was never the issue. I guess I decided I didn't deserve you, that you deserved someone who had a lot more to offer than I did."

"Oh, I can't wait to hear this. What do you think I deserve?" she asked.

"Jamie—"

"No," she reconsidered. Why would she give him a chance to try to talk her out of this? Lay it on the line, she told herself. It was time. Time to tell him exactly what she wanted. "Let's skip that part altogether. It isn't an issue. Let me tell you what I want."

"Okay."

Gathering her courage, she told him, "I want a man who respects me, one who's honest, one I can trust. One who can make me laugh and smile. One who can take my breath away. One who can make me melt with just a look and make magic with a kiss. I want a man who'll never leave me, one who wants to have children with me. One who has the patience and gentleness to be a good father to those children."

His hand, which had been making lazy circles along the side of her hip, slid beneath the shirt she wore once again, resting flat against her skin, fingers splayed wide across her abdomen. "Children."

She never hesitated. "Yes."

He looked worried then. "Jamie, we didn't use anything yesterday. I'm sorry. But I never meant to take things that far."

She hadn't even thought of that, hadn't thought of anything but having him inside of her, finally. Jamie tensed, knowing it was an irresponsible risk to take but knowing she'd never regret having his child. But how would he feel about it?

His hand still lingered against her skin, low on her belly, his touch exquisitely gentle, his expression wary. "I didn't even think about it until sometime last night, but it could have happened already."

Jamie's heart lurched crazily at the image he painted. Would it make him happy if she had his baby? Or would he push her away again?

"What else do you want?" he whispered, giving nothing else away.

You, she thought. I just want *you.*

But she wasn't sure he would accept that. So she searched through her own jumbled thoughts, sifting through what she'd already told him and beyond that, to the stuff of her dreams.

"I want a big, old house," she explained, seeing it in her head. "Three stories, with a porch that goes on forever, all sorts of odd-shaped rooms, and hardwood floors and a fireplace. I want a big yard with lots of trees, somewhere out in the country, and once I find it, I don't ever want to move. When I was growing up, we never stayed in one place. And I always dreamed of a place where I'd stay. I've been seeing this house in my head forever."

"What else?"

There wasn't much else. "A rosebush. No, lots of rosebushes. Climbers that get all tangled up in the side of the house, like they're never going to let it go. Fern baskets hanging from the porch. A porch swing. A puppy."

"It can't be that hard to find a man willing to give you a puppy or a big, old house in the country."

"I want a man who loves me." She took a deep breath. Her ribs protested, but she didn't care. She needed the air now that she'd gotten to the hardest part. "A man who'll be a father to my children. And I want it to last."

"That's it?"

She nodded. "I should tell you—all those other things? They're all negotiable. Except for the last three."

He smiled beautifully, sadly, but said nothing.

Jamie bit down on her bottom lip, thinking this could go either way, wondering why he'd asked all these questions if he hadn't wanted to know the answers.

She was going to cry in earnest, she decided as the silence stretched out between them.

Finally, he said, "Jamie, all of this has happened so fast. We've known each other for years, but…until a few weeks ago…"

"I know."

"The last few days…you could have died on that street that morning. I thought…" He sighed. "Everything's been so intense. I don't…I want us to be sure, Jamie. We need to take some time, to be sure."

Her emotions were rubbed raw, her tears were falling faster. He bent to wipe them away.

"I'm not trying to back away from this. I swear," he insisted, and she couldn't tell if she'd scared him with her talk about loving him and babies and old houses in the country, or if he was giving her one last chance to change her mind because he still thought that would be best for her.

Jamie tried to smile, but it was hard. Tears clouded her vision, and she couldn't breathe and her ribs hurt. And she wanted to hold him so tight, like she'd never let him go. She didn't want to let go of this moment, of the dreams drifting through her head.

He wrapped his arms around her, stared down at her. "Stay here with me," he whispered urgently. "I just need another week or so here with my therapists, until I'm getting around a little better with the cane. You need the rest, and I need to have you here. I'm going to keep you safe, Jamie. Stay with me."

"I will," she said.

"Like this?" he said, kissing her again. "In my bed?"

"Yes."

"We'll find out who hurt you, who shot me. And then we'll take some time just for the two of us. We'll figure everything out. Do you trust me?"

"Yes."

With her life. She hoped she could with her heart as well.

Chapter 15

They had eight glorious days together. Jamie felt truly pampered. She stayed in bed, sleeping much of the time away, soaking in the hot tub, resting, daydreaming. Dan was getting stronger every day, moving more freely and easily, though still using the cane.

She teased him, telling him he looked rather sexy with it, that he wore the wounded warrior look well. But she still worried that the damage to his leg was weighing on him more than he let on. And she was still afraid he didn't quite believe that it didn't matter to her if he never walked without the cane. But he wasn't trying to push her away anymore, either.

Still, they had to deal with the mess they'd left behind in D.C. eventually. She wasn't surprised one morning when Dan said Josh was on his way to the cabin so the three of them could plan their next move. She wanted it over with, but she was scared, too. Dan wasn't scared, but something was bothering him. She knew him too well not to recognize the signs.

She walked over to where he stood, with his back to her as he looked out one of the cabin's windows. She slipped her arms around his waist from behind, rested her head on his shoulder and said, "What's wrong?"

"Nothing," he insisted.

"You frown like this over nothing?" she said.

"Well…" He hedged. "Sometimes."

She remembered her mother's warning, that emotional intimacy was simply beyond some men, and tightened her arms around him. He'd been trying. She thought he honestly wanted to let her inside that thick skull of his. She'd hoped that would be enough.

"Tell me what's wrong."

He said nothing for the longest time, then admitted, "I'm being petty, all right."

"Oh." Intrigued, she pressed on. "Then we've got a problem here. I don't recall that being on the list of annoying habits I'm willing to overlook. I'm afraid you'll have to stop."

He turned around, leaned back against the windowsill and pulled her into his arms. "You want to talk about annoying habits?"

"We could." She smiled as sweetly as she dared. "But you'd just be doing it to distract me, and it wouldn't work. At least, not for long."

He kissed her lightly. "You are a truly annoying woman."

"Mmm. Want to renegotiate our deal? You can be petty, and I'll be annoying."

"No," he insisted. "I'm not renegotiating anything."

"Then you have to talk to me. What's wrong?"

He looked truly uncomfortable, and she started to really worry, wondering what else he might be keeping from her. Finally, he said, "When you were in the emergency room, the nurse who was with you offered to call someone to come and be with you. Do you remember that?"

"Maybe. It's all hazy. Why?"

"You asked her to call Josh."

"Oh." Was he still jealous of Josh? After the last eight days? "Dan, I told you—there's nothing between me and Josh."

"I know. And I believe you. But when you were hurt, he was the one you wanted with you."

"No," she insisted, knowing this must have been bugging him for days and thinking he deserved to suffer if he simply refused to ask her about it. "Josh was just closer. His apartment is about fifteen minutes from the hospital."

"That's it?"

"Yes. I was drifting in and out of consciousness, and I had to tell someone what happened. I knew I shouldn't stay in the hospital, that someone needed to wipe out any record of my being there. And I suspected someone at the agency was involved in everything. I also knew I'd be putting my life into the hands of the person I called."

"You were," he agreed.

"Believe me, you're the one I wanted with me," she reassured him. "But I thought you were an hour and a half away, and I was scared. Josh was just closer."

He looked annoyed. Whether at her or himself, she couldn't tell. He frowned again and said, "You're sure? That's it?"

"What other reason could there be?"

"You tell me," he invited.

"That's it."

He looked unconvinced, but all he said was, "This mess isn't over yet."

"I know."

"If you want to go somewhere else... If there's some

other place where you'd feel safer. Someone you want to be with now—''

"No," she insisted. "Don't you dare even think that. I trust you. I feel safe with you."

And then she just held on to him, refusing to let go, refusing to let him have any doubts. They climbed back into the bed and made love, like they had all week, but hastily, greedily. Yet he was still careful of her injuries. He left her there with a kiss and a promise to be back in an hour and a half, when he finished his workout in the pool. Josh should be here by then, and they would make their plan. One way or another, they were going to end this.

Thirty minutes later, Jamie had just gotten out of the shower. She was slipping a T-shirt over her head when the alarm sounded.

Jamie jumped at the high-pitched, whirring sound, her nerves shot. She didn't want to come face-to-face with the men who'd taken such pleasure in tying her up and beating her, and she didn't want to have to raise her gun to someone she'd considered a friend from the agency.

But she wasn't going to be caught unarmed, either. Dan would know about the alarm, she told herself. He'd be here in seconds. There was a guard outside, too, and she wasn't helpless. She reached for the nine-millimeter pistol Dan kept beside the bed. She'd barely gotten it into her hand when someone kicked in the back door and came charging through.

Jamie screamed and took aim with the gun, her index finger squeezing back on the trigger.

The man burst through the opening, his weapon drawn. Tense seconds followed when they stared at each other, struggled for long, deep, soothing breaths and waited for the adrenaline to stop surging, then finally lowered their weapons.

Jamie's hands were shaking as she put the gun down on the table and walked into the man's arms.

"Where the hell have you been?" he growled.

"Right here," she said, still trying to catch her breath and wishing she'd taken the time to silence the alarm.

She was just starting to relax when she heard a crash behind her. The front door was kicked in, and Dan came charging inside, gun drawn. Jamie's visitor still had his weapon in his hand, and the next thing she knew, she was the only thing keeping them from shooting each other.

His arm tightened painfully around her rib cage and he pulled her to the right—no doubt to shove her out of the way—but she refused to go, planting herself between him and Dan in an effort to get both of them to stop.

"Wait!" she yelled. "Both of you. Just wait a minute."

She reached for the control unit on the alarm, shut it off, then turned to make the necessary explanations before there was any bloodshed.

She turned to Dan, who still looked ready to commit murder. "Dan, this is my brother, Sean."

He stared as if he didn't quite believe her. She remembered that it took a minute after Sean burst through the door for her to believe what her own eyes were telling her. She turned to her brother, who still hadn't lowered his gun. "Sean, Dan and I work together. He's not going to hurt me, and you're not going to shoot him."

She stayed between the two of them until they finally lowered their guns. Dan swore. Sean started yelling.

"What the hell happened to you?" he said.

"It's a long story."

He reached for the side of her face, which still held traces of bruises. "Why didn't you call me?"

"I'm sorry," she said. "What are you doing here?"

"Looking for you."

"You found me." She managed a weak smile and turned

to Dan. She held out her hand to him, his closed tightly over hers, and she knew he'd been as scared as she was when the alarm went off. She whispered, ''Sorry.''

Her hand was trembling, so she couldn't be sure, but she thought his was as well, and she could just imagine how he felt when the alarm sounded.

''I'm all right,'' she reassured him, then remembered the guard and turned back to her brother. ''Sean? The guard? Outside the cabin? You didn't...''

''He'll be fine,'' her brother shrugged. ''In a couple of hours.''

Dan went to check on the guard. In the middle of that, Josh arrived. She introduced him to her brother, filled him in on what happened. Josh fussed over her bruises and gave her hell for causing so much trouble. Dan came back and reported that the guard was going to be fine, and through it all, Sean stood there seething. She could just imagine what was in store for her, once he finally had his say.

A few moments later, Sean, looking her over from head to toe, asked, ''What does the bad guy look like?''

''There were five of them, Sean. Do you think you would have gotten away if five guys jumped you?''

''I don't know, but I damned sure wouldn't have been wandering around down there by myself where somebody could grab me and do God knows what to me and then throw me out of a moving car,'' he yelled. ''Damn it, Jamie, did you or did you not get thrown out of a car on Burns Avenue twelve days ago?''

''She did.'' Dan came to stand beside her, slipping an arm around her waist.

Jamie saw the speculative gleam in her brother's eye as he looked over the two of them and decided to see if she could salvage something of this, their first meeting. ''I'm sorry,'' she said. ''I didn't take the time to introduce the two of you, properly. Dan, this is my brother, Sean Patrick

Douglass.'' She turned to her brother. ''Sean, this is Dan Reese.''

Reluctantly, they shook hands, sizing each other up as if they might still duke it out at any moment. Then Sean's eyes narrowed and gave a hint of a smile. ''Dan Reese?'' he said. ''Weren't you...?''

''Yes, Sean,'' she groaned.

''One of her instructors,'' Sean nodded. ''I've heard a lot about you.''

''Shut up, Sean,'' she said, reverting to threats.

''I've got to warn you,'' he continued. ''She looks like a sweet little thing, but she knows how to hold a grudge. And she has a nasty temper.''

''So does Dan,'' she countered.

''Now that I think about it, so do I.'' Sean turned back to her. ''I can't believe I had to hunt you down to find out what happened to you.''

''I'm all right,'' she said.

''This happened twelve days ago,'' he fumed.

''I'm sorry,'' she said again. ''I knew you'd worry, and I really didn't want to explain this to the family until the worst of the bruises faded.''

Exasperated, Jamie looked at Josh. He just shrugged his shoulders. Then she turned to Dan, who was smiling.

''I like this guy,'' he leaned toward her and whispered. ''I like the way he operates.''

''You would. The two of you are so much alike, it's scary. And Sean's just like my father. I'm sure the three of you are going to get along just fine.''

''Hey,'' Sean, impatient as always, interrupted. ''What *is* going on here?'' He was staring at the two of them with new interest, took his time about looking around the cabin, as well, as if he knew exactly what they'd been doing here.

Jamie groaned. ''Give it a rest, Sean. Why don't you tell us what you're doing here?''

"Well, it was the oddest thing. I'm sitting at my desk, minding my own business—"

"You?" she scoffed.

"—when I start hearing odd complaints from the Marshal's Service. You can imagine how happy they are to have people running around D.C. claiming to be their agents. Letting people who are supposedly theirs get beaten up and thrown out of moving cars. Checking people in and out of hospitals under false names, misleading the police and then disappearing. When I started nosing around and dug up the bit on the six-millimeter slugs, and I knew this had to be connected to Alex Hathaway's disappearance. I knew Division One lost him, and I worried that you," he pointed to Jamie, "were right in the middle of it. You weren't home, you weren't returning anyone's calls and you weren't on assignment, as you claimed to be. I have enough clout these days to check, you know."

Jamie nodded.

"And when I started asking questions about the witness who supposedly got thrown out of a speeding car, what do I find? She sounds a lot like my baby sister."

"Oh," she said.

"That was four days ago. It took me this long to find you," he complained. "Damn it, Jamie, I shouldn't have to play detective to find out you're in trouble."

"I'm sorry—" she said.

"You damn well should be."

"But this had to be kept quiet."

They fell silent for a moment. She thought the worst of her brother's anger had faded. "So," she said, trying to be civil. "You're trying to find Hathaway, too?"

"Everybody and their mother's trying to find Hathaway," he said, brushing his fingertips along her bruised cheekbone. "I think I'll leave 'em to it. Right now, I intend to find the bastards who did this to you."

"You'll have to get in line for the chance," Dan said.

"And I'm right behind him," Josh said.

Sean perked up. "Know where they are right now?"

Dan and Josh shook their heads.

"I do." Sean smiled.

Everything moved quickly from there. Dan could see that Jamie's brother had clout and knew how to use it. The four of them took a helicopter to the outskirts of D.C., drove in an unmarked van to what looked like an abandoned building, and met two men dressed all in black and armed to the teeth, ready and waiting. They'd argued about calling in anyone to help. Sean, once he heard their story, was as paranoid as the rest of them. In the end, they settled for using the three men who'd been tailing their suspects all day, and no one else.

Josh looked over the equipment they'd taken from the helicopter and whistled appreciatively. "You think you've got enough firepower here? You could take over a small country."

"I don't believe in taking unnecessary chances," Sean said, turning to Jamie. "Unlike some members of the family."

"Jump off any barns lately, Sean?" she countered.

If Dan hadn't been so tense, he would have laughed. He did like her brother. He was intrigued by the relationship between the two, wondered if her entire family bickered back and forth like this. He wondered if the love between the rest of them was so obvious, as well.

Sean would walk through a wall of fire for his sister. That had been painfully obvious when he saw the bruises on her face, when he was chewing her out for keeping him in the dark about what had happened to her. And he suspected Jamie was going to catch hell from her entire family—if the entire truth of what happened to her ever came out.

He suspected her family was too close-knit for it to remain a secret. Sean would tell. He, like Dan, would think he knew best for her and squeal on her. He'd think it was too important a thing not to tell the family. Jamie would be furious, but he figured she'd be too busy reassuring the rest of the family to take time to sink her claws into her brother. At least, not right away. Dan eased closer to her as they stood around the map of the neighborhood her brother was explaining.

Dan had a better understanding of a lot of things now. When Jamie told him he couldn't push her away, couldn't maintain any walls between them, this was why. She'd grown up with this kind of closeness, and she wanted the same thing for the family they would make together.

Dan stood beside her, feeling the tension in her body, wishing he could take her in his arms right here and tell her there was no reason to be afraid, that he wasn't going to let anybody hurt her, and neither would her brother or Josh. He also wasn't going to let her anywhere near the warehouse where her brother thought the gang members were holed up.

After Sean had finished his explanations, he took Dan aside for a private conference, while Jamie was talking to Josh.

"You and I need to talk. I know you want to go with us," Sean said, his gaze sliding over the black cane in Dan's hand. "Because they're the ones who did this to you, too, right?"

"Because I couldn't do anything but watch when they shoved your sister out of that car," Dan said. Because she wouldn't have gone after them in the first place, if it hadn't been for him.

Sean stood back and studied him. "I'd like to wring their

necks myself, but there's one little problem. We can't question them if they're dead. I hope you understand that.''

"Yes.''

"It's a damned shame, I know, but even I have to follow orders sometimes.''

Dan nodded toward Jamie, and said in a low voice, "How are we going to keep her out of it?''

"I'll hog-tie her if I have to. I've been doing it since she was seven and too curious for her own good.''

Dan did laugh then. So did Sean.

Jamie swung around to face them. "What are you two doing?''

"Nothing that concerns you.'' Sean ruffled Jamie's hair. "You're still in bad shape. Do me a favor. Stay out of trouble until I get back.''

"I'll try.'' She turned to Dan. "I suppose you're going with him?''

"They took you. And they hurt you,'' he groaned.

"Dan—''

"Excuse us for a minute,'' he said to her brother.

Dan pulled her into the shadows at the corner of the room and kissed her soundly. Pulling back, he marveled again at how very far they'd come, at how much she meant to him.

"I can't help this,'' he said. "It's personal. They hurt you, and they're going to know they'll answer to me if they ever touch you again. That's something you're just going to have to understand.''

"Dan—''

He tugged on the black turtleneck sweater she wore tucked into the waistband of her jeans until the ends came free, and then he slid his hand beneath the fabric, finding her soft skin.

"Please stay here,'' he said, switching tactics. If she didn't want to take orders from him, he'd have to find some other way of getting what he wanted, and he was certainly willing to consider asking nicely. "Do it for me. Because I asked you to."

"Why do you—"

"They've gotten away from me twice now," he said grimly. "They're not going to do it again. They're going to be behind bars, and you're going to feel safe again."

"I don't—"

"You've been sleeping in my arms every night, Jamie." He put his hand to the side of her face, the sight of the bruises still enough to make him murderously angry. "I've heard you cry out in your sleep. I know what your nightmares are made of."

She sighed. "You don't fight fair."

"No," he said unapologetically. "I don't."

She braced her hands against his chest, stretched up to kiss him softly on the lips. "All right." She gave in. "Go."

Dan nodded, kissed her one last time, and went to find her brother.

Chapter 16

They gave her a submachine gun and a headset, so she could hear what was happening inside and call for backup, if needed, then left her in an old building three blocks from their target.

Sean's voice was calm, rattling off instructions as they moved in. She heard the faint sounds of scuffling feet, confirmation that all six of them were in place, that the suspects were in sight, then they moved in. There was shouting, then a few rounds of gunfire that startled her badly.

The radio erupted with chatter. She had a sinking feeling that told her something was going wrong. Drawing her weapon, she headed for the scene, hampered by ribs that were still sore, but irritated with herself for letting them talk her into staying behind.

It was pitch-black, the area eerily reminiscent of the alley where Dan had been shot, the building reminding her of the place where she'd been held hostage for a day and a half. She felt sick to her stomach at the thought of getting anywhere near the people who'd beaten her, but she was afraid everything was unraveling, and she couldn't just stay back and not help the people she loved.

Through the headset, she heard Sean counting suspects as they were rounded up. They'd gone in believing there were four men inside, although they had no way to be sure. The three men Sean had on their trail couldn't watch all the exits and entrances to the building. By the time Jamie got to the building, they had five people in custody and were looking for more. She hadn't heard Dan's voice in fifteen long seconds.

Jamie paused, her back pressed against the side wall of the building. She checked her weapon one more time. It was ready to fire. Her heart was pounding. She waited until the last second to tell anyone what she was going to do, because she didn't intend to argue about it. They needed her, and she was going in.

She took a breath, hit the mike button and told the rest of the team she was at the southwest entrance off the alley and coming inside. Sean started swearing. Josh got her oriented to the scene, telling her where he and the rest of the team was, where they were holding their suspects. She finally heard Dan's voice; he sounded like he was running, something she didn't think was possible given the condition of his left leg. He was chasing a suspect, moving toward her, he thought.

She opened the door just wide enough to slip inside, stood with her back pressed against the wall. It was pitch-black. She heard the sound of footsteps, moving fast, not far from her. Two sets of footsteps, she decided. The unfamiliar weapon felt strange in her hand, the whole scene seeming unreal to her.

This morning, they'd been safe in the cabin. She'd awakened in Dan's arms, after they made love long into the night. She'd believed everything was going to be fine. The danger seemed so far away. And now they were in the midst of it once again.

The footsteps were coming closer. She crept along the side wall, then went right, along a row of tall crates toward the center of the building. Toward Dan and whoever he was chasing.

"Jamie?" His voice came through the headset. "He's climbing. Watch up top."

Her eyes scanned the rafters on one side. She was turning to look at the opposite side when someone fell on top of her. She heard him coming at the last second and lurched to the left, catching only a glancing blow to her head and shoulder. Still, she went down hard, the breath knocked out of her from the pain that shot through her ribs and the force of the impact. She lost her grip on her weapon only for a second, but that was enough. It went clattering against the floor.

When she opened her eyes, her assailant was beside her, on his knees, with his weapon in her face, snarling, before he recognized her and gave her a leering grin.

"Well, did you miss me?" he asked, adding a particularly vile name for her. "Did you think you'd come back for more?"

"No," she said, an icy calm settling over her as she got to her knees. "I came back for you."

The overgrown boy laughed softly and reached for her.

"Steady." Dan's voice came through her headset. "I'm coming. I'm almost there."

She marveled at his voice alone, steady as a rock, never wavering. It calmed her, as nothing else could have at the moment.

"Okay, on my count," he said. "Dive right."

She never saw him coming, never heard him move, but suddenly he was there, seemingly falling out of the sky, landing between her and the suspect.

Jamie heard grunts of pain, heard them both swearing and the sickening thud of fists on flesh. She turned away long enough to grab her gun, and by the time she turned around, it was all over.

Dan had the suspect immobilized on the floor. She didn't know what he'd done, but the suspect wasn't moving.

Sean and Josh were there seconds later, and the realization that she'd come face-to-face again with one of her assailants was starting to set in. Jamie was shaking again. Sean knelt down beside her, his hand on her shoulder. "You all right?"

"Yes." She nodded, surprised he wasn't giving her hell about coming inside. "I just need to sit here for a minute."

"Okay."

He turned and said something to Dan, then he and Josh hauled the last suspect away, toward the center of the building. She heard Dan moving beside her, then he pulled her against his side.

"You sure you're all right?"

She nodded, glanced up at the top of the crates on either side of them, marveling at what he'd done. "How in the world did you get up there?"

He kissed her forehead. "I don't know. He was coming after you, and I just did it."

She'd seen him struggling with his cane in the last week. She knew how difficult it was for him to walk. But she should have known nothing could stop him from getting the job done.

Dan's hand moved gently along her rib cage. "Sore? It sounded like you went down hard."

"It's fine. Just knocked the breath out of me." She had to stop to breathe, to tell herself it was all right now.

He must have needed to do the same, because he pulled her head down to his chest. When he finally spoke, she heard an odd quiver in his voice.

"God, Jamie. What am I going to do with you?"

"Keep me out of trouble?" she suggested.

"That would be a full-time job."

She laughed, finally feeling better. "Well, you're un-employed at the moment, right?"

"For the moment. Your brother seems to think I could be useful to his team at the Pentagon."

"Oh, great. The two of you together? I'd never have a moment's peace."

He kissed her then, quickly, soundly, then held her for another minute before they went to find Sean and Josh.

Dan wanted to take her home, but Jamie knew the job wasn't done.

They had six people in custody. Jamie recognized four of them from the time they'd held her hostage. Dan picked out the three people he'd seen the night he was shot, in-cluding the one who shot him and the girl he and Geri had tried to save.

Sean pulled some strings and arranged to have their sus-pects held at the nearby Marine Corps training center at Quantico, Virginia. Jamie and Dan stood in front of a one-way glass, watching and listening as, one after another, the five males in custody denied any knowledge of Alex Hath-away or where he might be. But the girl told a different story.

Looking scared and terribly young, she said she went for a drive with two of the teenagers now in custody, one of whom she considered her boyfriend, although he tended to get a little rough with her from time to time. They were acting strangely that night, watching the time, waiting for something, then drove down the street in front of the ware-house. They started arguing with her, pushed her from the car, started hitting her. She'd been afraid, had tried to run away. Dan had caught her, but she'd still been scared.

When she had the chance, she ran again. She heard gunshots moments later, saw blood on the boys' hands and their clothes when they caught up with her a few blocks away.

She claimed she didn't know the name Alex Hathaway, hadn't seen anyone that night but Dan and Geri and the two boys she was with.

"Do you believe her?" Dan said.

"I think I do," Jamie replied.

The girl said the gang had grown increasingly uneasy after hearing a federal agent had been shot and killed that night. Their deal wasn't about killing a federal agent. It was about being decoys. They were just doing a job for someone who had access to weapons they wanted. They had the prototype weapons they'd taken from the agents at the warehouse that night, but that was all. They wanted more of those same guns, and so far, they hadn't been paid.

The girl didn't know who hired them, but she picked up their instructions on the hit on the warehouse from a private company that rented mailboxes. She'd seen the man who dropped it off, a tall, lean man in his late twenties with short, dark hair and glasses. He wore a suit and tie. Apparently, they'd taken the precaution of following him, and weeks later, when they still hadn't gotten paid for the job they'd done, they went to find him. That was when they saw him with Jamie, outside FBI headquarters.

They'd snatched her off the street later that day, after she showed up at the liquor store asking questions, because they were tired of being kept in the dark, tired of not getting their guns.

Jamie knocked on the glass to get Sean's attention, then backed away from the window. Dan came with her, put his arm around her waist. "You okay?"

She nodded. When Sean came out, she said, "Ask the girl when they saw me with the man at FBI headquarters."

The day before they grabbed Jamie off the streets.

"It was the day I came to the office," Dan said. "What else did you do that day? Who did you see?"

"Geri and I argued about the Section 123 report. Tanner and I argued. I got a copy of the report..." she paused, remembering, stunned. "I know who it is. Rob Jansen."

"Who?"

"Rob Jansen. He's with the FBI, some kind of computer wizard. I asked him to look through the FBI computers for any inquiries about unidentifiable weapons or bullets. I met him that day to ask him in person." She frowned. "Wait. Why would he tell me about the liquor store robbery if he was part of this? If he knew that information would lead us to the two men he hired to help Hathaway get away?"

"Maybe he knew you were trouble, at that point. That they'd have to deal with you. Maybe he figured if he fed you that information, you'd go down there. They were probably waiting for you. I doubt they intended to let you out of there alive."

Sean walked out of the interrogation room and joined them. They filled him in on what they believed happened. Sean asked if Jansen had the kind of access it would take to find out Hathaway's whereabouts.

"He was inside Division One for months last year," Jamie said. "There's no telling what he had access to in that time. And if he set up the link with the FBI...who's to say what else he might have done when he was inside our computer system."

"Or what he might have been able to get out of Tanner's secretary without her knowing it," Dan added. "They're engaged."

"She was in the office that Saturday when we were briefed on the assignment at the warehouse," Jamie remembered. "I doubt her security clearance is high enough for her to know much about what was going on, but if Rob knew we were getting Hathaway, I bet he could have gotten enough out of Amanda to piece everything together."

"Okay," Sean said. "Let's pick him up."

They picked up Rob Jansen without incident. Jamie simply called him and said she needed to see him. If he was surprised that she was still alive, he didn't show it. Or maybe he came to get rid of her once and for all.

Whatever the reason, he showed up at the meeting place she suggested. He looked nervous and not terribly surprised to find himself being taken into custody. Jamie and Dan stayed a bit while he was questioned, heard strange mutterings about things they simply wouldn't understand, about secret missions and higher callings and protestations of innocence.

And then he shut up and demanded to see a lawyer.

Sean was making arrangements to search Jansen's car, his apartment, his banking records, phone records, etc. Jamie was exhausted. She'd been on her feet all day, and she didn't argue when Dan insisted on taking her home.

They went back to her apartment. He filled the tub for her, scrounged through her cupboards and found something for a late dinner while she soaked. Then he fed her and put her to bed.

She slept for a few hours, woke shortly before midnight when the phone rang. Dan was beside her in the bed and grabbed the receiver. Shivering, she pressed closer to him and waited. He finished his conversation and replaced the phone receiver.

"Tanner's coming over to fill us in on what he found out," he said.

She sat up gingerly, her ribs a little sore, and reached for her bathrobe. Dan made coffee. She was sipping her first cup when her boss arrived. If he was surprised to find them together, at this hour, at Jamie's apartment, he kept it to himself.

He looked over the fading bruises on Jamie's face with some concern. "Couldn't leave it alone, could you?" he said with a faint smile.

"I'm told that's a particular failing of mine."

Tanner laughed. "Don't worry. I've already forgotten the fact that you disobeyed a direct order from me."

Dan stepped closer, slid his arm around her waist. "You should thank her for that. You wouldn't have Jansen in custody if it weren't for her."

"I know," Tanner said. "Believe me, I'm grateful."

"What did Rob tell you?" Jamie asked.

"Not much yet. We've broken off questioning for the night, but we got our search warrants. At his apartment, he had a half-packed suitcase on his bed and a passport issued under a fictitious name. The passport shows he was in the Middle East a few weeks before Hathaway disappeared, in a real hot spot for terrorist activity. We checked departing flights using the name on the passport. Jansen had an airline ticket waiting for him at National. He was going back to the Middle East in the morning. He also had a bank account in the Cayman Islands under the same name. Somebody in Zurich wired him three million dollars today."

"This is still so hard to believe," Jamie said. "He's practically one of us."

"I know." Tanner said.

"Why would he use the kids from the gang to help him get Hathaway out?" Dan asked. " It seems like a foolish risk to take."

"I don't think he planned to use them," Tanner said. "I did some double-checking with the CIA. They knew some-one was after Hathaway, and they were watching a number of known terrorist organizations. Twenty-four hours before

Hathaway disappeared, the CIA detained two people we think were working with Jansen as they tried to enter the country. The CIA couldn't do more than hold them for forty-eight hours and send them back to the Middle East. I bet those two were supposed to get Hathaway out. When they couldn't get into the U.S., Jansen had to scramble for help at the last minute.

"Remember, Division One was only supposed to have Hathaway for two days or so. I'd say Jansen thought that was his best chance at Hathaway. Afterward he thought he'd be in a position to monitor the search for Hathaway, that if anyone got too close to figuring things out, he'd know and be able to get away in time."

"And I went to him for help," Jamie said.

"We got him because you wouldn't give up on this," Dan said, then he turned back to Tanner. "Why do you think Jansen did it?"

"Three million dollars, that's why. From what we've found so far, other than the money just wired to the Caymans, he was broke, which would explain why he hadn't been able to pay off the gang kids he hired."

"But he got Hathaway away from us months ago. Why wouldn't he have the money before now?"

"The explosives haven't surfaced anywhere yet. Before Hathaway disappeared, he claimed he was having trouble perfecting the chemical formula. The government thought he was stalling, that he didn't want to turn the explosives over to the U.S. But maybe he wasn't lying about that. Maybe he hadn't perfected the design yet or he wasn't able to do it right away. Who knows? Maybe we got lucky, caught them in time and we can keep those explosives off the market."

"What's so special about these explosives?" Dan asked.

"He added a chemical base that renders them virtually undetectable to any existing security devices. If somebody wanted to blow up a plane? A government building? We'd be at their mercy.''

Dan swore. Jamie felt dizzy at the implications.

''I know,'' Tanner said. ''Takes your breath away, doesn't it?''

Jamie nodded. ''So, this is it? You think Rob's the only one on the inside involved?''

''With the kind of access he had, I think he could have easily done it alone. He probably got some information through Amanda, but I believe he took advantage of her and their relationship. I don't think she was a part of this. We don't have any information to indicate anyone else on the inside was involved.''

''What about Hathaway?'' Jamie said. ''Do we know where he is?''

''I'm sure Jansen does. And with the evidence we have against him, he's going to talk. I think this whole thing's going to be over in the next twenty-four hours,'' Tanner said. ''Don't worry. I'll keep you posted.''

''Thanks,'' Dan said.

Tanner turned to Jamie. ''Good work.''

''Both of you.'' He looked back at Dan. ''I'm still trying to smooth some ruffled feathers with the D.C. police, the U.S. Marshals Service, St. Mary Margaret's…that's everybody, isn't it? I don't have any more surprises waiting for me, do I?''

''I don't think so,'' Dan said.

''We need to talk. About the reprimand. Given how this turned out, I can probably make the reprimand go away, if that's what you want,'' Tanner said.

Dan shook his head.

''Hate to lose you,'' Tanner said. ''What are you going to do with yourself?''

''I've got some ideas.'' Dan looked at Jamie and smiled. ''And she is going to need some time off.''

Tanner nodded. "Take it, Jamie. As long as you need. We'll be here when you get back."

Jamie walked him to the door, locked it behind him. Dan came to stand beside her. His hands encircled her waist.

"You're trembling," he said.

She sagged against him. "I can't believe it's over."

"You heard Tanner. It's done." He kissed the side of her face.

Jamie sighed.

"Tired?" he asked.

"No. Just shaky."

"What can I do?"

"Take me to bed," she whispered.

He did, held her for a long, long time, until she wasn't shaking anymore, until she made a tearful confession.

"I was so scared today. I was sure something would go wrong. Because every time I thought you and I were finally going to be together, something happened."

"Hey—" He turned her in his arms, until she was lying on her back and he was leaning over her. "You don't have to be scared anymore. It's over."

She shivered in his arms. He held her for a long time, then pressed his lips to hers. Long, deep, drugging kisses followed. She wound her arms around his neck as he worked his magic on her body, taking the fear away.

There was such heat in him, such strength. She couldn't seem to get close enough, though she fought each time they came together to take him closer, until he was a part of her, until they could never be completely separated again.

She'd never felt this way about a man before, never completely understood the power of the bond between two people, the need that rose like a fever, consuming her and pushing every other thought out of her head, except him.

He soothed her, stroked her, stripped her bare and slid his naked body against hers, until she was begging him to come to her. He went to pull her on top of him, but she stopped him.

"Like this," she said, rolling onto her back and pulling him to her instead. "Please."

One of his thighs slid between hers and then the other, but he was careful to kept his weight on his forearms, not on her. She pulled him down, until her breasts were nestled against his chest, until she felt him, big and hard and strong, teasing against the opening of her body.

"Are you sure?" he groaned, kissing her again.

They hadn't made love this way yet, because of her ribs. But she thought it would be okay now. Besides, she wanted him this way, wanted to feel surrounded by him, wanted to feel his big, solid body on top of hers, wanted to find herself pinned beneath him with him thrusting into her.

"Yes," she said, moving against him, opening her body to his, and taking him inside. "Just like this."

She was indeed surrounded by him, consumed by him. She loved the power, the determination that drove him on. She loved the sensation of being taken by him, filled by him. She loved that he pushed her to the point where she would let him do anything he wanted to her, where she could do nothing but hang on to him and go where he led her. She loved trusting him enough to let him do all of those things to her.

She let her thighs fall open, as wide as she could, and used the muscles in her legs and abdomen to arch her body against his, taking him even deeper. She felt sweat dampen his chest, saw the straining muscles in his arms. She wanted him to let go, too, wanted him to think about nothing but his own pleasure this time, wanted him to take for a change, not give.

She pulled his mouth down to hers, rocked her body against his. Her arms went around his back, pulled at him, her nails sinking into his back.

"Please," she said. "Dan, please."

He moved faster, pushed harder, until she broke right through that steely control of his, and she had him. He groaned out her name and what she thought was an apology, and then he was moving against her, as he never had before. Fast and furiously, in quick, deep strokes. He was in a frenzy, and she had a second or two to concentrate on the look of pure need in his eyes, the immense concentration on his face, before she was too caught up in her own sensations to do anything but feel.

The feel of him, moving this way inside her, was amazing.

Dan groaned out her name. He went rigid for a second, and then started thrusting again. She felt the rippling climax move through him and into her, until she shuddered and cried out his name, as well.

She lay beneath him shivering and struggling for breath.

He rolled off her, lying flat on his back beside her. She heard a string of curses, and then he was leaning over her, running his hands over her ribs, whispering urgently to her.

"I'm fine," she reassured him.

"God, Jamie, I can't believe—"

"What?"

"That I did that to you."

"I think you were provoked," she said, smiling. "At least, I'd like to think I managed to provoke you."

"Provoked? Lady, you make me crazy."

"I do?"

"Yes. I don't lose control like that. At least, I never have before."

She smiled wickedly.

"You're sure you're all right?"

"I'm sure. I wanted you. Just like that."

He settled her against his side, kissed her lazily, soothingly, until her heart rate was back to normal and she could breathe again. Then she was snuggled against his big, warm body, wrapped tightly in his arms.

She could hear his heart still pounding heavily, heard the sound of the wind kicking up outside. It could storm tonight, and she wouldn't care. He'd be right here with her. Then she heard a strange scraping sound—a tree against the side of her apartment?

"Did you hear that?"

"What?" he said, the sound rumbling up from deep inside his chest.

She waited, tense and edgy all over again, but heard nothing.

"What did you think it was?" Dan said.

"Maybe a branch scraping against the bedroom wall? I don't know."

"Want me to check?"

She hesitated, thinking she was being silly, thinking she was comfortable and didn't want him to move. "I'm getting paranoid."

He tugged on her hair, until she lifted her head from his chest and looked him in the eye. He was grinning, an endearingly sexy grin unlike any she'd ever seen from him.

"Maybe you are. Maybe you aren't," he said, giving her a quick kiss. "Roll over. I think I need to check this out."

She rolled away from him, pulling the sheet around her, watching as he took three awkward steps to the window and looked outside.

When he turned around, he was still smiling. "All clear."

"You're up to something," she said.

He sat down on the side of the bed. "Maybe."

Then she heard a strange whimpering sound from the next room and her heart started pounding. She reached for the gun she kept in the nightstand. "Someone's in here."

"Hang on." Dan took the gun from her hand and returned it to the drawer. He pulled on a pair of boxer shorts and grabbed his cane. "I think I know what the problem is."

She watched in disbelief as he walked to the bedroom door without her gun and disappeared.

"Dan!"

"Close your eyes," he ordered.

"What?" Her heart started pounding even harder, but from somewhere came the realization that she didn't have to be afraid.

"I'm not coming back in there until you close your eyes," he insisted.

Oh, God. She thought she knew what the whimpering sound was.

"Are they closed?"

"Yes," she said breathlessly.

She was sitting in the middle of the bed, her back against the pillows and the headboard, the sheet wrapped tightly around her, her heart hammering so hard she could hardly hear anything else, except—whimpering. Pitiful, fussy whimpering.

She felt the bed give with Dan's weight. He settled in beside her on the bed, put a basket in her lap, kissed her softly, sweetly on the lips. "Open your eyes, babe."

She felt something warm and wet and smooth sliding against her fingertips, which were curled around the edge of the basket. Opened her eyes and found a trembling, little ball of fur huddled against one corner of the basket, licking her fingers and pawing at the edges to try to find a way out. Its eyes were barely open, its hair long and curly and golden, its ears long enough to drag on the ground when it walked.

Jamie couldn't breathe.

He'd gotten her a puppy.

"Sean said you had a cocker spaniel one time, when you were living in Germany."

She nodded, unable to speak, then looked more carefully at the bottom of the basket. It was lined with rose petals, a half-dozen shades of pink mingling with creamy whites.

"I wasn't sure what color you liked. So I ordered some of each," he said. "Climbers, right?"

She nodded. Vines to entangle themselves to the house, from the foundation up. Her puppy was still whimpering and licking her fingers. She could smell the roses now.

"They won't ship the rosebushes until spring. We need to have a place to plant them by then," Dan said, handing her a glossy magazine with one corner nearly chewed off. "Sorry. The dog and I had an eventful evening while you were off in dreamland."

Dreamland? She laughed weakly. This was dreamland. He was about to make it all come true.

Dan opened the book, a real estate book, she realized, to a page near the middle where the corner had been turned down. She saw lots of trees, a wide porch, a big fieldstone chimney on one side, a roof that went this way and that at all sorts of interesting angles.

"It's in Maryland, near the Bay. You can pick whatever you want, of course. I just flipped through the book a few times and I thought you might like this one. I thought you might like being on the water."

"Yes."

Tears ran down her cheeks and dripped onto the page. Dan eased her against him until her head was lying against his chest. The puppy was crying, too, and she watched Dan stroke him gently, trying to soothe him as well.

The gentleness always surprised her and pleased her.

"When did you do all this?" she asked.

"While you were sleeping. I had Josh come over and stand guard, to make sure you didn't get away, and I went and picked up a few things. The puppy's been crying for hours. He finally wore himself out and fell asleep right before Tanner called and woke you up. And once Tanner left, I got sidetracked when you dragged me off to bed.'' He pulled a small cardboard box from the back of the basket—a home pregnancy test. ''This is my backup plan. In case things don't go the way I planned, you can take this in the morning. Maybe the results will persuade you to give me what I want.''

Jamie tried to sort through the jumble of thoughts running through her head to find the most important things to ask. ''You want me to be pregnant? I thought…that first morning…''

''It threw me a little.'' He hugged her gently. ''Just for a little bit. I shouldn't have taken the choice out of your hands that way. It was unfair of me. I was still hung up on walking around with the cane. But…the more I thought about it, about you carrying my baby, the more I hoped it was true.''

He shifted away from her just a little, looked down into her eyes and said, ''I had a lousy father, Jamie. He was never there. Never. You're going to have to help me a little.''

''I will,'' she whispered.

''I love you,'' he said harshly. ''I just couldn't help myself when it came to loving you.''

Her tears flowed freely. She could barely breathe. Oh, God, she'd waited so long.

''And I need you,'' he confessed. ''I need you desperately.''

''I need you, too.''

''I'll make you happy, Jamie. I swear it. I'll cherish you, worship you. Probably spoil you rotten, too.''

She smiled, imagining his particular brand of spoiling.

''And I don't see how I could live in this world without

you beside me. Say it," he coaxed. "Say you love me, too."

Jamie felt sheer happiness bursting inside of her, spreading and filling her. "I do. I love you. I always have."

"I know I promised you some time. I know it hasn't been that long, but I don't have any doubts. Not where you're concerned. Not about the way I feel." His palm pressed flat against her belly. "I want it all. Everything we talked about that morning. I want to give you everything."

She smiled, hoping his baby was tucked safely inside of her.

"There's just one little detail we haven't discussed," he said.

"What's that?"

He went fishing for something in the rose petals in the corner of the basket, then tucked a strand of her hair behind her ear. When he pulled his hand away, there was a big emerald-cut diamond, stunningly clear, winking at her from the end of his index finger. It sparkled and shimmered and absolutely took her breath away.

"I'm an old-fashioned kind of guy," he said. "If you're going to live with me in some big old house in the country and have my babies, you're going to have to marry me."

"I'll *have* to?" she managed. "You're telling me? Ordering me?"

"Babe, you've got me on my knees. You know I'd do anything in this world for you. You're going to have to do this for me."

She lay beneath him, the world turned blurry from all her tears. She took his face in her hands, kissed him softly, urgently.

"Say it," he demanded. "Say you'll marry me."

"I will."

He slipped the glittering diamond on her finger. She held

her hand up in front of her to admire the sight of his ring, and cried some more.

"I'm going to make you so happy," he promised.

"You have," she said, wrapping her arms around him. "You already have."

* * * * *

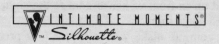
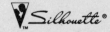

If you enjoyed what you just read,
then we've got an offer you can't resist!

Take 2 bestselling
love stories FREE!
Plus get a FREE surprise gift!

Clip this page and mail it to Silhouette Reader Service™

IN U.S.A.	**IN CANADA**
3010 Walden Ave.	P.O. Box 609
P.O. Box 1867	Fort Erie, Ontario
Buffalo, N.Y. 14240-1867	L2A 5X3

YES! Please send me 2 free Silhouette Intimate Moments® novels and my free surprise gift. Then send me 6 brand-new novels every month, which I will receive months before they're available in stores. In the U.S.A., bill me at the bargain price of $3.57 plus 25¢ delivery per book and applicable sales tax, if any*. In Canada, bill me at the bargain price of $3.96 plus 25¢ delivery per book and applicable taxes**. That's the complete price and a savings of over 10% off the cover prices—what a great deal! I understand that accepting the 2 free books and gift places me under no obligation ever to buy any books. I can always return a shipment and cancel at any time. Even if I never buy another book from Silhouette, the 2 free books and gift are mine to keep forever. So why not take us up on our invitation. You'll be glad you did!

245 SEN CNFF
345 SEN CNFG

Name	(PLEASE PRINT)	
Address	Apt.#	
City	State/Prov.	Zip/Postal Code

* Terms and prices subject to change without notice. Sales tax applicable in N.Y.
** Canadian residents will be charged applicable provincial taxes and GST.
All orders subject to approval. Offer limited to one per household.
® are registered trademarks of Harlequin Enterprises Limited.

INMOM99   ©1998 Harlequin Enterprises Limited

INTIMATE MOMENTS®
™ *Silhouette*®

invites you to join the Brand brothers,
a close-knit Texas family in which each
sibling is eventually branded by love—
and marriage!

MAGGIE SHAYNE
continues her intriguing series

with

THE BADDEST BRIDE IN TEXAS, #907
due out in February 1999.

If you missed the first four tales of the irresistible
Brand brothers:
THE LITTLEST COWBOY, #716 (6/96)
THE BADDEST VIRGIN IN TEXAS, #788 (6/97)
BADLANDS BAD BOY, #809 (9/97)
THE HUSBAND SHE COULDN'T REMEMBER, #854 (5/98)
You can order them now.

™ *Silhouette*®

Available at your favorite retail outlet.

COMING NEXT MONTH